The

Wedding

Dance

Missy and Dan's Wedding– Summer Lake Book Eight

SJ McCoy

A Sweet n Steamy Romance

Published by Xenion, Inc

The Wedding Dance Copyright © SJ McCoy 2015

Published by Xenion, Inc.
First Paperback edition 2017
www.sjmccoy.com

This book is a work of fiction. Names, characters, places, and events are figments of the author's imagination, fictitious, or are used fictitiously. Any resemblance to actual events, locales or persons living or dead is coincidental.

Cover Design by Dana Lamothe of Designs by Dana
Editor: Mitzi Pummer Carroll
Proofreader: Aileen Blomberg and Kristi Cramer

ISBN 978-1-946220-16-5

Dedication

For Sam. Sometimes life really is too short. Few xxx

Happy Birthday.

Acknowledgments

This is the eighth book in the Summer Lake series. Add two more in my Remington Ranch series and this is the tenth book I've written. Today, December 22, 2015, is my son's twenty-third birthday. His deathday was August 14, 2011.

If it weren't for Sam, you wouldn't be reading this, because I wouldn't have written it. After he died, I wanted to escape the world. Instead I chose to honour a promise I made to him a long time ago. I used to talk about writing my books someday—he made me promise that someday I'd stop talking about it and actually do it. In honouring that promise, I have escaped into my fictional world. He gave me that gift. If Summer Lake is an escape for you, too, then please consider it a gift from Sam. He'd like that.

These books wouldn't be what they are without my editor extraordinaire, Mitzi Carroll, who translates the ramblings of this odd little English mind of mine into Amerikish. More than that she gets me through the tough days. The word 'editor' used to conjure up images of a stern lady with a red pen. Now, in my mind at least, 'editor' means the same as my friend—or "frined"—and my comfort. Thank you.

These books wouldn't make it out into the world without the amazing Dana Leah—my cover designer, graphics guru, PA, and most of all my friend. We've come a long way in the last couple of years. We're still at the beginning of our journey—it started about books and along the way it became about life—long may it continue. It's been over a year since we sat at that café in Vegas and talked about this story. It's finally here—bring on the goosebumps. We made it. Vegas baby;

Chapter One

"Mom? Are you nearly finished?"

Missy smiled and shut down her computer. "I am; come on in, sunbeam."

Scot rolled his eyes at her as he came into her office and plonked himself down on the easy chair that faced out to the lake. "Don't you think that, by fifteen, you could maybe drop the baby names?"

Missy laughed. "Maybe, but you're not fifteen yet."

"I'm not far off."

"I know." Although she knew it, she still couldn't quite believe that fifteen years had gone by since she'd held him in her arms for the first time.

"So, any chance of dropping the baby names?"

She smiled. "I'll try. I've been doing better, and I never use them when anyone else is around, do I?"

"No. I guess I should be grateful for that, at least."

She laughed. "I guess you should, because you know, even if I stop using the names, you'll always be my baby."

He shook his head at her with rueful smile. "I know, I know. And no matter how big I get, you can still stand on a chair to tell me who's boss."

She laughed. "I can and I will." He was already a good few inches taller than she was. "What did you want, anyway?"

He shrugged and stared out the window at the lake.

"Well, if you're not going to tell me, I can't help you."

He met her gaze for a moment, then stared back at the lake before he spoke. "Jarret said the best man at a wedding has to stand up in front of everyone at the reception and give a speech."

Missy's heart melted for him. "Yes, but we already figured out how to handle that, didn't we? Uncle Jack is going to do the speech, so you don't have to. I think Dan feels a bit bad about not asking him to be his best man. This way we don't leave him out—and you don't have to worry about that part."

He looked at her for a long moment. "Mom, I'm not a little kid anymore. I know you're trying to make it easy on me, but I'm not really the best man if I don't do the speech, am I?"

Missy wrinkled her nose at him. She and Dan had thought that letting Jack make the speech was a win-win. Scot struggled to talk to anyone other than her and Dan most of the time. Standing up to speak in front of a room full of people would be a huge ordeal for him—or so they'd thought. "So what are you saying, son?"

"That I think I should do it."

"Do you want to?"

She watched him mull it over. His answer told her just how fast he was growing up. "It isn't always about want, is it? I think I should; I think it's important."

She nodded, even as she swallowed the lump in her throat. He was right, he wasn't a little kid anymore. He was becoming a young man; a young man she was very proud of.

"If that's how you feel, then you should."

He nodded. "Thanks, Mom." He stared out at the lake again. Missy waited, knowing there was more to come. "What about Uncle Jack, though? I don't want to leave him out."

She smiled. "Let's talk to Dan when he gets back, shall we? Maybe you can both make a speech?"

"Okay. He should be home by five. We'll talk to him then."

Missy smiled. She didn't know what time Dan was due home. She loved that he and Scot kept in touch as much as they did. That they had their own relationship that had continued to grow after they'd all moved into this house together.

~ ~ ~

Dan smiled as he pulled into the driveway. He was so glad to be home. He cut the ignition on his Jeep and sat there a moment. Home. It was such a wonderful place, such a wonderful feeling. This time last year he'd never have believed that he'd be living the life he was now. Home was in this great house, right on the water in Summer Lake. Home was here because Missy and Scot were here. His beautiful little lady and his son. He loved them both so much. A year ago, he wasn't sure he was even capable of love. He'd thought it was a strange emotion—one that defied the logic and reason by which he navigated through life. Now he knew that it did defy logic and reason, but he also knew that he was as susceptible to it as anyone. Perhaps even more so, since it seemed that the love he felt for Missy grew exponentially with each day that passed. Scot had become his son in all but genetics and he couldn't be happier. In a week's time, they would enter into a commitment he had also believed was illogical—marriage. Now it made all the sense in the world. He couldn't wait to marry her.

"Hey, Dad!"

Scot's voice brought him back from his musings and reminded him that he was still sitting outside in his Jeep. He climbed out and ran up the steps to the front door where Scot greeted him with a hug.

"Hey, champ. How's it going?"

Scot grinned up at him. "It's going great. I need to show you those files later. I found the bug and I think I fixed it."

Dan smiled. "You only think so? You didn't test it?"

"Of course I did, but I know I won't have thought of everything." He grinned. "At least not all the weird scenarios you'll come up with."

Dan laughed. "I have taught you well, Grasshopper."

"Yeah, you have. Come on in, though. Mom and I wanted to talk to you about something."

Dan followed him through to the big kitchen. Missy was sitting on a stool at the island, but slid down when they came in.

"Hey, beautiful." He closed his arms around her and she put her hands up on his shoulders as she pecked his lips.

"Hi. I missed you."

He held her closer. "I missed you, too, but I'm glad I went. It was fascinating to meet some of Ryan's team." He smiled down at her. "And I won't get chance to go again for at least a month now."

She smiled back. "Well, you could if you want to, but I might get lonely on our honeymoon by myself."

He laughed. Missy was perhaps even more excited about the honeymoon they had planned than about the wedding itself. They were going to tour Europe. Their itinerary spoke of just how different they were. Missy's highlight was four days in Ireland, where she hoped to learn more about her heritage. Dan's own highlight was a couple of days in Switzerland—to visit CERN! He had to admit he was excited to visit the Large Hadron Collider.

"You know there's no way that would happen," he replied. "Scot said you wanted to talk to me about something?"

She nodded and looked at Scot.

"How do you think Uncle Jack would feel if I wanted to make the best man's speech?" he asked.

Dan rubbed his hand over his cheek. "Do you want to?"

Scot nodded. "I think I should."

"Then you should."

"What about Uncle Jack? I don't want to take everything away from him."

Dan nodded slowly. Neither did he, but shocked as he was that Scot wanted to make the speech, there was no way he'd tell him no.

"I said maybe they could both do one," suggested Missy.

He nodded. That could work. It would also take some pressure off Scot. "That'd be great." He looked at the kid. "Perhaps you could work on your speeches together?"

Scot thought about it. "I'd like that. You don't think he'd mind?"

"I don't think he'd mind at all." In fact, he was pretty sure that Jack would be thrilled at the idea. Scot was going to stay with Jack and Emma while he and Missy went on their honeymoon. Emma was one of his favorite people in the whole world. It might be good for him to have some time bonding with Jack, too, before he spent a couple of weeks with them. "Do you want to call him?"

Scot looked uncomfortable. He was getting better about being around people, but he still avoided talking on the phone whenever he could.

"How about we invite them over for dinner?" asked Missy. "I'd love to spend some time with them before the wedding, and next week is going to be crazy."

Dan grinned, then looked at Scot. "I'd love to have them over; what do you think, champ?"

"Yeah, that'd be great." He smiled. "As long as you'll come look over those files with me before they get here?"

Missy laughed. "Go on then. You two go do your thing. I'll give them a call."

~ ~ ~

Emma didn't even make it through the front door before she wrapped Missy in a big hug.

"Hey, Miss. I'm soo excited! This time next week, we'll be in Vegas. And a week from tomorrow you'll officially be my sister-in-law, the other Mrs. Benson."

Missy laughed. "Hey, Mouse. Come on in. Why do I have the feeling that at some point we're going to have some crazy mix-up over both being Mrs. Benson?"

Jack laughed as he followed them inside. "Because knowing the two of you, and given the fact that we live in such a small town, it's pretty much bound to happen, isn't it?" He gave her a hug, too.

"You and Dan never get mixed up though, do you?" she asked. "And you've both been Mr. Benson your whole lives."

Dan came running down the stairs to join them. Scot was close on his heels. "I'm going to be Mr. Benson, too, after next week," he said.

Jack smiled at him. "Well, you and Dan might get into a mix-up, considering you're both geniuses, but I think I'm safe."

Missy was surprised that Scot went straight to the point. "What about which Mr. Benson is going to be the best man, at this Mr. Benson's wedding?" he asked.

Jack smiled. "Well, there's no room for confusion there. That would be you—Mr. Scot Benson."

Missy knew the look on her son's face. He was worried. "And you don't mind?" he asked.

Jack put a hand on his shoulder. "Mind? I think it's awesome. Don't get me wrong, if Dan had asked anyone else in the world to be his best man, I would have been pissed."

"Jack!" Emma slapped his arm.

Missy bit back a smile as Jack winked at Scot and continued. "In front of the ladies I might have been upset, but between you and me…" He shot a grin at Emma. "I would have been pissed."

Scot laughed.

"But to be perfectly honest, I'm glad it's you and not me." He looked at Dan. "Pete was my best man, and that was partly because I know your dad hates to have to stand up and speak." Missy caught Dan's eye. She'd thought it was strange when Jack hadn't asked him, but he'd explained later that Jack knew him too well. They'd talked about it and Dan had been relieved to let Pete have the honor.

"I hate it too," said Scot. "But I think I need to do it."

Jack gave him a puzzled look. "You do?"

He nodded solemnly.

"Then you should. I'll be glad to help if you want me."

"Thanks. I think we should both do one, but I'd like it if you'd help with mine."

"Tell you what," Jack offered, "why don't we work on them together?"

Missy was relieved to see Scot smile. "Thanks, Uncle Jack. That'd be awesome."

After they'd eaten, they took their drinks outside to sit on the patio overlooking the lake. Scot disappeared to his room, eager to work on the suggestions Dan had made to him earlier as to how he could fix his bug. Missy smiled to herself. Although the two of them tried and tried to explain their work, computers and programming languages were all gobbledygook to her. Every time they talked about fixing bugs she wanted to hand them a flyswatter.

Emma looked at her. "So how are you feeling with just a week to go?"

She laughed. "Impatient! I just want to get there and get on with it."

Dan looked at Jack. "Why is it, it took me months and months to persuade her to do this and ever since she agreed, nothing can happen fast enough? Anyone would think it was a shotgun wedding with the hurry she's in."

As Missy laughed, she didn't miss the look that passed between Emma and Jack. They knew as well as she did that there wasn't a chance in the world of her being pregnant. She narrowed her eyes at Emma, but her friend just gave her an innocent shrug.

"What are you complaining about?" asked Jack. "You're in just as much of a hurry yourself."

Dan's eyes twinkled as he smiled at her. "I am; I can't wait. It's just that Missy here is more interested in the honeymoon!"

She laughed. "I am not! I'm excited about it that's all." She looked at Jack. "And for the first time in my life, I'm not worried about going somewhere without Scotty."

Jack nodded. "He'll be fine. We'll have a great time." He gave her a puzzled look. "Do you really want him to have to make a speech though?"

She shook her head. "He came up with that one all by himself. I'm as surprised as you are, but I guess he's growing up even faster than I thought."

Emma nodded. "He really is. I'm so proud of him."

Dan nodded. "He's a fine young man." He looked at Jack. "And you really don't mind him making the speech?"

"Not at all. I think it's great. I'll be happy to help him with it." He smiled "Can I still at least make a toast though?"

"Of course you can! You can still make a full-blown speech, if you want to."

"Nah, I don't need to do that; I just want to make a toast."

"Well, you can do whatever you want to," said Missy.

Jack raised his glass. "In that case, I'd like to make a toast now. Here's to family."

Missy grinned as she realized that they really were going to be family. She chinked her wine glass against his and Dan's. As she turned to Emma, it dawned on her that Emma didn't have wine. She had a glass of water. That was all she'd had all evening. Missy froze with her own glass held up, as her grin grew even bigger. "Mouse?" She raised her eyebrows.

Emma gave her a sheepish grin and touched her glass to Missy's. "Yep, to family!"

"Oh, my God!!!" Missy leapt up. "That's amazing! Why didn't you tell me?"

Dan gave them a puzzled look. "Tell you what? What's amazing? What am I missing?"

Poor clueless man! Missy turned to him. "She's pregnant!!"

Dan's face was a picture. "What? How?"

"If you don't know how..." laughed Jack.

Dan laughed with him. "Not that! I mean how do you know, Miss? I don't get it. We're toasting to family, but I thought that meant all of us becoming family. How did you know it meant them starting a family? Am I really so clueless?"

Missy patted his arm. "No, hon. You're not. It's a girl thing. See, Emma's drinking water instead of wine, and that's a miracle in itself. She only picked at her dinner—which isn't like our Mouse."

Emma stuck her tongue out at her, but didn't argue.

"Add to that the fact that Jack looks so damned pleased with himself, and it all points to... they're having a baby."

Jack nodded. "We don't want to tell everyone yet." He took hold of Emma's hand and she smiled up at him. "It's still really early. But we've told Gramps and my mom, and we wanted to tell you."

Missy looked at Emma who nodded. "Yes, we're going to tell Pete and Ben. The four of us may as well be family."

Missy was glad. She'd considered Emma, Pete, and Ben to be family since they were all eight years old. They'd been the first people she'd told when she found out she was expecting Scot. She was so happy that their lives had drawn them all back to each other—and back to the lake—in the last year.

Dan caught her eye. "How are those two doing? I've hardly seen Pete lately, and, when I do, he's never with Holly. And I think Ben's avoiding me."

"Oh, he'd never do that!" cried Emma.

"I don't know, hon." Missy shook her head sadly. "I feel as though he's been avoiding me as well." She looked around at the three of them. "Ever since I told him I wanted to invite Charlotte to the wedding."

"Oh," Emma's face fell.

Missy shrugged. "I took Megan's advice and decided I should just go ahead and talk to him about it."

"What did he say?" asked Emma.

"You know what he's like. He said it was fine. That he'd be fine. That whatever I want is most important." She blew out a big sigh. "And I haven't managed to talk to him for more than two minutes since then. He seems to get incredibly busy the second I stop by or call him. I don't know what to do. I want Charlotte there, but I don't want to hurt Ben."

"I'll talk to him," said Emma.

"Thanks." That was the only cloud hanging over Missy's head. She and Charlotte had promised each other when they were kids that they would each go to the other's wedding. Of course, in those days they'd still believed that they'd both live in Summer Lake when they grew up—and they'd also believed that Charlotte would marry Ben.

Chapter Two

The next morning Missy grabbed the keys to her van and headed out. She'd told Dan to go ahead to meet the others at the Boathouse for breakfast. She'd catch up with him there, but she wanted to stop in to see her dad first.

"Is that you, Miss?" he called as she let herself in the back door.

"No, I'm a burglar," she replied with a laugh.

She found him in the front room, still in his pajamas. "Are you getting lazy in your old age?" She tried to make a joke of it, but she'd been worried about him lately. He seemed to have gotten old all of a sudden.

"It's looking that way, isn't it?"

She frowned. He'd normally make a joke or at least tell her off. Mild mannered acceptance just wasn't his style.

"Are you feeling okay?"

He nodded and gave her a gruff smile. "I'm just fine. What are you doing here anyway? I thought you'd be running around getting everything ready for next weekend."

She smiled and held up the bag she was carrying. "I made that beef stew last night. I thought you'd like some."

"Thanks, honey. Stick it in the fridge for me, would you?"

Missy went through to the kitchen and opened the fridge. There wasn't much of anything in there. She tried to look after him as best she could, but he refused any help most of the time.

She turned as he appeared in the doorway. He was moving slowly and looked stiff. "I haven't had a chance to get to the grocery this week."

She nodded. "Well, I have to go this afternoon. Do you want me to pick up anything for you?"

He held her gaze for a long moment. How many times had they had this conversation? How many times had he scolded her that he could look after himself?

"If you want to get me some basics, since you're going anyway? Milk, bread, coffee?"

"Of course I will!" She'd get him a damned sight more than that, too. Part of her was pleased that he was finally accepting her help. Part of her was sad and a little worried that he would.

He smiled. "Don't get carried away though. I'm not a feeble old codger who can't do for himself, yet. I've just been a bit under the weather this week. I figured I'd best rest up so I can be in top form to walk my girl down the aisle next Saturday."

Missy felt tears prick her eyes. "Exactly! I'm not trying to coddle you. I'm just making sure you'll be able to keep up when I sprint toward the altar!"

He laughed. "I'd hardly call it a sprint, Melissa. You're a middle aged woman with a near grown son. You've sure taken your time getting there."

She laughed with him. "I am not middle aged! You're right about Scot being near grown though. He's decided he wants to make the best man's speech."

She loved the way he smiled. He was so proud of Scot. "Good for him! He's come a long way in the last year, hasn't he?"
She nodded.

"You're a great mom to him, Miss, but having a dad now... well, having Dan has made the world of difference for him. Dan's the right one—for both of you. You may have taken your time getting to the altar, but I'm glad you did. He was worth the wait."

Missy blinked away the tears again. She knew her dad approved of Dan, maybe even loved him, but he'd never put it into words before. She nodded.

He shook his head and made his way back to the living room. She'd swear he dabbed at his own eyes once he had his back to her! "Anyway, thanks for the stew, and if you can remember to pick me up some milk when you're at the grocery, that'd be great." He was putting his shoes on. "You'd better get going, though. I want to get out to the shop. I can't sit around here talking to you all day."

She went and wrapped him in a hug. "I love you, Dad."

"Yeah, you too. See you later." He stepped neatly aside.

She should have known better. He wasn't a hugger. He may have opened up a little about the wedding, but she couldn't go expecting miracles. "See you later. I'll drop your groceries off this afternoon."

"Thanks," he didn't look back, just waved over his shoulder as he went.

At least he was going out to spend some time in his woodworking shop...even if he was in his pajamas!

~ ~ ~

Dan smiled at Jack as he took a seat next to him at one of the big picnic benches out on the deck of the restaurant.

"Yo, bro," said Jack.

"Morning." He looked around the table, surprised that so many of the gang were here already.

Ben mumbled a greeting and stood up. "I'll be back in a few," he said. "I just need to run up to the lodge."

Jack raised an eyebrow.

"See what I mean?" asked Dan.

"I'll talk to him after breakfast," said Emma with a reassuring smile. "Where's Missy?"

"She should be here soon; she wanted to see her dad first."

Smoke checked his watch. "I hope she hurries up. I need to get going and I wanted to talk to her about the arrangements for Thursday."

"Where are you off to this time?" asked Michael

"Just picking Holly up from LA. I'll be back this afternoon."

Laura pushed at him. "You had better be! I've hardly seen you for weeks."

Dan smiled to himself as Smoke snaked an arm around Laura's waist. "Oh, I will be. And I'll be home all week now." He looked at Dan. "At least until the madness starts on Thursday with getting everyone to Vegas."

Dan nodded. The logistics of getting all their family and friends to Vegas by Thursday night were quite daunting. He was grateful that Smoke enjoyed organizing the schedule. He'd be flying Papa Charlie, and he had Jason lined up with the second plane. Dan wished again that he'd found time to complete his own flight training. It would be cool to fly to Vegas himself. Not that Missy would hear of it. She was scared to death of flying at all. She had faith in Smoke, but she hated the idea of Dan flying.

"Have your nerves kicked in yet?" Michael asked him.

He shook his head. "Nope. Nothing to be nervous about. I'm a happy man. I'm a little impatient, but not nervous." He cocked his head to one side and gave Megan a little smile as he asked, "Why, Michael, are you nervous?"

Megan smiled back as Michael slid an arm around her shoulders. "Me? I don't do nervous, mate! I'm like you. Impatient, that's all. I finally get to make this little lady my wife. Saturday can't come soon enough!"

Dan nodded. He loved that Michael and Megan were going to get married on the same day as them. It made sense that they should make the most of having everyone together. Michael had been uncertain when he'd first run the idea by him and Missy—he hadn't wanted to steal their thunder. Dan had encouraged him though, and Missy absolutely loved the idea. Michael and Megan were going to have their ceremony first in the chapel at the Bellagio, and then later in the afternoon Dan and Missy would take their vows out on the balcony overlooking the fountains.

"I don't know how you pulled it all together so fast, Michael," said Pete. "I've still got another month to go and it's been nothing but a nightmare."

There was an awkward silence around the table. Everyone was fully aware that Pete and Holly were having a rough time. Even Dan knew that it was down to Pete getting carried away with his need to plan everything down to the last detail and the last minute of the day.

Jack looked at Pete. "Maybe you could learn something from Michael, huh, partner?"

Pete frowned. "Something like what?"

Jack laughed. "Like how to relax and enjoy it?" He smiled at Megan. "And how to keep your lady smiling."

Pete scowled. "Holly's not into smiling at the moment."

Laura shook her head at him. "Exactly! Why do you think that is?"

"Geez!" Pete looked about as rattled as Dan had ever seen him. "What is it? Let's pick on Pete day or something?"

Emma patted his arm. "No. We just love you and we hate seeing you mess things up."

"I'm not messing things up. I'm getting things organized so that we can enjoy our big day!"

Megan smiled at him. "I...I...I..."

Dan felt for her. She'd come out of her shell so much in the last few months, but she still struggled sometimes to talk in front of everyone. She struggled, but it didn't stop her from speaking up when she felt something was important. He watched her take a deep breath before she tried again.

"Maybe you both need to enjoy getting to the big day, too? I can't speak for Holly, but I can tell you that working with Michael to plan our wedding has been so much fun for me."

Pete stared at her for a moment. Dan wondered if he even understood the point she was making. He'd known Pete for years and when the guy got an idea in his head he was a man on a mission. His need to plan and organize the details sometimes blinded him to what was really important. Dan waited, wondering what his reaction would be.

He smiled. "Thanks, Megan. At least you put it gently."

She smiled back at him.

"Hey guys!" Missy called as she made her way across the deck to join them.

Dan moved up to the end of the bench so she could sit between him and Jack. He dropped a kiss on top of her head as she smiled up at him.

"So what have I missed?" she asked.

"Not much," said Pete. "Mostly just everyone getting on my back."

Missy laughed. "Well, you deserve it. How poor Holly puts up with you, I do not know!"

Pete scowled at her. "Thanks, bud. Love you, too!"

She laughed. "If I didn't love you, I wouldn't worry about you screwing things up, would I?"

He shook his head. "Seems that's exactly what I am doing, though."

Dan felt bad for him. The conversation moved on, but Pete continued to scowl out at the lake, saying nothing.

Smoke looked at Missy. "I'm going to have to leave in a minute, but can we get together later?"

She nodded. "Yes, please. We need to figure out who's going in which plane and when."

Smoke nodded. "Okay, great. I'll give you a call when I get back from LA." He leaned in to kiss Laura. "This is me gone. See you later."

Dan loved that Laura stood and went to walk Smoke to his truck. He knew his cousin was happier than she'd ever been since she'd met Smoke. He also knew that it wouldn't be long before they, too, announced a wedding date.

~ ~ ~

Missy looked around at their friends. Emma and Jack, Michael and Megan, Smoke and Laura, Pete...she wrinkled her nose. Pete, but no Holly—again. Most of the gang were here. Kenzie and Chase rarely made it to breakfast. Gabe and Renée were supposed to be coming, but they weren't here yet. There was no sign of Ben.

"Have we seen Ben yet this morning?" she asked.

Dan shook his head. "He got up and left as soon as I arrived."

So he was still avoiding them, then? Missy hated that.

Emma gave her a worried look. "I'll find him and talk to him once we get done here."

Missy stood. "Thanks, hon. But I need to do it myself. This is getting ridiculous."

"What is?" asked Pete.

Missy scowled at him. He was so caught up in his own stuff he hadn't even noticed. Normally she would have turned to him for help before now. "I told him I've invited Charlotte to the wedding. I haven't seen him for two minutes since then."

"Ah." Pete sighed. "That's not going to be easy for him."

"I know! I'm almost thinking I should un-invite her."

Pete shook his head. "Don't do that; he'd feel even worse."

Missy nodded sadly. "I need to talk to him though."

Dan looked up at her. "Do you want me to order for you?"

She smiled. "Yes, please."

He laughed. "The full Boathouse Breakfast, right?"

"You know it."

Michael laughed. "I still have no idea where you put that much food, critter!"

She laughed and smiled at Dan whose eyes twinkled back at her. "Well, I don't have hollow legs."

Dan laughed as she left the table and made her way into the bar, hoping to find Ben.

He wasn't in there, but she found him coming down the steps from the lodge. He smiled, but didn't meet her gaze.

"Good morning, bud."

She shook her head at him. "It isn't a good morning though, is it, hon?"

He finally looked her in the eye. "Why, what's up?"

"My oldest friend is avoiding me and I'm starting to get upset about it."

He rubbed both hands over his face and blew out a sigh. "Sorry."

She smiled. "At least you're not denying it; that's a start."

He shrugged. "I'll be fine with it, okay?"

She shook her head. "You're not fine with it now! What are you going to be like once you're in the same room with her?"

He sighed again. "It'll be a big room. There'll be lots of other people there, too. I'm sure we'll be able to stay out of each other's way."

Missy wrinkled her nose at him. "You couldn't just talk to her? I'd love to think that my wedding could be the turning point where the two of you put the past behind you?"

He shook his head sadly. "I couldn't handle that, Miss. I'm sorry. I'll stop hiding from you…"

"And from Dan?" she asked. "Even he's noticed that you're avoiding us!"

That was the first genuine smile she'd seen on his face in a long time. "Damn! I was making it that obvious?"

She laughed. "You were."

"Okay, I'll stop it, but I need you to promise me that we're not going to talk about it either. She's coming to your wedding. Fair enough. I understand that, and I wouldn't want to get in the way of it. But, I have no intention whatsoever of talking to her, and I'm sure she feels the same way."

Missy frowned at him.

He shook his head. "I'm not looking for a discussion about it, Miss. I'm looking for your understanding."

"So, how about you help me understand something?" She was tired of pussyfooting around—she wasn't very good at it.

"What?"

"Why can't you go with an open mind? Be prepared to talk to her. You two could be friends. She'd love to come back to the lake to visit, you know, but she won't come because of you."

He shook his head sadly. "If she wants to come visit, you figure out when and let me know. I'll go on vacation."

"But you don't need to do that. Why can't you leave the past where it belongs? Why can't you get over it? Be friends with her?" Missy asked all the questions that had troubled her for years. She didn't want to hurt him, but she needed to understand. Charlotte had been one of the gang; she still should be.

Ben met her gaze, and the pain she saw in his eyes answered her more eloquently than his words. "I can't do it, Miss. Because...me and Charlotte? We don't belong in the past. I can't get over it; I can't be her friend because...I still love her."

Missy's eyes stung. She knew that. Why had she needed to make him say it? She touched his arm. "I'm sorry."

He shook his head as he rubbed his arm over his eyes. "No, I'm sorry. I'm the dumb fuck who can't get over it. I've had long enough. She's been married for how many years?" He stared out at the lake then looked back at her. "I don't want to be around her because I don't want to be reminded of the future I thought we were going to have...the life we missed out on... Is her husband coming?"

Missy looked back at him wondering what she could say. She decided it was best to stick to the simplest fact. "No."

He nodded. "Good."

Chapter Three

Ben sat on his balcony over the lake. He should get down to the bar; it was Saturday night—band night. It was going to be a busy one and he was already half an hour late. He didn't want to go, though. He'd sooner just sit here. It was a whiskey night kind of night. He rubbed his hands over his face; except there was no one to drown his sorrows with him. He shrugged. And that was a good thing; all his friends were busy living their lives. Missy would be at home with Dan and Scot—the three of them excited about officially becoming a family one week from now. Emma and Jack would be home, too, making plans for their family...for the baby they had coming. He downed his whiskey at that thought. Pete might be around, but hopefully Holly would be back by now and the two of them could get around to sorting themselves out. Pete's plans had nearly screwed them over before—surely they wouldn't let it happen again.

He stood up. He needed to pull himself together and get on with it. He needed to snap out of it, to put the past back in its box, put a smile on his face, and go get on with his own life. He blew out a sigh. What life? He had a business to run, guests and staff to take care of. But a life? He hadn't had one of those in a long time.

He started at the sound of a knock on his apartment door. Kenzie had probably sent someone to come get him. It wasn't fair of him to leave her down there to run the bar by herself. He hurried to open the door and was surprised to see Smoke standing there.

He held up a six pack with a questioning smile. "What do you think? Is it time for one of our little chats?"

Ben had to smile. Despite the fact that he didn't know that times like this called for whiskey, not beer, Smoke had become a real friend. He shook his head and grabbed his keys. "Thanks for the thought, but I need to get to work. Kenzie's probably cursing me by now.

Smoke grinned. "Kenzie curses all the time. I wouldn't worry about her. In fact, she's the one who suggested I come see you. She's got the bar under control. She's got Laura, Holly, and Renée perched at one end to keep her company and the two new guys seem to know what they're doing. Looks like she's trained them well."

Ben nodded. She had. He'd been impressed with the way Kenzie had taken to her new management role as they brought in more staff for the upcoming busy season. He looked up at Smoke and then down at the beers in his hand. "Can we take a rain check on them?" he asked. "I'm pretty sure I'm going to want to take you up on the offer sometime soon, but I've just pulled myself together. I'd sooner get to work than open the box tonight."

"Sure thing. I just wanted to give you the option if you need it." He raised an eyebrow. "Are you okay?"

Ben shrugged. "I'm going to have to be. You know how that goes."

"I do; that's why I'm here." He handed Ben the beers. "Why don't you put them in the fridge on standby?"

"Thanks." Once he'd put the beers in the fridge, he came back and pulled the front door closed behind him. "Come on, let's go have some fun. I'm glad Pete and Holly made it out tonight; I've been worried about them."

Smoke pursed his lips. "Holly's here. No Pete."

Ben blew out a sigh. "Maybe we should take those beers and go find him?"

Smoke shook his head. "I called him. He's hiding in his work. He's pissed that everyone gave him a hard time at breakfast this morning. And Holly's pissed at just about everything he does right now. I picked her up from LA this afternoon, and, when we landed back here, she didn't want to go home. She hung out with Laura and then wanted to come here with us. It's not looking good."

Ben sighed again. He wanted to help them get back on track on somehow. Pete was his oldest friend. Holly was awesome. The two of them were perfect together—or they would be if Pete could just let go of his need to plan everything to death. He started down the steps. "Let's get down there. Maybe we can get him to come out, or at least we can try to talk Holly down. Remind her that he only goes overboard like this about things that are the most important to him."

Smoke gave a short laugh as he followed him down the steps. "Yeah, good luck with that. What do you think we've been trying to do all afternoon?"

~ ~ ~

Holly sat back and listened while Laura and Renée chatted. It sounded as though the Women's Center Renée was working on was coming together great. Holly knocked back the rest of her drink as she thought about it. She shouldn't be feeling like this—as though she might need a women's center for help and advice soon. Even if she did, though, it would be back in LA, not here. She loved her life here in Summer Lake, but it was all about Pete. She rolled her eyes and shook her head. Damn that man! She loved him, but right now she kind of hated him too. He made her feel worthless. He didn't value her opinion, didn't want her input. He needed to be in control. He claimed it was all for her, but if it was, surely to God he'd listen to her?! She shook her head again.

"If you're going to sit there shaking your head and rolling your eyes, I might have to cut you off."

She looked up at Kenzie who was leaning on the other side of the bar.

"Do you want to talk about it? Or do you want to go home and see that man of yours? Go work it out?"

She shook her head. "None of the above. I don't want to talk about it, because all I'll do is bitch and whine. I don't want to go home, because there's no talking to him. He only sees what he needs to do to feel good about himself. He can't see why I'm so fed up with it all. He doesn't understand that he's lost track of us while he's so hung up on planning and details. Anything I say to him, he thinks I'm being difficult—just for the hell of it! Which makes me wonder who he really thinks I am!"

Kenzie shook her head sadly. "I'm sorry. I have no clue what to say. I listen well, but I don't do advice. Even if I did, I'm clueless when it comes to relationship stuff anyway."

Holly smiled at her. She liked Kenzie. She kind of envied her right now, too. She had a great relationship with her fiancé, Chase. The two of them seemed so happy-go-lucky. She couldn't imagine them ever fighting over wedding arrangements. Hell, they probably wouldn't even arrange one! They'd just go do it on a whim one day. "You're not clueless at all. You're much better at it than I am. And besides, you've got Chase. Seems to me that he'll do anything and everything to keep your relationship on track."

Kenzie looked up at the stage where Chase was singing. She smiled when he caught her eye and winked as he launched into the chorus.

"Can you get me another?" Holly asked. She needed one.

Kenzie turned back to her with a stern look. "I can, but consider yourself warned. I will cut you off if you get any more miserable than you already are. Just because the boss man isn't around to steer you straight, doesn't mean I won't."

Holly spotted Ben coming through the bar with Smoke. "You're safe," she said to Kenzie. "The boss man's here to back you up."

As Holly watched them approach, she appreciated just how hot those two were. This place really was overrun with hot men. She sighed. Pete was the hottest of all of them as far as she was concerned. She pictured his face. He was gorgeous— his dark blond hair, his piercing blue eyes, his chiseled features. The little dimple on his chin that softened his imposing persona and gave a hint of all the laughter that… She sighed again. All the laughter they no longer shared.

Ben came straight over to her and gave her a hug. Poor guy. It sounded as though he had enough misery of his own at the moment with the thought of having to see his ex at Missy's wedding. Even with that on his plate, he was still coming to make sure she was okay. She felt bad as she reached up to hug him. Her problems were temporary—she hoped. It seemed as though he'd been living with his heartache for years. She shuddered at the thought.

"It's good to see you, Holly," he said. "It'd be better to see you with Pete though." He raised an eyebrow.

What did he want her to say? She shrugged. "You know what he's like."

Ben nodded. "And so do you. You know he's just getting carried away."

"So, what? I'm supposed to make allowances for him being the way he is? What about him making allowances for the way I am? I'm a woman who just wants to have a say about her own wedding, for God's sake!" She regretted it as soon as she'd finished. "Sorry, Ben. I didn't mean to snap at you."

He smiled. "I know. I understand. I've had a lifetime of him, remember? I know how frustrating he can be."

"Frustrating is a mild word."

Ben laughed. "I know. I just want to see the two of you happy again."

"So do I."

"I guess once the wedding is over with…"

Holly gave him a sad look. "Or if we call it off…"

Ben looked stunned. So did Smoke who was standing by his side.

"You don't mean that, do you?" asked Ben.

She shrugged. Did she? She didn't even know anymore. She loved Pete. She wanted to be with him, wanted to spend the rest of her life with him. But if this was an indication of what the rest of her life would be like…? Was this really what she wanted?

Smoke gave her a questioning look. She wasn't about to start pouring her heart out to these two! Laura and Renée had already tried to get her to open up. She couldn't! She shouldn't have said that much out loud. It felt disloyal to Pete. She could bitch about what he was doing; that was okay. But if she really was going to call it off, he should be the first to know. She smiled back at Smoke. "Just ignore me. I need another drink." She didn't miss the worried look he exchanged with Ben as she turned away from them. She needed to watch her mouth. She shouldn't be saying anything to anyone until she knew what she wanted. And when she did, it was Pete she should be talking to.

She saw Gabe come in through the main door. Renée had said he was still working but would join them later. He was another one—all organized and busy planning things. She watched as he approached the bar. The way Renée smiled when she saw him, the way he smiled back made her heart hurt. She was happy for them, she just wished she and Pete still smiled at each other at all—let alone like that.

~ ~ ~

Gabe smiled at the sight of Renée sitting at the bar chatting with Laura. The two of them were smiling. He'd guess Renée was talking about her women's center from the look on her face. She lit up whenever she talked about it. It made him happy that she'd found something to do with her life that met her need for meaning and purpose, while at the same time allowing her to stay here and contribute to the town where she grew up. And most importantly, to be with him. Things were moving along well for them. He was making great progress with the Development Committee. They were living in the house up at Four Mile while their new one was being built on Renée's land. All they needed now was for her divorce to finally come through. He couldn't wait for them to join the list of happy couples who were getting married around here.

He spotted Holly sitting next to them, looking grumpy as usual. He didn't know her that well, but he had to wonder what Pete saw in her. Sure, she was beautiful, but she never seemed happy. He'd hardly include them in the list of happy couples. He shouldn't judge, but he did have to wonder why they were getting married.

Ben was there with Smoke. He nodded at Gabe, who nodded back. He leaned in to peck Renée's cheek and smiled at Laura. "Don't worry, I won't interrupt your girl talk. I just wanted to say hi."

"Hi," Renée spoke into his ear sending shivers down his spine and making him hope she didn't want to stay out too late.

Laura smiled at him. "Hey, Gabe. You can have her back in a minute. We're just talking jewelry-making class details."

He nodded and turned to Holly. He felt bad for her. "Hi, Holly."

She nodded and gave him a sad smile. "Hi, Gabe. How are you?"

Wow! She was attempting conversation? "I'm doing great, thanks. How are you?" He didn't really want to know, but he had an idea he was about to find out.

She shrugged. "I'm okay. Just feeling sorry for myself, I guess."

Gabe would much rather turn away and join Ben and Smoke's conversation, but she looked so down. "I'd have thought you'd have a lot to smile about? You're taking one of the spaces in the plaza up at Four Mile aren't you? And, from what Renée says, it sounds as though your business in LA is thriving? And you've got the wedding coming up." Oh shit! Why had he brought that one up? The look on her face said her wedding was nothing to smile about. "Sorry. I'm just trying to cheer you up, but evidently I'm not doing a very good job of it."

She met his gaze. "Can I ask you something?"

He nodded, wondering what was coming.

"When you and Renée get married, what will your wedding be like?"

He didn't get why she wanted to know, but he thought about it. "I guess it will be whatever she wants it to be." He could tell Holly was looking for something, but he didn't know what it might be, and he could only tell the truth.

She stared at him for a long moment. "What about you, though? What do you want for yourself? What's important to you?"

He considered that. "That is what's important to me. That she gets what she wants." He thought about it a little more, believing he might understand what she was getting at. "For me personally, what's important is that my family should be there. My folks and Michael. That's about it really." He met her gaze. "Why, Holly, what's bothering you?"

"Just ignore me. Sorry, Gabe. I thought you were like Pete, and I was trying to understand what might make you tick."

He nodded. "Well, if I can make a suggestion, you'd be better off talking to him than to me."

She glared at him for a moment. He held her gaze. He wasn't going to back down. She needed to hear it from someone.

After a long moment, she smiled. "Thank you. You're right." She slid down from her stool and said her good-byes.

Kenzie came down the bar. "Did you just scare her off, Gabe?"

He laughed. "Hi Kenzie, nice to see you, too. And no, I didn't. I just told her that if she's got problems, she might want to talk to her fiancé instead of people in the bar."

Kenzie narrowed her eyes at him for a moment, then she laughed. "Good for you! And thanks. Someone needs to bang their heads together!"

Gabe nodded. He'd rather keep things positive than get bogged down in other people's problems. "Are you all ready for next weekend?"

Kenzie grinned. "Yes, sir! Do you think you can stand to be officially related to me?"

Gabe smiled. Kenzie was not his kind of person at all, or at least that's what he'd thought, until he'd actually gotten to know the brash blonde. She was good people. Nowadays he considered her a friend. And when Michael and Megan got married they would, as she said, be related…somehow? In-laws of some description, if his brother married her sister then…yeah. He had no clue. He nodded. "Stand it? I'll be happy to call you family. Almost as happy as Ethan will!" Michael's son was thrilled about the wedding and thrilled that Kenzie and Gabe would soon officially be his auntie and uncle.

The way she smiled back at him reminded him again that she was so much more than the brash blonde that first met the eye. Her whole demeanor seemed to soften as she nodded. "Me, too. And I really do feel as though I'm becoming part of the family. Your parents are awesome; they've been so kind to me, as well as to Megan."

Gabe grinned. "They're good people. As far as they're concerned, they're gaining two daughters." He didn't know the whole story of Kenzie and Megan's own family life, but it sounded as though it had been pretty awful. He loved that his folks were welcoming the two of them into the family. He shot a quick look at Renée; he was even happier that they were excited to welcome her as a daughter-in-law, too.

"How do they feel about Vegas, though?" asked Kenzie. "Don't get me wrong, I think it's awesome that so many of the oldies are coming, but it must be kind of weird for them."

Gabe laughed. "You would think so, wouldn't you? But, no. My parents are excited about a trip to Vegas. Missy's dad says he hasn't been there in years…"

Ben leaned in to join them. "Joe and Gramps are like a pair of teenagers at the prospect of a weekend in Vegas."

Laura looked up. "So are my mom and Aunt Christine."

Gabe gave her a puzzled look. "Aunt Christine?"

She smiled. "Dan's mom."

"Ah, right."

Kenzie laughed. "See, there are so many oldies coming!"

Ben nodded. "Yep, Pete's parents are going to be there, too."

"They are?" asked Kenzie, looking puzzled.

"They wouldn't miss it. Missy's been like a daughter to them since we were in Kindergarten—and Michael."

Gabe laughed.

So did Ben. "You know what I mean! Not that Michael's like a daughter! That we're all like brothers and sisters."

Kenzie smiled. "I envy you all that. And you said your parents might even make it?"

Gabe watched Ben for his reaction. He looked uncomfortable for a second, but covered it almost immediately with a smile. "Yeah. I spoke to them yesterday. They reckon they're going to be there."

Gabe held his gaze for a moment. Ben rarely mentioned his folks. He gave the slightest shake of his head. Fair enough. He didn't want to talk about it? Gabe wasn't going to push.

Chapter Four

Smoke reached for Laura's hand as he drove them back up East Shore. He was glad that she'd wanted to called it a night. Ben seemed to have pulled himself together and was back in full-on work mode. Holly had taken herself off home—hopefully to talk to Pete. Gabe and Renée would have stayed and hung out for a while; that might have been fun. Smoke liked them, but all he'd really wanted was to bring his lady home.

"So what do you want to do for the next few days?" she asked.

He smiled through pursed lips, but said nothing.

Laura laughed. "I take it we're not getting out of bed until Thursday then?"

"I've missed you. We've got some making up to do."

"I've missed you, too. It seems as though it's been forever since we had a couple of days at home together."

Smoke nodded. "It does, doesn't it?" He loved the life they were building. He got to fly and Laura got to travel and design her jewelry. She spent a lot of time out in the workshop in the orchard behind the house. He spent a lot of time at the airport setting up the flight school. The first batch of students were due to arrive next week. Life was good; he and Laura were both free to come and go as they pleased. They'd both maintained their independence and rather than feeling trapped—as they'd each feared they might—they enjoyed their busy lives and looked forward to whenever they could snatch some downtime together. "We can do whatever you want to. My only request is that we get some alone time, just you and me. Next weekend is going to be crazy; I just want my lady to myself for a while before the madness starts."

His heart thundered in his chest at the way she squeezed his hand and smiled back at him. He loved that she still made him feel that way every time she smiled at him. "And I want you to myself, too. Let's close the world out for a couple of days, shall we?"

He nodded. "Yeah, let's do that."

He turned off the main road and onto Cottonwood Creek. He was surprised to see an SUV parked in the driveway outside their house. Laura gave him a puzzled look. "Who the hell is that?"

Smoke frowned. He had no clue, but he didn't like it. He pulled up and cut the engine. "Wait here. I'll go see."

Laura laughed. "Yeah, right. Stay in the truck, little lady? Ha!" She opened her door. "I'm coming with you!"

Smoke blew out an exasperated sigh—of course she was. He hurried around the truck, needing to at least get in front of her. He drew her to his side as the vehicle's door opened and a man stepped out.

"Hey guys! Sorry to land myself on you, but I'm here! I finally made the move."

"Nate!" Smoke and Laura both spoke at once.

He laughed. "Yeah, glad you still recognize me."

"What the hell are you doing here?" asked Smoke.

Nate grinned. "I'm making the move, like I said."

"But I thought I was picking you up in LA on Thursday?"

"Sounds as though you're going to have enough people to ferry around next weekend." Nate shrugged. "And I got finished up ahead of schedule. I thought I may as well come up here and start looking for a place, get settled in." He raised an eyebrow at Smoke, "Plus, I thought my friends might be pleased to see me a couple of days early."

Damn! Smoke was glad to see him, but his plans for the next few days hadn't included a house guest. "You could have let me know."

"Sorry," Nate looked apologetic.

"No need." Laura dug Smoke in the ribs as she smiled at Nate. "We are pleased to see you. It's just a bit of surprise. Come on in. I'll make up the spare room."

Nate started grabbing his bags from the car. "Thanks, Laura. It's good to see you."

Once they were all settled in in the living room in front of the big windows overlooking the lake, Smoke turned to Nate. He still didn't quite get why he was here.

"I'd have thought Jack would be your first port of call."

Laura pushed at him. "Don't be an asshole, Smoke." She smiled at Nate, "We're glad you're here."

Nate laughed. "Thanks. Sorry. I probably should have called or something, but you know what I'm like. I got a wild hair up..." he stopped short and smiled at Laura. "...and here I am. I figured Jack and Emma would be busy helping with wedding stuff. Pete, well, I saw Holly last week, and I didn't want...I thought I'd best not land on them. You two are easygoing, spur-of-the-moment types; I didn't think you'd mind. I can go get a room at the resort if it's a problem though?"

"Oh, no, you won't," said Laura. "We're happy you're here!"

Smoke pursed his lips. He was happy to see Nate. It was about time he moved up here, but having him stay with them for the next few days wasn't ideal. Hadn't they just been saying they wanted time together—alone?

Nate raised an eyebrow at him and Smoke smiled.

"You're a pain in the ass, Nate. You're lucky that my lady is such a sweetheart." He smiled at Laura. "If it were down to me you'd be in a room at the resort."

Nate laughed. "Sorry. I'll go see Ben tomorrow. Get a room while I house hunt." He turned and winked at Laura. "But tonight you're stuck with me."

Laura laughed with him. "And we're happy to be. So, come on. Catch us up. What's going on with you?"

"Well, like I said. I got finished up early in LA. Everything's finally come together for me to move up here. Nothing much else going on except a wedding to go to next weekend. I don't suppose you have any pretty single friends lined up for me, do you, Laura? It seems odd to go to a wedding without a date. And from what I hear, the only bridesmaid is married to my boss, so that's not going to work out for me."

Smoke chuckled. "You don't need a date. And you're going to have to tone yourself down if you're going to live up here; so leave the local girls alone. We'll be in Vegas for Christ's sake. You'll find plenty enough mischief to get into."

"Yeah. Ben and I can go out on the prowl. We had fun at Pete's stag night."

"I wouldn't bank on that." Smoke thought about it. He didn't know if Ben would be eager to go off partying with Nate or whether he'd be too preoccupied with his ex. He shrugged and looked at Laura. The way her eyes shone with mischief as she smiled back at him made him a little uneasy.

"Slow down, Smoke. Maybe we could find Nate a date."

He shook his head rapidly. He didn't want any of Laura's friends falling prey to Nate's charms. If Nate was going to be living here, he really would need to tone himself down—or at least have his fun elsewhere. Nate liked women, but he wasn't exactly good boyfriend material. The women around here all seemed to want to settle down and live happily ever after. That wasn't Nate's deal at all.

"Don't worry," said Nate. "I can be a gentleman."

"I'm sure you can," said Laura. "I think it'd be fun for you to go with someone; it'll get you off on the right foot to get to know more people, if you're going to be living here."

Smoke scowled at her. "Who do we even know that's single? Everyone seems to pair off as soon as they get here."

"There's April, for starters."

Smoke didn't like that idea. He didn't know April too well, but he did know the poor girl had been through a lot. She'd come here to escape an abusive husband. She didn't need to be falling under Nate's spell and having her heart broken. He looked at Nate. "She's not your type."

Laura laughed. "We're talking about a date to go to the wedding. That's all."

Smoke laughed and jerked his head toward Nate. "You don't know him like I do. He's on the triple F plan."

She raised an eyebrow at him, making him laugh again. "Find 'em, fuck 'em, and forget 'em."

Laura looked at Nate and he hung his head with a sheepish grin. She laughed and looked back at Smoke. "I know someone else who was on that plan when I met him."

It was true. Smoke had lived that way for years. It was different though. He'd had good reason. He didn't want to get close to a woman because of the hurt he'd been through, and because he'd believed that being with a woman would mean giving up who he was. Nate wasn't like that. Nate just wanted to have fun. He lived life to the fullest and made the most of every moment—before he moved on to the next. Smoke shrugged. It wasn't really any of his business. "Yeah, but meeting you changed it all. Changed me. There's only one of you. Nate's not going to get as lucky as I did."

Nate laughed. "And no offense, Laura, but I wouldn't want to." As he smiled, even Smoke could see why women fell for him so easily; he was a good-looking guy. "I just want to get lucky!" he said with a laugh.

Laura nodded, but Smoke could tell she was still scheming something. He'd have to have a word with her when they went to bed. She didn't understand what she was dealing with when it came to Nate.

"Anyway," said Nate, "I want to hear what you two are up to." He looked at Smoke. "How's the flight school coming?"

"Great." Smoke was relieved to change the subject. "We've got the first batch of students coming in next week."

Laura smiled. "I'm glad Michael was able to fit them all in in time."

Nate raised an eyebrow.

"You met Michael at the fundraiser," said Smoke. "He's the Aussie, the doctor? He took the training so he can issue medical certificates that they're fit to fly.

Nate nodded, looking thoughtful. "Yeah, he seemed like a good guy."

"He's the other one getting married next weekend," said Laura.

"Yeah, right."

"But what?" asked Smoke.

Nate grinned. "You just got me thinking about the fundraiser." He looked at Laura. "Is that blonde friend of yours coming? Leanne."

Smoke groaned.

Laura cringed. "Yeah, she is. She and Dan have been big buddies since they were at Berkeley together." She looked at Smoke. "She's not Smoke's favorite person though."

"Ah, shit! She was the one…" Nate shook his head. "Sorry, dude."

Smoke blew out a sigh. "It's okay. She meant well." He gave Laura a pointed look. "Or so somebody is always telling me."

Laura laughed. "She did. I wish you'd just get over it."

Smoke scowled. "I have."

Nate laughed. "Sorry, I didn't mean to cause a domestic. I could always keep her out of the way—keep her occupied in my room so you don't have to run into her."

Smoke had to laugh. "Yeah. I wish you luck with that one."

Laura laughed as well. "If you set your sights on Leanne, then that is nothing to do with me. It sounds as though you may be a match, but I take no responsibility—for either of you!"

Smoke was grateful that at least she wasn't trying to set them up. He did understand that Leanne had just been trying to look out for Laura, but he still didn't like her. She'd caused him too much pain...even if she had, as Laura always told him, made them stronger for it in the end. "Didn't Dan say her ex is going to be there, too?" he asked.

"Yeah. Ryan." She shook her head. "It's going to be quite a weekend. We've got two weddings and two, long-overdue reunions."

Nate gave her a puzzled look.

"Leanne and Ryan were a big deal for a long time," she explained. "They were engaged. And then, Ben's ex, Charlotte, who he hasn't seen for years is going to be there, too."

"Wow. Sounds as though I'll be better off hitting the clubs and staying away from the drama," said Nate.

Smoke nodded. It wasn't so long ago he would have felt the same way. "It'll be whatever it is. For now, though, I'm ready to turn in." He stood and held his hand out to Laura. "I'm glad you came, Nate. We'll take you down to the resort for breakfast in the morning."

"Thanks, that'll be great."

Smoke grinned. "And while we're there we can talk to Ben about finding you a room!"

Laura pushed at him. "Asshole!"

Nate laughed. "Thanks, guys. Goodnight."

Chapter Five

Megan smiled as Ollie pulled on his leash. "We're nearly there, boy."

He turned and looked back at her and gave two short, sharp barks. He loved their Sunday morning walks on the beach. Megan loved them, too. She loved to come out early while it was still quiet everywhere and just walk the beach and enjoy the silence.

Michael had taken Ethan over to April's house where he was going to spend the day with her son, Marcus. The two of them had gotten really pally over the last few weeks. Megan was happy about that. Ethan loved to spend time with Missy's son, Scot, but Scot was that much older and as he grew into his teen years, the difference between him and Ethan became more apparent.

She stopped at the edge of the parking lot and Ollie sat, knowing what was coming. He grinned up at her and wagged his backside even as he sat on it.

"Good boy. Now you listen, Oliver. When I take this leash off, you need to be good, okay? You can play, but don't go in the water, and you come back to me when I call you."

He offered her a paw to shake, making her laugh.

"Yes, it's a deal," she said as she shook it. "You do as you're told and you can have your treat when we're done." She unfastened his leash.

Ollie gave his trademark two short, sharp barks and ran off down the beach. Megan shook her head as he ran straight out into the water. He was such a good dog; he was pretty well behaved with most things, but he did love the water. She shrugged. It made him happy. Everyone should be able to do what made them happy. She was finally happy. She loved Michael with all her heart and soul, she knew he loved her the same way. She loved Ethan, loved the family that they were becoming. She took a deep breath. She couldn't wait for them to grow their family. Well, actually, she could. She was desperate to have children, but she wanted it to happen when they were married. She took another deep breath. She mustn't get herself worked up. She was just being silly. She was probably emotional because she was hormonal. That must be it. Her period was way overdue.

And another deep breath. She picked up her pace as she went after Ollie. She wanted to grow their family, she wanted a baby so badly. But she did not want to be pregnant when they got married. Maybe that was silly, but it was deeply engrained in her. It was Adrian's fault. Yet another of the mean things he'd drilled into her head when she was with him. He'd told her he would never marry her. Of course, she'd been grateful of that! But he'd told her and told her that no one would ever want to marry her. That the only way any man would ever marry her would be because he had to, if she was stupid enough to get pregnant. She did want to get pregnant, she did want to have Michael's baby, but she wanted him to marry her—just for her—first. It didn't help knowing that Michael had married Ethan's mother Kay when she was pregnant—because she was pregnant. Look how that had worked out for him!

She reached the water's edge and called Ollie, who was happily chasing leaves. She mustn't let her mind go there. She wasn't pregnant; she was just late. That was all. She turned at the sound of a shout from the parking lot. She smiled when she recognized the guy standing there. It was Chase. She called Ollie again, but he'd spotted Chase, too, and was already racing back up the beach toward him. By the time Megan reached them, Chase was squatting down and Ollie had a paw on his shoulder.

"Good morning, Megan."

"Hi, Chase. How are you?"

He nodded. "I'm great, thanks. Just getting a run in while I can."

Megan laughed. "Let me guess. Kenzie is still sleeping?"

"Yeah. She works hard."

Megan loved that Chase obviously loved her sister so much. He was always quick to defend her. "I know. I'm really proud of her."

Chase smiled. "Me, too. For a while I didn't think either of us were capable of this—of living together, settling down—you know?"

Megan nodded; she did know. She'd had her doubts about the two of them herself, but she was so happy for them. "But look at you now. I just can't wait for the two of you to set a date and get married."

"Neither can I. We'll do it when the time's right. How about you? How are you feeling about your big day?"

To Megan's surprise, she felt herself start to shake. "I...I...I" Oh no! Was she really back to stuttering?

Chase looked concerned. "Are you okay?"

She nodded, but realized just how far from okay she really was as she felt tears roll down her face. She brushed them away as Ollie looked up at her and started to whine.

"Megan, what is it?"

She shook her head. "Ap…Apparently it's something about bumping into you out here that makes me cry." She gave him a weak smile. He and Kenzie would never have gotten together if Megan hadn't run into Chase out here once before and given him Kenzie's number.

He smiled. "Well last time that happened, you told me what was going on and it worked out pretty well for both of us. So what do you say, do you want to try again? Tell me what's up?"

She nodded. It was crazy. She did want to talk to someone, and Chase was a safe someone. Someone she trusted and who would be neutral.

"I…I…I…" Oh, for goodness sake! "I think I might be pregnant!" she blurted out and burst into tears.

Chase put an arm around her shoulders. "Hey, don't cry. Isn't that what you want? What Michael wants? I thought the two of you wanted kids?"

She nodded and blew her nose. "Yes. But…but…but…" A fresh wave of tears came. "I'm sorry, Chase. I'm just so stupid."

"Hey! You are not stupid! You're one of the smartest people I know. So, come on. Tell me what the problem is."

"I don't want Michael to marry me because I'm pregnant!"

Chase looked puzzled—as he had every right to. "But he's not. He's…"

"I know. I know. I told you I was being stupid. It doesn't make any sense. We're getting married anyway. Because we want to. It's just a stupid hang-up in my head. I don't want to get married because I'm pregnant! Can you understand that?"

He nodded. "I think so. I mean, I get it, but it's not like that, is it?"

"No, it isn't, but in my head, it feels like it is and it makes it feel all...wrong! Just. Wrong."

"But you don't know if you are?"

She shook her head. "Ridiculous, isn't it? I'm getting myself worked up about something that might not even be an issue. I know I should find out, but I keep putting it off because I don't want to face it. And besides, what would I do? Go to the doctor? That would mean Michael or his dad. Even one of those test things...I'd have to get it from the pharmacy. How long do you think it would be before the whole town knew?"

She wondered what he must think of her. What must be going through his mind as his brow creased and he stared out at the lake. "I'm sorry. I shouldn't have said anything. It's not your problem."

He tightened his arm around her shoulders. "I'm glad you did. We're almost family; we will be soon. I'm glad you told me. I'd like to help."

He was so sweet! "Thanks, Chase, but there's nothing to be done about it."

"Well, I see three options. And I'll be honest, I like the first one the best."

She blew her nose again and looked up at him. "And what would that be?"

He smiled gently. "Talk to Michael about it. Let him do the test and you two decide together."

She shook her head. "I know you're right. That's the right thing to do, but I don't want to face it."

Chase nodded. "So option number two is that you don't face it."

"I don't understand. What do you mean?"

"I mean, do nothing. Don't even think about it. Your wedding is less than a week away now. You forget this, you get married, and if you are pregnant, you'll find out for sure soon enough."

She shook her head. "I see what you mean, but I'd know."

He nodded. "Okay, option number three is the one I like the least; but if you won't go for the others then it seems like this is all you have left."

"What is?"

"Kenzie and I will go get you one of those test kits from the pharmacy."

"You would?"

He nodded. "If that's what you want. But, Megan, I still say you should talk to Michael."

"I know I should! But I don't know what to do! What if I am? How could I not marry him now? And what if I'm not? Then I've put him through all that for nothing!"

Chase shrugged. "You're going to need to figure out what you want to do if you are. And even if you're not, I'm sure he'd rather go through it with you than be left out."

She nodded. That was true. She should be turning to him, not away from him. She didn't know what to say.

Chase smiled gently at her. "You don't need to decide right here this minute. Think about it; just know that you've got options. You're not alone." He narrowed his eyes at her. "You've got Michael, and you've got Kenzie and me, too, okay?"

She nodded again. "Thank you, Chase. Thank you so much."

He shrugged. "That's what friends are for and we're not just friends, we're almost family." He laughed. "Just ask Ethan."

That made her smile. "I don't need to, Uncle Chase."

He grinned. "Where is he this morning, still in bed?"

"Oh, no. He's gone to spend the day with Marcus."

"Marcus? Is he the kid that came from Montana with his mom?"

"Yes. April. Have you met her?"

"Not really. I've seen her around." He smiled. "So has Eddie."

"Oh!" Megan liked Chase's bandmate, Eddie. He was nice.

Chase shrugged. "Hopefully, we'll get them in the same room at some point. For now, though, you've got more important things to think about, and I need to get back."

"I do. We're going to go over to the Boathouse for lunch if you and Kenzie want to come?"

"Maybe. I'll see how she feels. But you come over or call whenever you want, okay? We're here for you."

"Thanks, Chase."

He bent to make a fuss over Ollie then ran back up through the parking lot. Megan mulled it all over as she watched him go. It really shouldn't matter. If she was pregnant she should be ecstatic. It was what she wanted, what they both wanted. Why did she have to be so silly about it?

Ollie pawed at her leg, bringing her back to reality. For now, she needed to forget about it. Enjoy her walk with Ollie, not get herself into a state.

~ ~ ~

Chase ran back through town. He hoped Megan would sort herself out. It didn't make any sense at all to be upset about getting pregnant a week before her wedding. She and Michael were getting married anyway. They wanted babies anyway. He kind of understood though. Kenzie had told him snippets about Megan's life with Adrian. He could understand that she might have some weird hang-ups left over from that. What he couldn't understand was why she didn't want to talk to Michael. That didn't make sense. Michael knew her better than anyone and had helped her though a lot of those hang-ups. He shook his head as he ran on down Main and turned into the square at the resort. It wasn't any of his business. Strange as it was though, it felt like his business. She was a friend. She was almost family. And whatever strange spell it was that Summer Lake cast over people, it had affected him too—he cared!

He slowed his pace as he approached the bakery. He wanted to pick up some brownies for Kenzie. She loved those things. If he could get back and bring her coffee and brownies in bed before she got up…who knew? They might get to stay there all morning.

"Happy Sunday, Chase!" Renée greeted him with a grin as he opened the door.

"Hey, Renée. How're you doing?"

She smiled. "Just great, thanks. Do you notice anything different about the place?"

Chase looked around, though it was obvious what she was talking about. The side wall of the bakery was hung with a big banner that said,

Watch this space! Summer Lake Women's Center coming soon!

He grinned. "Are you getting close?"

She nodded. "We're going to be closed next week while they knock through. By the time we all come back from Vegas, the bakery and the space next door will all be one. We'll have dividing doors right where the banner is, to close off the bakery for business as usual whenever we need to."

Chase smiled. "You're doing a great job. I think the center will be a useful service."

"I hope so. I'm so excited about it."

Chase eyed the sign again.

Renée pushed her hair out of her eyes and groaned. "You don't even need to say it; I know what you're thinking."

"What?" Chase felt guilty, but the name really was quite utilitarian.

"The name?" she asked.

He nodded. "Sorry, but yeah. It's not very imaginative, is it?"

Renée sighed. "I know! But I just can't come up with anything. It should sound friendly, inviting, encouraging. But I have no idea what would work. For the moment, Summer Lake Women's Center it is. Unless there's some imaginative person out there who can come up with something else, then that's what it will stay."

"Sorry, but I'm no use. I have no idea what would be good. I just know that isn't!"

She laughed. "Yeah, me too. But what can I do?"

"Well, you can get me some of those brownies for Kenzie."

Renée smiled. "I can see why she loves you so much. You take the best care of that girl."

Chase grinned. It was still a new feeling to him—to be so in love with his woman, and so happy that the rest of the world could see it. "I do my best."

"You are the best! The best thing that's ever happened to her. I can't wait for you two to get married."

"Neither can I. We'll get there. And you and Gabe will, too."

She nodded. "I know. But there's nothing stopping you. I have to wait for my divorce to finally come through. It feels like it's taking forever."

"Any idea how much longer it will be?"

She shook her head. "Not yet. I just keep my fingers crossed and try not to think about it. One day I'll get a nice surprise."

She turned as the front door opened and Missy walked in. "Morning!"

"Good morning, Miss. Have you come for your last donuts as a free woman?"

Chase laughed and so did Missy. "No," she said. "I'm sure I'll be back for more later in the week." She looked from Renée to Chase. "Neither of you are going to be free for much longer either. You're just jealous that I'm getting married before you!"

Renée laughed. "You got me. I'm not going to argue with you."

"Nor am I," said Chase. "Though I am going to ask you when we can get together to go through the set lists for next weekend. I know you're going to get crazy busy, and I don't want to be the detail that gets overlooked."

"Thanks, hon. I'll be honest. I already had forgotten about that! Are you around at lunchtime? We're going to eat at the resort. If you and Kenzie are coming down I could grab you afterwards?"

He nodded. It seemed as though the reasons for them to come out for lunch were mounting. "I'll have to check with Kenzie, but I think so. I'll call you if not." He took the brownies. "I'd better get going, but I'll see you later, hopefully."

"See you later, hon," said Missy.

"Say hi to Kenzie for me," called Renée.

~ ~ ~

Missy smiled at Renée. "He's a sweetheart, isn't he?"

Renée nodded. "I want to say I wish I had a guy who would buy me chocolates and pastries all the time, but if I ate all the goodies Kenzie does I'd be huge!"

Missy tutted. "You would not!"

Renée laughed. "I would, but I don't care. I am what I am. It's all I ever have been; all I ever will be."

"And all Gabe wants," said Missy with a smile.

She loved the way Renée smiled back. "And that's another reason I wouldn't want a Chase—I already have a Gabe."

"He's good for you. You're good for him."

Renée nodded. "We are. It's funny how we've both come back here and found each other."

Missy smiled. It seemed everyone was coming back here to find their happiness.

"How's Chance?" asked Renée. "I feel as though coming back here gave me him back, too. We were all so close growing up."

"He's doing fine." Missy wished Chance could come back here and find his happiness, like so many others were doing. Not that that was likely to happen. At least he was coming to the wedding though. "He's going to meet us in Vegas on Thursday. I had hoped he would come here first, but he says he can't take the time away."

Renée nodded. "It sounds as though he gets really busy with the cattle. I wish he'd come back here though. I feel as though it did him some good."

"Oh, it did him a lot of good. The two of you helped each other out when he was here, if you ask me." She laughed. "Not that anybody did."

"You're right. I know he helped me enormously. I just hope it did something for him too."

Missy nodded. "It did." She wasn't going to say that talking things through with Renée had helped heal all his wounds, but it had certainly eased his pain in some respects. She just wished there was some way to heal the rift between him and their dad.

"Are you okay?" asked Renée.

Missy nodded. "Yeah. Just thinking about the wedding. Hoping that Chance and my dad might have the same kind of breakthrough that you and Chance did, but knowing that's not going to happen." She shrugged. "Sorry. Anyway, do you have any of those cheesy loaves left? I think I'll take my dad one. He loves them." She'd loaded him up with groceries yesterday, but she knew a cheesy loaf and some doughnuts would bring a smile to his face—and give her reason to check in on him again.

Chapter Six

Pete shut down his laptop and sat back. He didn't need to be working; it was Sunday morning! He didn't know what else to do with himself, though. He'd been up since six. Holly was still sleeping when he got up. Or at least pretending to be—he had a feeling that was more like it. He'd tried to hold her, but she'd rolled away from him. He hadn't felt like lying there staring at her back—or her cold shoulder.

He could take a walk down the beach, see if Jack and Em were around, but that didn't feel right. They were happy, all caught up in the excitement about their baby. They didn't need him bringing his grumpy self into their happy home. Besides, Holly would be pissed at him if he went without her. He shrugged and put his feet up on his desk, steepling his fingers under his chin as he stared out at the lake. He loved the view from his office, he loved the house they'd built. He blew out his cheeks in a sigh. He loved Holly; he just wished she'd understand that the wedding was important to him. He wanted it to be perfect—for her! Perfect didn't just happen out of nowhere. It took planning, organization, hard work. Why didn't she appreciate it? He just didn't get it.

He looked up when he heard her come down the stairs. He could hear her in the kitchen, making coffee. He wanted to go see her, go wrap her in his arms and tell her how much he loved her. But he didn't. He'd learned from experience lately that it wouldn't work. They'd just end up arguing, and that hurt even more. So he stayed put. After a while he heard her talking on the phone—laughing, chatting away, sounding happy. Someone could still make her laugh. He had to smile himself when he heard her say, "Damn you, Berto! You have such a dirty mind!"

Roberto, her visual display manager at the store in LA was a good guy. Pete wondered if he should talk to him. He shook his head. He should be able to figure it out himself, not go talking to her friends about their problems. He heard her say goodbye and hang up. He stood. Call him a sucker for punishment, but he had to try again. He had to try to get through to her.

She didn't even look up when he came into the kitchen. She was sitting at the table with her coffee, tapping away at her cell phone.

"Good morning," he said.

"Morning." She still didn't look up.

"Do you have any plans for today?"

She let out that bitter little laugh that drove him nuts. "I prefer not to plan. I figure you'll tell me what we're going to do."

He shook his head, regretting the decision not to stay in his office and hide. "Holly, that's not fair..."

She laughed. "I couldn't agree more. I don't think it's at all fair that you decide everything and tell me what I'm doing." She finally looked up at him. Her amber-colored eyes flashed, but this time he understood; it was pain, not anger, that he saw in them.

He resisted the urge to snap back at her and instead sat down across the table from her. "I'm sorry you see it like that. I don't mean to tell you what to do. I just..."

"You just have to be in control of everything, to plan everything, to…oh, you know what? Forget it, Pete. There's no point talking about it."

He reached for her hand, but she didn't take hold of his. Instead, she glared at him. "But I want to talk about it. I want to try to make things right."

She snatched her hand away. "Well everything isn't about what you want all the time. What about what I want?"

He sighed. "That's what I'd like to talk about. I want to know what I'm doing so wrong; I want to change it, so that you can have what you want."

Her expression softened slightly. "Do you really? Or do you just want to talk me into seeing things your way? That's how this usually goes. I start out telling you what I want, and you end up telling me why I shouldn't want it, how all this planning is necessary and how your way is best so that's what I should want."

Pete thought about it. He could be pretty determined when he believed he was doing the right thing. That trait of his was a large part of why Phoenix was so successful. "Honestly? I don't know, sweetheart. All I know is that I love you. I want to make you happy, but all I seem to do these days is make you miserable. And that makes me miserable." He held her gaze. "I would never have believed that you and I could be like this. We're constantly either at each other's throats or avoiding each other."

She looked so sad as she reached for his hand. "It's not what either of us signed up for, is it, Bigshot?"

He shook his head. "So how do we change it? How do we get back on track?" He felt relieved now. At least they were talking, acknowledging the problems. Now they could work together to find the solutions. Her next words turned his relief to shock.

"I don't know that we can."

He stared at her, holding her gaze, asking all the questions with his eyes. Since his lips refused to speak the words. She couldn't mean what he thought she did, surely?

He watched a tear escape and roll down her cheek. "Pete, we've been like this ever since you started planning the wedding. We don't laugh anymore; we don't have fun. Hell, we barely even talk, and when we do, it's just to argue. I don't feel heard and you don't feel appreciated. Is that really how you want to live the rest of your life? Because I can tell you right now, it's not how I want to live mine."

"But, sweetheart. We're forever. You and me. I love you. We're getting married—in a month."

There went that bitter little laugh again. "Yeah, and it'd sure screw up your plans if we were to call it off, wouldn't it?"

He felt as though all the air had been knocked out of him. She couldn't seriously mean that? He held her gaze.

"Don't do that!"

"Do what?"

"You know damned well what. Don't look at me like that, with your steely blue gaze, all demanding, all expecting I'll just fall at your feet and be all yes, Pete, no, Pete, whatever you say, Pete. I'm sick of it! I love you, you arrogant prick! But maybe that's not enough."

Pete stared at her in disbelief. "I love you, Holly. How can you say that's not enough? Isn't that all we really need?"

Damn, he wished she'd quit with that laugh!

"I thought it was all we needed, Pete. I really did, but you need so much more. You need a plan, you need to be in control, you need a freaking clipboard! Maybe love just isn't enough— for either of us. And maybe we both need to think on that for a while before you go making any more plans." She stood. "As for today, I plan to go horseback riding. You do whatever the hell you want."

He watched her stalk out of the room, wondering what had just happened.

~ ~ ~

Dan put an arm around Missy's shoulders as they walked down Main toward the resort. "I love you, little Miss Missy," he said with a smile.

She stopped walking and smiled up at him. "I love you more, Dan. Sometimes I wonder if I'm going to wake up one morning and discover that all this was just a dream."

He shook his head. "It is a dream, but it's a dream come true." Sometimes he had to wonder at the things that came out of his own mouth. Missy often told him he was a romantic. Who would ever have guessed? Certainly not him!

She wrinkled her nose at him as they carried on walking. "I never dream in this much detail. It seems like there are still a million details to take care of. I think I got all the flight stuff taken care of with Smoke. He and Jason are going to be hurtling around the skies all day on Thursday and then again on Sunday."

Dan nodded. "I'm glad Leanne and Ryan are going to fly commercial, that's one less headache to figure out."

Missy nodded. "Yeah, I don't know how we could have fit in extra trips to LA."

"Actually I was thinking more about the fur flying if we tried to coop the two of them up in the same small jet for an hour."

"You don't think they'll just get along for the weekend, for your sake?"

Dan shook his head. "I doubt it. I'm more concerned about keeping them away from each other."

Missy sighed. "Like Ben and Charlotte."

Dan nodded. "Yeah. I feel sorry for all of them. I can't imagine what it must be like."

"Me neither." Missy reached up and pecked his cheek. "I'm just glad I found my hero and we got it right the first time. I can't imagine losing you."

"That's okay, you won't ever have to. You're stuck with me. You've promised me forever, and I intend to hold you to that."

"I intend to hold you to it, too."

They'd reached the Boathouse now. Dan smiled when he saw Jack and Emma sitting out on the back deck. "Looks like we're early."

"Good. I want to talk to those two first."

Once they were settled at the table Jack grinned. "Did mom manage to get hold of you, Dan?"

"No, why? Have you talked to her?"

"Yeah, she's so excited. She's excited about the wedding. She's excited about the baby; she's been talking to Lexi and she's thinking about making the move."

"Making the move?" Dan grinned back. "You mean coming to live here?"

Jack nodded. "Yep. Pete and I are about ready to start operations out of the mini-HQ here. Lexi's moving up, Nate's coming after the wedding. Mom's thinking it's time for her to be near her boys—and grandkids."

Dan looked at Missy. He'd taken her and Scot to Texas to meet his mom after they got engaged. He knew Missy loved her, and she and Scot had developed a surprising friendship. Missy said it was because he'd never had a grandmother figure in his life.

She grinned. "We need to start looking for a place for her!"

Emma nodded. "That's what I said."

Jack laughed. "Because neither of you want your mother-in-law coming to live with you?"

Emma slapped his arm. "It's not that and you know it! Your mom would hate to have to stay with any of us. She's used to living her own life—just as much as we are."

Missy nodded. "She's more than welcome if she wants to stay with us for a while, but I can't see her wanting to live with any of us long-term. I'm just excited to go house hunting with her. It'll be a good chance to get to know her better."

Dan looked at Missy, "How would you feel about her staying at our place while we're gone?"

"Of course! If she's ready to move right now, then that makes all kinds of sense."

Dan looked at Jack. "What do you think?"

Jack nodded. "She said she's thinking it's about time, but you know what she's like. That just means she's already thought it over and she wants to do it; she just wants to make sure we're okay with it before she does."

"That's what I think," said Dan. "So if we ask her to stay at our place—to look after it—that will give her chance to be here and get to know the place. It'll give her a reason to be here that's not just about doing what she wants to. You know she's uncomfortable just doing what she wants."

Missy smiled up at him. "You're so smart."

Jack laughed. "Yeah, not bad for a guy who's not supposed to get people."

"She's my mom!"

He looked out at the parking lot where a familiar truck had just pulled up and three people were getting out. "Jack, didn't you say Nate was coming up here after the wedding?"

"Yeah. We're done with all the outstanding projects for a while. HQ is here now, and I want him working on Four Mile. Why?"

"Because there's a guy who looks an awful lot like him, who's headed this way."

Missy followed his gaze. "That is Nate. It must be. He's with Smoke and Laura."

"What the…?"

Jack grinned and held up a hand to greet them. "Nate! What are you doing here?"

Nate laughed as he approached the table. "People keep saying that to me! How about, Hi, Nate. What a nice surprise."

Emma laughed. "Hi, Nate. What a nice surprise!"

Nate leaned down to kiss her cheek. "Hey, Em. Good to see you. I knew I could rely on you."

Dan had to laugh as Jack scowled. "Hands off my wife!"

Nate laughed as he straightened up. "Don't worry, boss! I'm just showing affection to the only person who's been pleased to see me since I arrived."

"When did you arrive?" asked Jack.

"Last night," said Smoke. "He landed on our doorstep after dark and expected bed and board. We've brought him down here to see Ben—he's the one who provides those."

"See what I mean?" asked Nate. "Nobody wants me." He sat down next to Missy who patted his arm.

"Aww, poor Nate. We all want you. We're very happy you're here."

Nate winked at her. "Thanks, Miss. At least you still love me." He grinned at Dan. "Just unlucky for me that the best man got to you first."

Dan laughed. He liked Nate.

"Sorry. Nate. You never stood a chance," said Missy.

He shrugged. "Story of my life."

Dan looked out at the parking lot again. Here came Kenzie and Chase. He looked at Missy, "Did you say you were going to bring the lists of songs you wanted the band to play?"

"Oh, crap! I forgot!"

He smiled. "I'll go get them if you like?"

She shook her head. "You stay. I'll go."

"But we don't have the car here. I don't want you walking back by yourself."

Missy laughed. "It's lunchtime, Dan. Not midnight!"

"I know, but still."

"I'll tell you what. After we've eaten, you can walk me back. Then I'll come back in the van to talk to Chase and go on up to see my dad. I got him some goodies from the bakery this morning. I want to drop them off and check in on him."

Dan nodded. "Okay. Whatever you say. I'll come with you if you like?"

She shook her head. "You wanted to work this afternoon."

He nodded, he did. But she was his priority.

She smiled. "And you might want to call your mom, too? Ask her about staying at the house while we're gone."

"Yeah. I'll do that."

As the others arrived, they needed to pull two of the picnic benches together. Michael and Megan arrived shortly after Kenzie and Chase. Megan seemed troubled about something, but Kenzie was doing her best to keep her chatting and smiling. Gabe and Renée came next. Dan watched as Missy chatted with Renée. He liked that the two women seemed to be getting closer after Chance's visit. Their family history tied them together, but Missy said they'd never been close. It seemed like that was changing now, though. Pete came wandering out of the bar after they'd already started to eat. Holly wasn't with him.

"Hey, partner," called Jack. "I didn't think you were coming? Are you going to eat?"

Pete shook his head. Dan had never seen him look so miserable. "Nah. I just came out to say hi. I'm hanging at the bar with Ben."

So Ben was here, but not coming to join them either? Dan didn't like that. Missy had said that she'd talked to Ben and he wasn't going to avoid them anymore. This sure felt like he was avoiding them. He couldn't imagine how it would feel to be Ben. Not to be with the woman he loved. He felt bad that his and Missy's happiness was causing Ben so much sadness. Charlotte and Renée had been the two wedding guests he wasn't sure about. Things with Renée had worked out just fine since she and Chance had already made their peace. Charlotte and Ben? Dan doubted they would ever make their peace. There was only one way Ben would be happy, and that could never happen because Charlotte was already married to someone else.

"Where's Holly?" asked Missy.

Pete scowled at her. Dan himself wished that she didn't always have to be so forthright.

"She's gone horseback riding apparently. I thought she might have come for lunch."

That wasn't good, that he didn't even know what she was doing for lunch. Everyone made plans to meet up here. All the couples. Dan rubbed his hand over his cheek. That was Holly's problem with Pete though, wasn't it? She was sick of his plans.

"Looks like she's coming now," Emma said. She waved her fork toward the parking lot where Holly was getting out of her car and another woman climbed out of the passenger seat. Dan chewed the inside of his cheek. He knew her name. Missy had introduced them. She'd grown up here, too. She was friends with Chance and Gabe and Renée. Lily! That was it.

He watched Holly and Lily approach. They were chatting and laughing as they walked across the parking lot. It was the first time Dan had seen Holly smile in weeks. He looked up as Pete turned on his heel and went back inside. Dan felt bad for him. She certainly never seemed to smile at Pete anymore.

Holly looked around them. "Well, hello! Why are you all looking at me like that?"

"Because Pete was out here looking for you," said Emma. "He just went back inside."

Holly shrugged. "Well, I'm here to have lunch with my friends." She plonked herself down on the end of the bench.

Lily looked around apologetically. "Hi!"

Everyone greeted her. "I'm glad you're here," said Renée. "I want to talk to you about the center."

As they started to chat about riding and horsemanship lessons, Dan looked at Missy. "Do you think Pete's okay?" he asked.

Missy shook her head. "No. I'm going to go talk to him."

Dan nodded. "How about while you do that, I'll walk home and bring the song lists and your van back?"

He loved the way she smiled up at him. "You really are my hero! Will you bring that cheesy loaf and the doughnuts for my dad?"

"Yep. They're in the pantry, right?"

She laughed. "Unless Scotty found them."

Dan stood. "I'll see you back here in a little while then."

Missy got up and placed her hands on his shoulders as she reached up to plant a kiss on his lips. "Thanks."

He watched her make her way across the deck and into the bar. She cared so much about her friends. He loved that about her.

Chapter Seven

Missy pulled onto her dad's street. She was even more worried about Pete and Holly now than she had been. She'd never seen Pete so defeated; in fact, she'd never seen him defeated at all before—about anything. Yet there he was claiming that the best thing that had ever happened to him—his relationship with Holly—might be over. Missy just couldn't believe that. They were made for each other. It was plain to anyone with eyes in their head! Pete had almost messed them up before they even got started with his insistence on sticking to his stupid plan. Why couldn't he see that he was making the same mistake again? And why couldn't Holly see it? Why wasn't she bringing him back to reality? Reminding him what was most important, instead of taking it so personally and making matters even worse. She pulled up in front of her dad's house. That was easy to say as an outsider. What woman wouldn't take it personally if her fiancé was ignoring her and her wishes in the planning of their wedding?

She shrugged to herself and reached in the back for the loaf and the doughnuts. She wanted to bang their heads together! All she could do was hope that maybe a weekend in Vegas with all their friends, watching her and Dan and Michael and Megan get married would remind them both of what was really important.

"Hey, Dad! It's that pesky burglar again!" she called as she let herself in the back door. "Dad?" she called when he didn't reply. He must have the TV on too loud again. She could hear it murmuring away to itself in the living room. She went through. He was sitting in his chair staring at the box. Something wasn't right. She knew it immediately.

"Dad!"

He turned his head toward her slowly. "I'm not right, Miss. I feel a bit off." He didn't sound right.

She knelt down beside his chair, her heart hammering in her chest. "What is it? What do you feel?"

He gave her a puzzled look. "Confused."

Oh crap! One side of his mouth was moving fine, but the other seemed to be having trouble keeping up. She thought she knew what was going on. She grabbed the phone and dialed 911. She told the dispatcher she thought her dad was having a stroke. At least that was one good thing about living in a small town, the ambulance would be here in a few minutes. The hospital might be half an hour away, but at least he'd be under the care of the awesome paramedics on his way there.

She hung up. "Can you lift your arms up, Dad?"

He gave her a puzzled look and lifted his arms. His left arm came up above his head, his right reached shoulder height before drifting back down, causing his expression to become fearful.

"Talk to me," she said. "Tell me when I'm getting married."

"Next week."

The words came out okay, but the right side of his mouth didn't move in sync with the left. At least it moved.

"You think I had a stroke?"

She nodded. "Maybe. Just a little one. You'll be fine." How she hoped she was telling the truth! "So smile, would you?" It was another test. And it confirmed what she feared. The left side of his face was his usual self, the smile gruff, but there. The right side drooped, but there was some movement. It gave her hope; she knew the effects of a stroke were reversible if they were caught in time. "When did you start feeling like this?" she asked.

"Just right now. Before you came."

A wave of relief rushed through her at the sound of a siren. Thank God! She knew every minute counted with a stroke. She smiled at her dad. "That's good. You're going to be just fine."

"I don't need an ambulance," his speech was worse now. He tried to stand but his right leg gave out and he slumped back down in the chair.

"Yes, you do! I'm going to let them in. You stay there." She rushed to the front door to let the paramedics in.

Not five minutes later she was in the van following the ambulance to the hospital. She kept trying to calm herself. Thank God she'd gone to see him! He'd be fine. He had to be. She dug her cell phone from her purse, grateful for the first time for the hands free system Dan and Scot had rigged up in the van for her. She called Dan.

"Hey, beautiful," he answered.

"Dan can you come to the hospital? I think my dad's had a stroke. They're taking him in an ambulance; I'm going after him."

"I'll be right there. I'll get Jack to come hang with Scot."

"Thanks, honey." She loved him all the more in that moment. With Dan there was no panicking, no asking a million questions. Just straight down to business. He'd make sure Scot was okay and he'd be there for her. She realized she was gripping the steering wheel tight as she drove. She needed to make another call, too. Maybe there was no need, but it wasn't a risk she was prepared to take. It wasn't her place to decide what her brother might want. She hit Chance's number and waited.

"Hey, little Miss. This is a nice surprise."

"Chancey." She swallowed around the lump in her throat. She was probably overreacting.

"What is it? What's wrong, honey?"

"It's Dad. It might not be anything. But I think he just had a stroke. He's in an ambulance. I'm following him to the hospital. He's probably going to be just fine. I don't want to worry you, but I had to tell you." She swallowed again. "You just never know, and I…" she bit back a sob. She felt stupid. He was going to be fine; she was pretty sure of it, but just the thought that he might not be….

"I'll get there," said Chance.

"It might be nothing, though. I don't want to worry you."

"Yeah, but Miss, we both know you had to call me. Because…well, what if he's not okay? You drive. I'll figure out a way to get there as fast as I can. Is Dan with you? Are you all right?"

"He's on his way."

"Good. I'll call you back when I know what I'm doing."

"Thanks, Chance, bye." As she hung up and concentrated on following the ambulance down the two-lane highway she knew she'd done the right thing. Her dad was going to be just fine, she had to believe that. But she'd never forgive herself if he wasn't and she hadn't called Chance right away and at least given him the option to get there if he wanted to.

When she made it to the hospital she rushed in through the doors and straight to the desk. She was relieved to see a familiar face sitting there. She'd gone to school with Rachel.

"Hi, Missy. You'll have to wait here. They've taken him straight through. Doctor Morgan was here this afternoon visiting some of his patients. He's gone in with him."

Thank God for that! She knew her dad would be a lot more comfortable with Doc Morgan than someone he didn't know. "Thank you."

Rachel smiled. "It sounds as though you did great. Time is one of the most important factors with a stroke."

Missy nodded. She hoped so.

"The waiting room is empty; someone will be with you as soon as there's any news."

Missy went to the waiting room and sat down. Then stood up and began to pace. Why was it always like that when something bad happened? You had a mad rush and then had to sit around and wait for hours. Her phone rang and she fished it out of her purse.

"Hi, Dan. Is everything okay?"

"Everything's fine here. Jack's on his way to get Scot. I'm on my way to you. Are you okay? Have you talked to Chance?"

"Yeah, I called him. I had to Dan."

"I know, Miss. I was going to call him myself, but I wanted to ask you first."

"Ask me what?"

"If you want me to send Smoke to get him?"

"Oh, yes! Yes, please! If he can. Chance was going to try to figure out the fastest way to get here."

"Well, I can't think of anything faster than sending Smoke up to get him. I'll call them both, okay?"

"Thanks, Dan."

"It's going to be all right, Miss."

"I hope so. I just hate this waiting."

"I'll be there as soon as I can. I love you."

Missy had to swallow the lump in her throat again. "And I love you, so much."

Once she'd hung up she swiped at her eyes feeling a little ridiculous. She didn't need to go making a fuss.

~ ~ ~

Dan hung up with Missy and dialed Smoke. It rang and rang and then went to voicemail.

"This is Smoke. You know what to do."

"Smoke, it's Dan. Can you call me back as soon as you get this? Missy's dad's been taken to the hospital. I'm hoping you can fly up to Montana to get Chance. Call me back?"

He hung up. He knew Smoke and Laura had been hoping for a couple of quiet days together before the wedding, but this was an emergency.

It was only a couple of minutes before his phone rang.

"Hey, Dan. Where is he? When do I need to be there?"

"I'm guessing the Bozeman airport will be the closest place you can land Papa Charlie, and I haven't set anything up with him yet, because I didn't know if you'd be up for it."

"Of course I am. How's Missy's dad? What's happened?"

"She doesn't know yet. She thinks he's had a stroke. They've taken him in and she's just waiting to hear. I'm on my way there."

"Okay, well do you want to give me Chance's number and I'll figure things out with him?"

"Yeah." Dan told him the number from memory. "Give it ten minutes before you call him though? I'll call him myself and tell him to expect you."

"Great. Talk to you later."

Dan hung up and called Chance.

"Dan?"

"Yeah, it's me. No news yet. I just wanted to let you know that Smoke, the pilot, is going to call you to arrange to come get you."

"Oh. Wow. Great. Thanks."

"Is that okay?"

"It's great! I was just checking flights and there's no way to get there before tomorrow afternoon."

"Well, there is now. I'm going to hang up because I'm almost to the hospital. Expect a call in the next few minutes. You and Smoke can figure where and when is best for him to come get you."

"Thanks, Dan."

"No, worries. I'll see you tonight. We'll call you if there's any news before then."

"Okay. See you later."

Dan found Missy pacing in the waiting room. She flew toward him and he wrapped his arms around her. "No news?"

She shook her head. "It's frustrating as hell! There's hardly anyone around since it's Sunday afternoon. Rachel on the front desk is getting sick of me, and she's about to go home soon anyway."

Dan nodded. "I'm sure he's going to be fine."

She nodded. "I think so, too. It's just that I wish someone would come and tell me that! Apparently Michael's dad is here, so he's with him."

"They will, as soon as there's anything to tell. Right now they're better in there with him."

"I know. I'm just impatient. Did you talk to Chance?"

"Yeah, I put him in touch with Smoke and they're going to figure it out between them."

"Thanks, Dan. It's probably wrong to bring him all this way. Especially when he was coming on Thursday anyway, but I just couldn't...I hate the thought of..."

She didn't need to say it; he understood her fear. He hugged her close to his chest. "I know, Miss. It's better to get him here for this, than to risk him not being here."

She nodded. "That. Yes."

~ ~ ~

Chance hung up the phone and went into his bedroom. He opened his bag and threw in the suit he had ready for the wedding. He wouldn't be coming back before next weekend; he was sure of that. He'd need to take everything. He knelt down and pulled out the wedding gift from under the bed. He didn't want to forget that! His mind was racing. His dad was going to be okay by the sounds of it. He had to be! Maybe he didn't need to go at all, but he was grateful Missy had called him. What if she hadn't and the old man had…Nah. He wasn't going to think about that. He was just going to get his shit together and go talk to the hands. He had a good team. He knew he could leave Brody in charge, no worries. That had been the plan anyway while he was away for the wedding. This was just moving things forward a few days. He'd call Mason and Shane on his way to the airport. Let them know the score. And that was it. He closed up his bag and looked around. He had everything. And what he didn't have wouldn't have to matter.

He heard a knock on the front door of the cabin. Who the hell could that be? He went to open it and found Shane and Cassidy standing there grinning at him.

"What are you guys doing here?"

Shane grinned. "We were out riding this morning. We're headed to the Riverside for a late lunch and came to see if you want to join us for a beer and a burger? I would have come right on in, but the princess here says that's rude of me."

Chance stared at them. "I can't, I've gotta go."

Shane laughed. "Now that is rude!"

Cassidy picked up that something was wrong. "Got to go where, Chance? What's going on?" she asked.

"My dad's had a stroke. I need to get to the airport."

"Oh, shit! I'm sorry, dude. Let us take you."

"Are there any flights?" asked Cassidy. "Have you checked?"

"There's one coming to get me. My brother-in-law sent his pilot buddy."

"Great. Well, at least let us take you?" asked Shane. "There's no point leaving your truck at the airport until you come back."

Cassidy nodded. "You can't even know when you'll be back. It's your sister's wedding next weekend, isn't it?"

He nodded.

"Is there any news on how your dad is yet?"

"Not yet. It might not be that bad. But I want to be there. You know?"

Cassidy hugged him and for a moment it felt good to know that someone cared. "Of course you do," she said. "Now let's get going. Have you got everything?"

He nodded. "Everything I'm taking."

"Come on then," Shane walked into the cabin and grabbed his bag. "Let's get you out of here."

As they approached the airport exit, Cassidy turned to Shane. "Don't go to the main passenger terminal. You need to go to General Aviation."

Shane scowled at her. "Of course you'd know all about that, wouldn't you?"

She laughed. "Get over yourself, cowboy!"

Chance had to laugh at the look on Shane's face. "Anyone want to tell me the story?" he asked.

"Ask Cassidy about her pilot friend," said Shane. "Can you believe she dated a guy named Justin? Just in!"

"I did not date him! Asshole!"

Chance laughed at the two of them as they bickered. They were such a good match—and such good friends to him. He realized now that the drive over here had been a lot less stressful in their company than it would have been by himself. "You can just drop me in front of the building," he told Shane as they approached the building.

"No way!" replied Shane. "You get to fly off in a private jet? I want to at least see it."

Cassidy turned and rolled her eyes at Chance. "Do you want the company while you wait?"

He nodded. He did. And if it gave Shane a kick, then why not.

Shane parked the truck in the little parking lot and they walked over to the building. Once they were inside Cassidy headed for the ladies' room.

Shane grasped his shoulder. "Are you all right?"

Chance nodded. "Yeah. I really do think he's going to be okay. I think this trip is going to be more about making my peace with him. I've kept thinking I'm not ready to, but maybe this is life giving me a kick up the ass, you know? You can only put it off so long before you miss the opportunity completely."

Shane nodded. "Your last trip back to Summer Lake seemed to do you a lot of good. Hopefully this one will, too. I hope your dad's okay."

"Thanks."

Cassidy came back out to join them. She pointed out through the windows. "I saw a Learjet just land. Is that you?"

"Damned if I know." All Chance knew was that he would recognize the pilot, Smoke. He remembered him from Missy's birthday party. The guy had made it pretty clear that the girl with the long dark hair was with him. Chance smiled. They were engaged now—good luck to them!

A few minutes later they walked in through the door from the ramp. Smoke and…Laura, that was her name. She was Dan's cousin. Chance waved and went to greet them.

"Thanks for coming to get me guys." He shook hands with Smoke.

"We're happy to help," said Laura who leaned in for a hug.

Smoke nodded. Chance would guess that he was less happy, though whether that was about coming to get him or the fact that Laura was hugging on him, he wasn't sure. He turned back to Shane and Cassidy. "Thanks for bringing me."

Laura smiled at them and Chance knew he should introduce them all. It felt weird though. There had never been any crossover before between his life here in Montana and the life he'd left behind in Summer Lake.

Shane took matters into his own hands. He smiled back at Laura and tipped his hat. "Pleasure to you meet you. I'm Shane and this is my fiancée, Cassidy."

Smoke extended a hand and shook with Shane. "I'm Smoke and this is my fiancée, Laura."

Watching the four of them, Chance realized that if ever his two worlds did collide, this bunch would probably become fast friends. But right now, what he wanted to do was get out of here. He didn't know how to move the conversation along, so he didn't make any attempt to. "Thanks for bringing me," he said to Shane. "I'll let you know when I'm coming back."

"Let us know when you get there, please," said Cassidy. "We want to know how your dad's doing, okay?" She hugged him again and Shane smiled at him over her shoulder. Once again it felt good to feel like someone cared. He hadn't needed anyone to care—hadn't wanted anyone to—for years. It seemed as though things were changing; he was changing.

Twenty minutes later he was sitting in one of the big club seats in the jet, staring out of the window as they banked to right.

The Gallatins sparkled with snow; he caught a glimpse of the valley beyond them before the plane headed south.

Laura popped her head out of the cockpit. "Are you okay?"

He nodded. "Just fine."

Chapter Eight

Michael put the phone down and looked at Megan.

"What's wrong?" she asked.

"That was Dad. He's at the hospital. They brought Missy's dad in this afternoon. He's had a stroke."

"Oh, no! How bad is it? Is he going to be okay?"

"They hope so. Missy found him almost straight away by the sounds of it and called the ambulance. Time is so important with a stroke."

Megan nodded. "I know. I remember one of the men who used to come into the library where I worked before had a stroke. His face was all droopy afterwards, it was hard to understand him. You could tell he got so frustrated; he knew what he was saying, but his mouth just couldn't form the words properly." She stopped short and looked at Michael. "He couldn't walk very well, either. What do you think? Will Missy's dad be able to even go to the wedding? He's supposed to walk her down the aisle—well, out onto the balcony."

Michael hoped so. He knew how important it was to Missy that her dad should give her away. "I don't know, little one. All we can do is hope and wait for news. If they got to him in time he might be just fine. Missy and Dan are there with him."

"Where's Scotty? We can have him come stay here, if they want."

"I reckon they'll have something sorted out for him if they're both at the hospital already, but I'll call her and check." Megan seemed distraught. "It'll be okay, Meggie."

"I hope so, Michael." She wrung her hands together.

He gave her a puzzled look. She seemed more upset than he would have expected. "Are you okay?"

"Yes, of course."

He wasn't convinced. "Come here and give me a hug, then."

She stepped into the circle of his arms and he held her close, loving the way she felt—the way she always felt—as though she was made to measure, just for him. "Even if her dad can't get there, maybe Ben can do double duty. After he gives you away, he can do the same for Miss."

Megan looked up at him, her eyes big and troubled.

"What?" He knew something was bothering her.

She shook her head and buried her face in his chest. He waited, knowing she'd speak only when, and if, she was ready.

"It means the world to me that Ben is going to walk me down the aisle, but I think Missy would be more likely to ask her brother, if her dad can't."

"Yeah," Michael nodded his agreement and waited some more. He wanted to know what was really troubling her, but she didn't speak again, just squeezed her little arms around his waist and rested her cheek against his chest. She'd tell him when she was ready—he hoped.

~ ~ ~

Missy stood up as Doc Morgan came into the waiting room. Dan stood, too, and put his arm around her shoulders.

"How is he?" she asked.

"He's comfortable. He's going to be okay. You did a good job getting him here so quickly."

A rush of relief swept through her. She'd kept telling herself he was going to be okay, but the nagging doubt had refused to go away. "How bad was it?" she asked. "His face was droopy. He couldn't hold his arm up." She took a deep breath. "His leg gave out on him."

Doc Morgan nodded. "His right side is affected."

"Is that hemiparesis?" asked Dan.

Missy looked at him. He'd been reading up about strokes on his phone while they waited.

Doc Morgan nodded. "The left side of his brain was affected and that is reflected in the right side of his body."

"Will he be able to get back to normal?" asked Missy. She didn't need to know the why. She needed to know the practical.

Doc Morgan's face gave her less hope than his words. "We'll have to wait and see. There's a lot that can be done to regain strength in the affected muscles. He'll have a lot of work ahead of him."

Missy nodded. Her dad wasn't afraid of hard work, especially if it would get him back to normal. She had to ask the selfish question that had been plaguing her while she'd been sitting here waiting. "Will he be able to walk me down the aisle next week?"

Doc Morgan patted her shoulder. "I wouldn't get your hopes too high for that, Missy. He's going to have to learn to control his muscles. It's going to take a little while, but knowing your dad, he'll be quicker than most." He gave her an encouraging smile. "He might have to wheel you down instead of walking."

Missy's heart sank. She knew her dad. He was too damned proud and too damned stubborn. No way on earth would he go down the aisle in a wheelchair!

Dan tightened his arm around her shoulders. "We'll figure something out."

She nodded. "I know. What matters is that he's okay. Can we see him?"

Doc Morgan nodded. "You can. Come on through."

It was a shock to see him looking small and pale in a hospital gown. Missy went straight to him and hugged him. He grunted, but didn't push her off. She leaned back and smiled at him. "I think I might make the most of this, I can hug on you and you can't stop me."

The left side of his mouth lifted in a smile, the right tried to follow. He pushed at her with his left arm. "This side still works just fine," he said. The words were a little slurred, but perfectly understandable.

Missy smiled. "I won't push my luck then! Doc Morgan says you're going to be back to normal in no time."

He frowned at her. "Don't get carried away. I'm not going to be walking for a while."

She knew he was thinking about the same thing she was. "So, you can use a wheelchair if you need to."

His eyebrows came down. "You know better than that, Melissa."

"We don't need to decide right now," said Dan. "Who knows how you'll be by next Saturday."

Missy hated the sadness in her dad's eyes as he said. "I'm not going to be able to do it."

"Don't say that, Dad! We'll work something out."

"I already have."

"What?" she had no idea what he might mean.

"Your brother should do it."

Missy met his gaze. He nodded. "I want him to."

"Well I want you to!" She knew she sounded petulant. She was stunned and pleased that he would even suggest Chance should do it, but didn't every girl want her dad to walk her down the aisle?

He chuckled. "It's not always about want; is it, Melissa. It's about what can happen. What should happen. If I can't then your brother should."

His words reminded her of how Scot had talked about making the best man's speech. She stared back at him. "Well, since you're so keen for Chance to do it, you can talk to him about it later."

His eyes widened. "He's coming?"

She nodded. "He'll be here tonight."

"How? Why?"

She shook her head at him. "How? Smoke flew up to get him. And why? Well, because stubborn as you both are, he loves you. Just like you love him. When I told him what was going on with you, he wanted to come."

Her dad's eyes glistened as he nodded and looked away.

She swallowed that lump that was in her throat so often these days. "I'm going to leave the walking down the aisle thing to you two. You'll have to talk to each other to work it out. And I'm not playing go between. I've got too much else on my plate!"

Her dad looked at Dan. "Are you sure you want to marry her, son? She's a bossy little madam."

Dan laughed. "You know I do."

Missy was surprised to see her dad's eyes close. He drifted off to sleep. She gave Dan a worried look.

He smiled back at her. "It's okay. It's only to be expected. He's going to need lots of rest. I'm surprised he was as with-it as he was. We've probably worn him out."

She nodded. "I guess we should talk to the nurses, see what we can expect."

Doc Morgan popped his head around the door and ushered them out. "I waited. I wanted to get you in to see him while he was awake. You need to be prepared for a long, hard road ahead though."

Missy nodded. "How long do you think he'll need to be in here?"

"At least a few days."

"The average stay in the hospital after a stroke is five point two days," said Dan.

She bit back a laugh. He was so good about researching useful information to reassure her. He just wasn't so good at knowing how much of it was actually comforting.

Doc Morgan smiled at Dan. "I'm afraid averages don't tend to apply in medicine. Every case is unique, just as every patient is."

Dan looked sheepish. "Sorry. Do you think he'll be able to go to the wedding? Will flying be an issue for him?"

Doc Morgan looked at Missy. "It might be too soon for him to travel at all. You need to prepare yourself for that possibility."

Missy's heart sank. She'd been so concerned about him being able to walk, she hadn't considered that just getting to Vegas might be too much for him.

"It'll only be about an hour's flight time each way in the jet," said Dan. "Maybe less. I'll have to ask Smoke."

Doc Morgan nodded. "We'll have to see how he gets on this week. I don't want to make any promises. And I don't want you to get your hopes up, okay?" He put a hand on Missy's shoulder.

She nodded. Her heart was heavy. Not having him walk her down the aisle was one thing—getting married without him being there? She didn't know if she would even want to!

They went back to the waiting room. Smoke was going to bring Chance to the little airfield out here. He and Laura were going to drive him over to the hospital and then he could ride home with Missy tonight.

Dan closed the door behind them; there was no one else around. He wrapped her in a hug. "It'll be okay, Miss."

She looked up into his eyes. He was such a good man. He might not have many words, but he was such a comforting presence. When he said it would okay, she believed him—even though she didn't see how. "What are we going to do though?"

"Wait and see, just like Doc Morgan said. That's all we can do."

"But Dan, honey. There's so much to think about."

He cocked his head to one side. Clearly not understanding.

"I don't mean with the wedding." She couldn't even make herself think about that just yet. "I mean with him going home. What's he going to do? He can't be by himself when he can't walk, or use his arm properly, can he?"

"Ah. I hadn't even thought of that." Dan rubbed his hand over the stubble on his cheek. "He's not going to want to stay anywhere else though, is he?"

She shook her head. "No way! You heard him when we talked about moving him closer to town. The only way he'll leave that house is in a box!"

"That's not going to happen for a long time yet."

"I hope not, but he can't be out there by himself." She wrinkled her nose. She hated the idea, but now she thought about it, it seemed like the only solution. "Do you think we need to cancel the honeymoon?"

"No!" Dan shook his head vigorously. "No. you can't give up your honeymoon to go and take care of him. He'd hate that! And be honest, the two of you would drive each other nuts inside a day. You're too much alike. You can't be the one to take care of him."

"Who else is going to? I'm all he's got. It's not like Chance could do it, even if he could stay for a while."

Dan shook his head. "We need to hire someone. That's the only way to do it."

Missy stared at him. She couldn't imagine her dad letting some stranger take care of him. That'd be worse than letting her do it.

Dan smiled. "We don't need to decide right now; we just need to consider the options. He's no doubt going to have an opinion about what he wants, and we need to be prepared to tell him what alternatives we see."

Missy nodded and blew out a big sigh. There was so much to think about!

~ ~ ~

Dan started when the waiting room door opened. Missy jumped up when she saw Chance standing there.

"Hey, honey. How are you holding up?"

"I'm fine. Dad's doing okay. He's sleeping. He's going to be all right, Chance."

Chance nodded. "Good." He turned to Dan. "Thanks for getting me here."

"No worries. We want you here."

"So what's the score with the old man?"

Missy explained everything she knew and told him about the weakness on his right side. Dan knew she was holding it together well, but at some point she'd need to let go. That point came at Chance's next question.

"So is he going to be all right for the wedding?"

Missy burst into tears. Dan held back, knowing this was a moment Chance needed to share with her. "I don't think so!" she wailed. "He can't walk very well and he says he won't go down the aisle in a wheelchair."

Chance hugged her to him and stroked her hair. "He's a tough old bastard, honey. He might be back on his feet in a week."

She shook her head into his chest. "I don't think so, Chancey. Doc Morgan doesn't even think he'll be able to go!"

Chance looked at Dan over her shoulder.

Dan shook his head sadly. He had to admit that Doc Morgan hadn't sounded too hopeful. "He said we'll have to wait and see, but no matter how he is, flying so soon may not be the best idea."

Chance kept on stroking Missy's hair. "We'll figure something out, honey. Maybe I can drive him over there."

Dan shrugged. "I don't know which would be worse. It won't take long in the plane; it'd be more like four hours on the road."

Chance nodded. "Either way, we'll get him there, Miss. And he'll get over the wheelchair thing if he has to. He'll get you down the aisle."

She shook her head again. "He says you'll have to do it."

Chance froze. "He said that?"

"Yep, so you know how adamant he must be that he's not going to."

Dan watched the struggle on Chance's face. He knew some of the history between Chance and his dad, but not all of it. He could tell that there was pain, confusion, and something else... perhaps the hint of a smile in there as Chance worked through his reaction to that news.

He pulled himself together. "And you're crying that you might have to walk down with the aisle with me?" he asked. "Thanks, lil sis!"

She pulled back and looked up at him with a smile. "Course I am! If you do it, no one will even notice my dress. Everyone will be looking at you! The mysterious Montana man will steal my thunder!"

Dan smiled as the two of them laughed together. "Don't worry, I don't want to steal anything. You can imagine how eager I am to walk out in front of a bunch of people to give my sister away." He grinned at Dan. "If it were up to me, I'd sell you. I'm pretty sure this guy would pay whatever I asked."

Missy slapped his arm and Dan laughed. "Damned straight, I would. Just name your price."

"Nah, you can have her. Seeing as you're such a good guy."

Dan beamed at that. He and Chance had become friends, and that meant a lot to him. Having Chance's approval of his relationship with Missy meant even more.

"Can I go in and see him?" asked Chance.

"I think so," said Missy. "We've been waiting out here for you because he was sleeping. Let's go to the nurse's station and ask."

~ ~ ~

It was late by the time Missy pulled up outside the house. Chance had ridden with her and they'd followed Dan back down Route Twenty. She'd called Emma to say they'd pick Scot up, but Em had insisted that she and Jack would bring him home. Missy smiled; she knew her friend was looking out for her, wanting to save her from driving any more than she had to. But she also knew that Em would take any opportunity she got to see Chance. She'd had a crush on him since she'd first met him when they were eight and Chance was twelve.

She showed Chance to his room and came back down to the kitchen. He joined her there a few moments later and she opened the fridge and handed him a beer. "I'm guessing you need one of these."

He took it with a smile. "Thanks. I'm guessing you do, too?"

She nodded and pulled out another for herself.

Chance peered into the fridge and laughed. "I never noticed before. I knew Dan lined 'em up with all the labels to the front, but he keeps them in alphabetical order, too?"

Missy did a double take as she looked at the bottles. "Well, damn! So he does. I'd never noticed either. God, I love that man!"

Dan appeared in the kitchen doorway. "I hope you're talking about me, when you say that?" His eyes twinkled as he looked at her.

She went to him and slid her arms around his waist. "You know it, hero! I don't know what I would have done without you today—or any day for that matter."

He closed his arms around her and smiled down at her. "Good thing you'll never have to find out then, isn't it?"

She nodded. She couldn't imagine her life without him anymore.

Chance raised his bottle to them. "You two deserve each other. You're the oddest couple I've ever met, but you're one of the best."

Missy wrinkled her nose at him. "Only one of the best? Who do you know that's any better than us?"

He narrowed his eyes at her with a smile. "No one better. I've just been surprised lately; a couple of my buddies have found their perfect women. Guys I'd never have expected to settle down with anyone. I thought you two were unique, but now I'm realizing that this love thing can strike anywhere."

Missy couldn't resist. "See, it might even strike you some day."

Oh, why had she done that? His eyes were still narrowed, but his smile was gone. His lips pressed together into a thin line. "I think it's like lightning. Doesn't strike in the same place twice."

"Sometimes it does though, Chance."

He shrugged.

She was relieved when the doorbell sounded. She smiled at him as she went to get the door. "Scot's going to be pleased to see you. He's growing up; I think you'll be surprised."

Chapter Nine

Monday morning saw Ben running around like crazy—as usual. Well, maybe even more than usual. He found that the busier he kept himself, the less time his mind had to dwell on things. The less chance he had to think about next weekend—about seeing Charlotte again. He needed to keep his mind the hell away from her. No matter what his heart had to say. She was the past.

He drained the last of his coffee and looked up when a head poked around the door to the bar. They weren't open yet. He smiled when he realized who it was.

"Hey, Nate. How was the cabin?"

"Awesome! Thanks, Ben. I don't know about house hunting. I think I want to stay right there!"

Ben laughed. "Sorry, bud. Through the winter I could probably offer you a deal on the place, but we're coming into busy season. I can make more in a week on that place than you would pay for a month on a rental house."

Nate nodded. "That figures. I appreciate you letting me have it for the week though. I doubt I'll find anywhere like that to actually live in."

Ben thought about it. "Come see me this afternoon. We'll go through the available rentals. I can't think off the top of my head what there is right now. If I don't have anything, I'll put you in touch with Austin. He usually has a couple of nice rental properties."

"Thanks. What are you up to today? Want to hang with me?"

Ben laughed. "You're kidding? I'd love to, but busy doesn't even come close. In fact, I have to run right now, but come find me later, yeah?"

Nate nodded. "Will do. You got any recommendations for what a guy like me can do with himself around here?"

Ben paused. He knew Nate didn't want to make a nuisance of himself. All the people he knew here had things of their own going on. Pete and Holly were hardly going to entertain him, Jack and Emma were at her gramps' today, he knew that much. He'd stayed with Smoke and Laura his first night in town, but they'd flown up to Montana yesterday. Ben knew they were long overdue some alone time. He shrugged. "Everyone's kind of busy this week. There's a lot going on."

Nate grinned. "That's okay. I don't need a babysitter, just wondering what there is to do. I can pretend I'm on vacation. What do people come here to do?"

"In that case, you can rent a boat, go out on the lake. Take a hike, there are maps at the front desk." A thought struck him and he smiled. "Go horseback riding. That might be your best bet. The stables are usually quiet on a Monday morning."

Nate grinned. "Now there's an idea! I haven't ridden for years. I might just do that. Thanks, Ben."

"No worries. Have fun. I'll catch up with you later. I've got to run." He had a long list of jobs he needed to get done today, but first on his list was nothing to do with work. He wanted to stop in to see Missy. Jack and Emma had come into the bar for a drink after they'd dropped Scot back home last night. It had really shaken Ben to realize that Missy had been at the hospital all afternoon with her dad and he hadn't even heard about it. Not so long ago he would have been the first person she'd call. He'd put a bit of distance between her and Dan and himself over the whole Charlotte thing. He needed to set that right. Their friendship was more important than his...his...whatever it was he was doing.

He stopped in at the bakery to pick up doughnuts and brownies. He knew Missy stocked up on them whenever she could, and her dad loved those brownies, too. He'd get some extra for her to take to him. Hopefully, he'd be up to eating them.

"Hi, Ben," called April when he stepped into the bakery. "I'll be right with you." She was serving a couple of tourists.

He watched her chat with them, load up their doughnut box, point out the brownies, and sell them a couple of sandwiches that they hadn't known they needed. He smiled. She was good. She was settling in really well and was a real asset. Not that she would be an asset to him for much longer. When Renée leased the bakery from him, April was going to work for her. She'd still be here, but she'd also be helping to run the women's center. That made sense to Ben. She'd been through so much herself, she had a lot to offer to other women needing help. Just as importantly, Ben had the feeling it would be good for her. For the first time in her life she'd be in a position to help others, not just be in need of help herself.

Once the tourists had gone, she smiled at him. "What can I get for you?"

"Doughnuts, brownies, a box of each, please."

She laughed. "Are you hungry this morning?"

He laughed with her. "They're not for me; well, not all of them. I'm going to see Missy."

"How's her dad? Megan told me what had happened when she came to pick Ethan up last night."

Ben shrugged. "I only heard about it from Jack and Emma. It sounds as though he's going to be okay, though."

"Good. How's Missy? It must be a shock right before her wedding. Michael seemed to think her dad might not be up to going; that'd be awful."

Ben stared at her. He hadn't even thought about that. He knew how much Missy wanted her dad to give her away. "It would, wouldn't it?" he said. He paid her for the pastries.

"Well, give her my love, would you? And let me know if there's anything I can do. She's been so kind to me. She didn't need to invite me to the wedding. She hardly even knows me."

Ben smiled. "Yes, she does. You're one of us now. You may as well get used to it. Missy is awesome, and she likes you. You're a friend—to all of us. So don't forget it."

"I'm just finding it hard to get used to. I haven't really had friends before."

"Well, you've got a whole gang of us now."

The smile on her face as he left told him how much that meant to her. He was glad she'd come here. Glad Chance had thought that the lake would be a good place for her. He wondered if she knew that Chance was here.

When he got to Missy and Dan's house Missy looked worn out. Her bright smile when she opened the front door couldn't hide it.

"Hey, bud. I came to see how you're doing." He held out the boxes of goodies. "And to bring you these. I'll go, if you're busy."

She wrinkled her nose at him. "Don't you even dare think about leaving, Ben Walton!"

He grinned. That was his Missy. "Good to see you've still got your bossy boots on."

She hugged him. "I always will with you. Now come on in. You're making the place look untidy standing there on the doorstep like that."

He followed her through to the kitchen. "Dan's in the shower. Scot's gone to school. There's no reason for him to stay home. Chance has gone for a walk. Do you want a coffee, and we'll make a start on those doughnuts?"

He smiled. "Sounds good to me. How's your dad?"

She nodded. "I called the hospital just now. They said he's doing fine. Better than you might expect, in fact. They're keeping him in for more tests and for observation."

"Did they give you any idea how long for?"

She shrugged. "They don't know themselves. It will depend on how he does, what the tests show. The last thing they want to do is to let him come home and have it happen again."

Ben nodded. "Will he be okay for the wedding?"

She gave him a sad look. "I don't know." She sniffed and turned away.

He put a hand on her shoulder. "I hope so, bud."

She nodded, but didn't turn around. "Me too. He won't be walking me down the aisle though. He says he won't do it in a wheelchair. That Chance will have to do it."

"Oh, Miss. I'm sorry."

She turned around and smiled at him. "It is what it is, right? He's still here, that's what matters."

He nodded. "But I know how much that meant to you."

She shrugged. "It can't be helped. I've just got to get on with it. I've got more important things to worry about, like what we're going to do when he comes home."

"What's he going to need?"

"I don't know yet, but he's not going to be able to be by himself. He's going to need help. I know he won't want to come stay here. He won't want to leave his house, but I don't see how he'll be able to stay there."

Ben rubbed his hands over his face as he thought about it. "Do you want me to put you in touch with Alice?"

Missy stared at him. "Alice? Oh, yeah! The woman who stayed with Joe after his fall. Is she still around?"

"No, she went back to San Francisco, but she keeps in touch now and then. She was awesome with Joe. I don't know if she'd want to come back up here, but if she does she'd be perfect."

Missy smiled. "A woman who could keep Joe smiling while he was housebound has to be a miracle worker."

"She is. She's awesome. Your dad's got plenty of room. She could live in."

"Yeah, if you could give me her number, that'd be great."

"I'll do better than that. I'll give her a call and find out if she's interested." He smiled. "She had a soft spot for me, so if I ask her nicely…"

Missy laughed. "Everyone has a soft spot for you, because you're such a good guy."

"You still think so?"

"Why wouldn't I?"

He shrugged. "I haven't been a very good friend lately, have I? I was avoiding you and Dan because of the Charlotte thing, and I wasn't there for you with your dad."

She hugged him. "It's not like that. I would have called you, it's just that things got crazy. You're always there for me, I know that. Just like I'm always there for you. That's never going to change."

He smiled. He felt better now. "Good. I just wanted to make sure."

Dan came running down the stairs. "Are you ready to go, Miss? Oh. Hi, Ben."

"Hey, Dan." He pointed at the doughnuts. "I brought breakfast and an apology. I'm sorry I've been hiding from you guys. I wanted to let you know that I'm here for anything you need."

Dan smiled. "Thanks." He looked at Missy and then back at Ben. "I feel bad about the wedding thing."

Ben shrugged. "Don't. There's no need." He smiled at Missy. "It is what it is, and there are more important things to worry about."

She smiled back and nodded. "That's right."

"Well, I'd better get going. I've got a full day and I'm sure you want to get going to the hospital?"

Missy nodded. "We're going to leave as soon as Chance gets back."

~ ~ ~

Chance wandered down Main. He hadn't wanted to sit around waiting while Missy and Dan got ready. He was too antsy for that. To Missy's surprise he'd taken himself out for a walk. Normally he hid out at her house whenever he came back to the lake. This town had too many familiar faces, too many memories lurking around every corner. He didn't want to bump into any of them. He felt different this time though. He was starting to think about making his peace with them—the memories at least. He wasn't so worried about the faces.

He'd walked the old road out by the river. That had been tough. It had been one of Chloe's favorite walks. He'd done it though. And had actually smiled at memories of laughing with her as they walked. Chasing her, catching her, kissing her. Those memories were sweet.

He knew now that his last visit here had done him good. And he knew that Renée was largely responsible for that. He decided to stick his head into the bakery and see if she was around. Even if she wasn't, April would be there. He wanted to make sure she was settling in okay.

April looked terrified when he walked into the bakery. "Does he know I'm here?" she asked.

It took him a minute to understand. She was talking about her ex, Guy. The asshole that Chance had brought her here to escape. "No. Don't worry. I'm not here about Guy. I'm here because of my dad."

"Oh!" Her relief was almost palpable. "Sorry. I must seem awful. I didn't even think. I'm sorry about your dad."

"He's going to be okay."

"Good."

"How are you settling in? How's Marcus doing?"

Her smile lit up her face. "He's doing wonderfully. He actually likes school here, if you can believe that! He used to hate it up there. And he's making friends; he and Ethan are really close. This was definitely a good move for him. Thank you for bringing us here, Chance. You've changed our lives."

He nodded. He didn't know what to say to that.

"How is everyone up there?"

That was easier to talk about. "Did you hear that Mason and Gina got engaged?"

"Oh, that's wonderful news." She smiled, but he could tell there was a touch of sadness in there, too. She'd dated Mason years ago.

He hurried on. "And if you can believe it, Shane just got engaged, too."

She stared at him open mouthed. "Shane, as in, Shane Remington? Mason's little brother, Shane? Ladies' man of the valley, Shane?" She laughed. "No, I don't believe it!"

Chance laughed with her. "I don't blame you. I've watched him and Cassidy get to know each other and get together, and I still find it hard to believe. But at the same time, when you see them together, you get it. They're two of a kind, made for each other."

"Wow! Cassidy Lane? The artist?"

"Yep."

April shook her head. "Actually, I can see that. They'd make a beautiful couple, and she's no shrinking violet."

Chance laughed. "She is not. She's good people though."

"Oh, I didn't mean anything bad. I don't really know her, but she seems nice, just…forthright, speaks her mind, doesn't take any crap?" She smiled, "If anything, I wish I could be more like that."

Chance shook his head. "Don't you go wishing you were more like anyone. You're great just the way you are. Now you're here, and away from…" he bit back the that bastard, he wanted to say and instead chose, "…that place. You can get to know who you really are and become more of you."

She smiled, seemingly surprised at his words; he was surprised himself. He wasn't one for saying much of anything, let alone giving advice or support.

"It is you!" He smiled as Renée came in from the back. She came around the counter and hugged him.

He was taken so much by surprise that he relaxed and hugged her back—for a second.

"I heard about your dad," she said. "Is he going to be okay? What's happening with him?"

"He's doing well, considering." He checked his watch. "We're headed to the hospital to see him. I should get going." He looked at the banner on the wall announcing the women's center. He looked back at Renée and raised an eyebrow.

"What?" she asked, she sounded defensive.

"I'm glad you're doing it." He really was.

She smiled. "So am I. And sorry; I think I'm getting a little paranoid about the name. I thought you were about to criticize it, like everyone else has."

Chance pursed his lips. "I'm not one to criticize. I'll offer alternatives if I'm asked for them and I see them, but that's about it."

Renée smiled. "Well, I'm asking. Can you think of anything better? Something warm, inviting? I'd love to come up with something better than Summer Lake Women's Center."

Chance laughed. "Damn! I will say you've got to do better than that, honey. That sounds like somewhere that smells of disinfectant. I don't know, formal, institutional. That's not what you're aiming for, is it?"

She rolled her eyes and shook her head. "No, it isn't! But it's all I can come up with. So help me out if you can?"

Chance thought about it. "I'm not seeing any alternatives right now, but I'll think on it." He looked at his watch again.

"I'd better get going, though. Miss is going to be waiting on me." He looked at April. "It's good to see you both."

April smiled. "You, too."

Renée hugged him again. "See you soon."

He nodded. He would; he was here for the week—strange as that was. Most important right now was to get to the hospital and see what the doctors had to say about his dad. He was in less of a hurry to actually see his dad.

Chapter Ten

By Wednesday evening, Missy was exhausted. She thought she had everything ready, but at this point she wasn't sure any more. She shrugged. Whatever was forgotten was forgotten. All that mattered was that she and Dan and Scotty would be in Vegas this time tomorrow. Their friends would all be there. She sniffed. Her dad and Chance wouldn't, but that couldn't be helped. Chance was going to stay with their dad until Friday when Alice would arrive. Ben had called her and she was happy to come back to the lake for a time. She was going to live in and take care of their dad—who knew how long for. They'd agreed on a month to begin with.

Chance would drive to Vegas Friday night. He would be the one to walk Missy down the aisle. She had to focus on the fact that that in itself would be special. She couldn't afford to dwell on the fact that her dad wouldn't even be there. Scotty had cheered her up a little. He'd given her dad one of his laptops and had set it up so that he'd be able to watch the wedding live on there—somehow. All that Missy understood was that Ethan was in charge of using Scot's phone to video the ceremony and somehow the pictures would show up on the laptop for her dad to watch. He would be with her in a way, and that was something.

She looked up as Dan came into the kitchen. "Are you okay, beautiful?"

She nodded and went to him. "I am. I'm tired. I wish my dad could come. I'm worried about going away on our honeymoon and leaving him, but I'm okay. If anyone knows about making the most of things, even when circumstances are working against you, I do."

Dan looked concerned as he closed his arms around her. "We can postpone it all if you want. Wait until your dad is better and can be there. We can go on our honeymoon later. I want it all to be perfect for you. And right now, it's not."

She shook her head, loving him all the more. "Real life isn't perfect. It never will be. We can't wait for the storm to pass; we just have to dance in the rain. Dad will be able to watch. Chance will be there to walk me down the aisle." She shrugged. "It's all good."

"If you really feel okay with it, we'll go ahead. If not, we won't."

She hugged him tight. "Do you still want to?"

He dropped a kiss on her lips. "You know I do. But, Miss, us getting married is about the rest of our lives. It's not just about one day in Vegas or a couple of weeks in Europe. It's about forever. We can delay the day, postpone the honeymoon. It doesn't matter to me. What matters is that you're happy."

Her eyes filled with tears. "I love you so much. I am happy. I'm happy with you. That's what it's all about. I don't want to delay the day. I want to be married to you." She wrinkled her nose. "Do you mind if we hang fire on the honeymoon, though? I want to know dad's okay before we fly a million miles away."

Dan's eyes twinkled as he smiled down at her. "I was hoping you'd say that. I wouldn't feel right leaving the country just yet either."

Scot came into the kitchen and smiled at them. "Can you two put each other down for a minute? You're going to be married soon; you're going to have to stop doing that!"

Missy laughed. "Wherever you got the idea that married people don't hug and kiss each other, you'd better change it."

Scot grinned. "I'm only teasing. I just want you to listen to my speech. I think I've got it right now. I talked to Uncle Jack on the phone again, and I think we nailed it."

Missy grinned. Jack had been helping the kid whenever he could, and, in between times, they'd been talking on the phone.

Dan grinned at him. "Tell you what, how about you help me finish packing and then we'll all sit down and hear it."

Missy smiled to herself. She knew Scot hadn't finished packing. If she asked him to, it would be considered nagging. The fact that Dan had to finish getting his own bag ready made them co-conspirators and Scot was happy to go along with it. She went back into the living room as they ran off upstairs.

The sound of the doorbell startled her and she went to see who it was. She was surprised to see Michael standing there.

"Hey, critter."

"Hi, come on in."

He shook his head. "I can't stop. I just wanted to drop these off. I don't know if you'll want them, but…" he shrugged. "You can borrow them if you like."

Missy's eyes filled with tears as she looked at the box he held out.

"Oh, Michael!"

"Now don't go getting all teary on me. Just tell me to bugger off if you don't want them," he said with a wink.

She smiled. "I'd love to borrow them. I just can't believe you remembered."

He shrugged. "Mom brought them out when Megan and I said we were getting married. Kenzie had already bought Megan some wedding jewelry years ago, apparently. She wants to wear those. As soon as I saw these, I remembered when we used to go to my Granny's and how much you used to love her pearls."

Missy nodded. "God, it has to be twenty years ago that she told me they could be my something borrowed when I got married."

He nodded. "I reckoned maybe you've already got earrings and a necklace and that lined up, but I thought it'd at least make you smile to see these again." He put a hand on her shoulder. "Thought you might need a smile after this week with your dad and everything."

She nodded and swallowed. "Thanks, Michael. Are you sure you don't want to come in?"

He shook his head. "I should get on home."

"Are you okay?" Something about him wasn't quite right, but she didn't know what. "How are the preparations going at your house?"

He smiled, but it wasn't his usual smile. "Everything's just great."

She wrinkled her nose at him. "I cry bullshit, Morgan. Tell me what's wrong, already. You know you can't fool me."

He shrugged and hung his head. "I dunno, critter. It's probably just me, but it feels like Megan's getting cold feet. She's not right. She's getting quieter and quieter by the day."

"She's probably just nervous. I know I am."

Michael lifted his head and raised an eyebrow. "You're not exactly quiet and withdrawn, though, are you? Even with everything else you've got going on."

She laughed. "I wouldn't know how to be quiet and withdrawn. It's not my way and you know it. I'm a chatterbox;

if anything, I'm talking even more than usual. I think we all do that when we're stressed or nervous. Our personalities become exaggerated. For me that means I talk even more; for Megan that would mean she'd talk even less." She was trying to reassure him, and though he smiled, she could tell it wasn't working. "Has she said there's anything wrong?"

He shook his head. "Nope, but she's hiding something that's worrying her. I know it. I know her, Miss."

"Do you want me to talk to her?"

The shake of his head said no, but his eyes said, yes please. "When would you even have time?"

She laughed. "I have no idea. But I'll make some. There has to be a minute where I can drag her off, just the two brides-to-be, for a chat."

Michael nodded. "If you can, that'd be great. Don't worry if you can't though. It's probably just me. Anyway…" He thrust the box into her hands. "Here you go. Mom sends her love with them as well. She remembered, too, as soon as I mentioned it."

Missy took them and smiled. "Thank you. I will wear them." She smiled up at him. "This means the world to me." She reached up to give him a hug.

She laughed at the sound of Dan's voice behind her. "Get your hands off my wife!"

Michael laughed and hugged her tighter. "She's not your wife yet, mate."

Dan laughed. "Why do I have a feeling of déjà vu about this moment?"

Missy smiled and went to put her arms around him. "Well you're not leaving this time," she said, remembering the first time Dan had walked her home and Michael had shown up on the doorstep and scared him off.

He smiled down at her and then at Michael. "Damned straight, I'm not. Never again."

Michael grinned at him. "You're welcome, by the way. Who knows how long it would have taken you to get your act together if I hadn't shown up."

Dan grinned back. "I would have gotten there, but yeah, thanks. Are you coming in?"

Michael shook his head. "I need to get home. I guess I'll see you guys in Vegas."

"You will, and don't worry. I'll have a talk with Megan," said Missy.

"Thanks, Miss. Good night, guys.

~ ~ ~

Michael walked back down Main with his hands in his pockets. He couldn't help but notice the difference between Missy and Megan. Missy was obviously happy and looking forward to getting married. Even with her dad just out of hospital and the fact that he wouldn't be at her wedding, there was no mistaking the fact that she was happy. Megan, on the other hand, didn't seem happy at all. It wasn't just that she was quiet—that wasn't so unusual—she really was withdrawn. She seemed lost in her own thoughts much of the time and jumped whenever he spoke to her. He'd asked and asked if there was anything wrong, but she told him no every time. She made excuses about being nervous, even tried to make him laugh, but he wasn't buying it. There was something going on with her and he needed to know what it was.

Instead of heading straight home, he decided to stop in at the Boathouse. Ben was always good for a word of advice when he needed it. He was giving her away after all. He wouldn't mind a word with Kenzie either. She might have some idea what was going on. He smiled to himself—once she got over giving him shit for coming out without Megan.

He walked in through the bar and was surprised to see Jack and Emma sitting there, chatting away with Ben. He grinned when they spotted him.

Ben raised an eyebrow. "I thought you'd be home getting ready for tomorrow."

He shrugged. "Good to see you, too, mate!"

Ben shook his head. "You're not getting all touchy on me are you?"

Michael laughed. "Course not. It'd just be nice if for once someone would greet me with a, hey, Michael, it's good to see you!"

"Hey, Michael, it's good to see you," said Jack.

Michael high-fived him. "Thanks, mate. It's good to see you, too."

Emma hugged him. "How are you? Are you excited yet?"

He nodded.

Ben gave him a puzzled look. "You don't sound it."

He shrugged. "I am. I'm just not so sure about Megan."

Emma laughed. "Don't be silly. She's over the moon. She could hardly contain herself last time I saw her."

"Yeah, but how long ago was that?"

Emma frowned. "Umm, it's been a couple of weeks since we had lunch."

Michael nodded. "Yeah, it's only gone south in the last week."

"What do you mean, gone south?" asked Ben.

He shrugged. "I dunno."

Kenzie came over to join them. She gave him a mock scowl. "Haven't I told you before that I will rip your balls off if I find you in here without my sister?" She couldn't help laughing.

Michael held a hand up. "Many a time! And no worries—I believe you. I wouldn't dare. Except..." he hesitated, but decided to go for it. "If I didn't come without her. I couldn't ask you what was up with her. Could I?"

Kenzie's smile was gone in an instant. "What do you mean? There's nothing up with her!"

Michael was a little taken aback. "Your reaction makes me think there's something—and it makes me think that you don't want to tell me either. What's going on, Kenzie?"

Her smile was back, but it was as fake a smile as he'd ever seen. "I don't know what you mean. She's fine. I just get a little defensive about her, sorry, but you do know that."

He nodded. She was fobbing him off, he knew it. "She's not right though. Something's up with her, I know it."

"She's nervous, Michael. What do you expect?"

He shrugged. "I don't expect anything. But I was kind of hoping that a couple of days before we get married, she might seem happy about it. Might, you know, smile occasionally?"

Kenzie's face softened. "Are you sure it's not you that's getting nervous? She's fine. She loves you to pieces. Get over it. If I were you I'd go on home to her."

He nodded. "Yeah, you're right." He looked at Emma and Jack. "I guess I'll see you guys tomorrow."

Jack smiled at him. "You will. And don't sweat it, Michael. Megan's probably just nervous."

"Yeah." He felt pretty dumb; maybe he was just looking for problems that weren't really there.

As he made his way back across the parking lot, he met Chase and Eddie heading into the bar. "Hey, guys."

"Michael." Chase nodded at him and kept on walking. That was weird.

"Have you got a minute? I wanted to talk to you about the set list for Saturday," he said.

Eddie stopped and smiled. "Yeah, what's up? Do you want to make any changes?"

Chase looked uncomfortable. "I thought we had everything covered?"

They did; Michael was just using it as an excuse to talk to him for a minute—to see if he knew anything. "I just wanted to make sure. Have you talked to Megan...?"

Now Chase looked guilty as hell! There was no mistaking it. "About what? Why?"

Eddie gave him a puzzled look. "Does she have any special songs she wants adding?"

Michael looked at him then back at Chase. "What's going on, mate?"

Chase shrugged. "I don't know what you mean."

Michael knew he was lying. He also knew he wasn't going to get anything out of him. "I think you do."

Chase met his gaze. "Michael, I'm sorry. I don't want to get caught up in the middle. I'll say the same to you as I said to Megan. You should be talking to each other, not to anyone else."

Michael nodded. It was true. The only trouble was, Megan wouldn't talk to him!

He blew out a sigh. "Easier said than done, mate. She's hiding something; I just don't know what."

Chase nodded. "Talk to her. That's all I can say, and it's the best way I can help."

Michael nodded. "Thanks, mate. I'll see ya." He started for home. Chase was right. He needed to talk to her. And this time he wasn't going to take any excuses. He needed to know what was wrong.

~ ~ ~

Megan made her way back downstairs. She'd let Ollie sleep in Ethan's room, though she wasn't sure they'd do any sleeping. She shrugged. They were both too excited. Ethan was excited that they were flying to Vegas tomorrow. Ollie knew something was up and was excited whatever it might be. She was a little concerned about leaving him up at the stables while they were gone, but she knew it was the best option. He loved going up there. He hung out with Lily's dog, Jake, whenever she went riding—but that was a couple of hours at a time, not a couple of weeks. After Vegas, she and Michael were going to Aruba for ten days. Ethan was going to stay with Michael's parents. He'd wanted Ollie to go with him, but she didn't want to disrupt their life that much. The girls who worked at the barn were going to care for both dogs over the weekend, and Lily would be back on Sunday. She was happy to keep Ollie.

She went into the kitchen and sat at one of the stools at the counter. Right now she wanted a drink! But that wasn't an option. She should be happy. This should be the happiest time of her life. She was getting married to the man she loved— making their family a reality. She covered her face with her hands. Their family. Michael, herself, Ethan…and the baby. She hadn't been able to stop thinking about it after she'd talked to Chase on Sunday. She'd had to know. She'd gone over to their place and Kenzie had gone to the pharmacy for a pregnancy test kit. She'd hated herself as she sat in their kitchen letting the minute tick by until the little stick would tell her. She'd hated herself because she knew she should be sharing the moment with Michael—not hiding it from him! She'd hated herself even more when she'd seen the word in the little box; Pregnant.

She should be so happy. Part of her was. Part of her just wanted to cry all the time. She didn't want to get married because she was pregnant! The little voice of reason kept telling her it wasn't like that. The logical part of her knew it wasn't like that. But not the emotional part of her, the part that still took over far too often. That part had been shaped— warped—by her childhood and by the miserable years she'd spent with Adrian. It kept repeating—screaming—I don't want to get married because I'm expecting a baby!

The sound of the front door opening brought her back to reality. She realized she was shaking. There were tears streaming down her face. She wiped them away quickly and tried to compose herself before Michael came into the kitchen. The look on his face told her that something was wrong—very wrong.

"What's the matter, Meggie?"

She shook her head. "Nothing. I'm fine. Just getting a little emotional."

He came to her and put his hands on her shoulders. "Look at me, little one."

She slowly looked up to meet his gaze. A fresh wave of tears came as she saw all the love and concern in his eyes. "Please tell me what's wrong? I'm scared. I'm starting to think that maybe you don't want to marry me." He gave her a weak smile. "But I learned my lesson about not assuming I know what you're thinking. So please, put me out of my misery? Just tell me. If you don't love me anymore, that's okay. You being happy is what matters most to me."

She flung herself into his arms. "You silly man! Of course I still love you. I do want to marry you…but…but…"

"But what, Meggie? Please tell me?"

"I'm pregnant!"

He stared at her in disbelief.

"I'm sorry!"

"Sorry? But why? Isn't that what we want?"

"Yes, but not until we're married!"

He held her shoulders and leaned back to look into her eyes. "I don't understand. We nearly are married. Just a couple of days to go."

She nodded; she couldn't stop the tears that were streaming down her face. "Yes, but Michael, I don't want us to get married because I'm pregnant."

He cocked his head to one side. "We're not. We're getting married because we love each other and because we want to spend the rest of our lives together."

She nodded. She was being ridiculous and she knew it. "I...I...I'm sorry. I think I'm just hormonal or something."

He hugged her to his chest. "You must be, Meggie. This is wonderful. It's something to celebrate, not something to cry over."

She nodded again. He was right. She needed to stop it, to get over her silly hang-up about it. As she rested her cheek against his chest, she just hoped that she could.

Chapter Eleven

Chase smiled at Kenzie when she came into the kitchen. "Good morning, lover."

She smiled, but didn't reply.

He knew better. He handed her a coffee. "Here, work on that. I'm making omelets."

She took the coffee and sipped it before smiling again. "Mmm, thank you."

Chase waited until the mug was empty; he knew there was no point attempting conversation before she was fully caffeinated. He poured her a refill and finished up the omelets.

Once they were both seated at the little table, he smiled. "How are you feeling?"

She smiled back. He loved how soft she looked when she smiled like that. "Almost human."

He laughed. "Well, that's a good place to start, I guess."

She nodded. "I'm worried about Megan."

"Me too. I ran into Michael last night."

She looked up at him, finally seeming awake. "What did he say? He was in the bar early on, asking if anything was up with Megan."

Chase nodded. "He was asking me the same thing. And I'm sorry, Kenz, but I think I made things worse."

She frowned. "How?"

"I told him he needed to talk to her! He could tell I knew something he didn't—and neither of us liked that! I said from the start that she should talk to him."

"I know. And you're right. But when she gets worked up about things, reason goes out the window. For such a smart girl, she can be pretty dumb sometimes."

"You're not mad at me?" Chase had half expected her to bitch him out for not keeping Megan's secret better.

She came around the table and sat in his lap. "If I wanted to be mad at anyone it would be Megan. But I can't be. She's coping as best she can, but after Adrian—well, she's a bit fucked up, I guess!"

Chase nodded. That about summed it up.

"I'm glad you're not mad at me. Megan put us both in a difficult situation," she said.

"She did, but at the same time, I'm glad she felt able to turn to us."

"Me too. I just hope things don't get too screwy. I want to see them get married and figure out the details later."

Chase smiled. He liked that idea himself—and not just for Megan and Michael. "They'll be fine, I'm sure." He looked up at the clock on the wall. "What time do we need to be at the airport?"

"Ten," said Kenzie with a sigh. "I'd better get my butt moving. I said we'd be happy to go later, but Megan thought it was best if we went with them."

Chase smiled. "It is. You want to be with your sister while she gets ready for her wedding, and Eddie and I want to check out the venue."

"I know, I know." She got up and made her way to the door. When she reached it, she turned and smiled at him. "It's weird when you think about it, isn't it?"

"What is?" he asked.

"That Megan and Michael, the librarian and the doctor, are turning to the two of us, the singer and the eternal fuckup, to help them sort themselves out."

He shook his head at her with a smile. "I resent being called a fuckup!"

She laughed. "I meant me! You're the singer!"

He narrowed his eyes at her. "You should be though. Have you decided if you're going to sing at the wedding? You know she wants you to."

Kenzie shrugged. She had that stony look that made him regret bringing it up. "I don't have to decide yet; she's happy to let me see how I feel on the day."

"Sorry, I know. I'd just love to hear you, that's all. I can't help encouraging you to sing whenever I get the chance."

Her face softened. "I know. You're too good to me."

"I just love you, that's all."

"I know," she smiled. "I really do know it. I just hope you know how much I love you."

He grinned. "Maybe you can show me when get to our hotel room?"

She laughed. "If you want to join me, I can show you in the shower right now."

He stood. He wasn't going to turn down an offer like that!

~ ~ ~

Gabe took Renée's hand as they walked across the parking lot at the airport.

"I wish it was us getting married," she said.

He nodded. "It will be, soon enough."

She laughed. "It won't be soon enough. It can't come soon enough. I just want my divorce to hurry up and come through."

He smiled at her. "It can't be too far away now."

"I hope not."

He gave her a puzzled look. "Would you want to get married in Vegas?"

She shook her head vigorously. "I would not! I mean, no offense to Megan and Michael or Missy and Dan, but it's not my style. When Eric and I got married it was a quick trip to the courthouse and that was it." She smiled up at him, "It didn't bother me, but with you, it's different. It does matter. I want us to do it right."

He smiled. "We will. We'll do whatever you want."

"Aw, thanks Gabe…Oh, look. There's Kenzie and Chase. Who else is coming with us?"

"Michael, Megan, you and me, Kenzie and Chase and, I think, Chase's bandmate Eddie…"

"And April!" Renée finished for him. "I wanted her to come with us, since she doesn't know too many people, and it means Ethan and Marcus will be together, too."

Gabe nodded. That made sense.

Once they were inside the FBO building, Gabe spotted April sitting by the windows with Marcus. She stood with a smile when she spotted them.

The others came to join them and it seemed everyone was talking at once. Gabe smiled at Chase and nodded at Eddie. They were like Kenzie. People he wouldn't have given the time of day to in his old life, yet now he knew them, he liked them. He had to wonder about how stuck-up he must have become in his life as a New York attorney. He smiled some more; there was no chance of him being stuck-up now, not with Renée around!

"How's it going, Gabe?" asked Chase.

He nodded. "I'm doing great. How about you? Are you ready to play us all some good music?"

Chase nodded. "We sure are."

He looked at Eddie. "I thought you'd have all your equipment?"

"We do. We just got finished loading it with Smoke."

Kenzie turned to them and rolled her eyes. "Yeah, no one warned me I was expected to be a roadie as well as a bridesmaid this weekend!"

Gabe laughed. "You're a woman of many talents; that's the trouble, Kenzie."

She made a face at him. "I guess."

Renée turned to greet Eddie. "Hey. Have you met April before?" she asked.

Gabe didn't miss Eddie's reaction, the slight hint of pink that tinged his ears as he smiled and held out his hand. "Not officially. Nice to meet you. I'm Eddie."

Gabe felt sorry for April as she shook Eddie's hand. She looked thoroughly embarrassed, but he wasn't sure why. "It's a pleasure," she mumbled.

Gabe saw the look Renée exchanged with Kenzie, but he didn't know what it meant. He'd have to ask her later. He spotted Michael and Megan enter the building, then Ethan barreled through the doors and came running over. He looked around at the group of them standing there.

"Hello!"

Gabe laughed. "Hey, monkey!"

Ethan grinned. "Hi, Uncle Gabe." He looked around again. "This is awesome! I've got two aunties and two uncles, and once Dad and Meggie get married it'll be official." Gabe loved the little guy. He watched him join Marcus who was standing shyly beside his mom. "And I've got a new best buddy, too."

Michael and Megan joined them. Gabe knew straight off the bat that something was amiss. He raised an eyebrow at Michael, but he just gave a little shrug, then smiled around at everyone.

"G'day, peeps. Are we all ready to go?"

Everyone murmured their agreement.

Smoke appeared at the doors to the ramp. "Is everybody ready?"

"Yep," said Michael, "let's get this show on the road."

They all followed Smoke out onto the ramp to board the plane.

~ ~ ~

Dan smiled at Missy. "Do you remember the first time we stayed here?"

She smiled back. "Of course, I do. I'll never forget it."

"Me neither."

There was a knock on the door. "I'll get it," called Scot.

Missy smiled to herself. It amused her how much like Dan he was becoming. The first time Dan had brought her here she'd been amazed at how the shy geek she thought she knew transformed into the confident man about town. Now it seemed Scot was doing the same. He'd chatted happily with George at the Concierge Desk, greeted him like an old friend. Now he was happy to go open the door to their suite, while at home a knock on the door sent him scurrying for cover.

"Hey, come on in."

It was Jack and Emma.

Jack grinned. "We're going to go pick up Mom from the airport. I wondered if you wanted to come?"

Dan looked at Missy. She thought about it. She'd like to, but she had so much to do. They were supposed to meet up with everyone at four o'clock to go through the details of the next few days. They were going to be quite a large group and she'd hate for anyone to miss out on anything by not knowing what was going on. She really wanted to catch up with Megan before then, too. "I'd like to," she said, "but I think I need to stay here. Do you want to go, hon?"

Dan nodded. "I'd like to, if you don't mind?"

"Of course I don't! You go."

Emma grinned. "What can I help you with, Miss?" She looked at Jack. "Bring your mom to our suite when you get back? I can't wait to see her, but I think you two boys should go meet her."

Jack smiled. "Okay, she'll like that."

Scot surprised Missy again. "Do you think she'd like to see me? I'd like to come."

Dan grasped his shoulder. "You know she would! She's been dying to see you."

Scot looked at Missy. "Is that okay, Mom? I want to see Nanna Chris."

"Of course it is!" She loved that he'd formed a bond with his new nanna. She smiled remembering how they'd decided between them what he should call her—asserting that he was too old, and she was too young for him to call her grandma.

"You guys get going. We can meet you with everyone else at four, if you like?"

"Okay, great." Dan came to kiss her. "We'll see you then."

Jack leaned in to kiss Emma, "See you later, baby."

Scot went to stand by the door. "I'm not kissing anyone! I'm just waiting to get out of here!"

Missy laughed as Emma gave him a sad look. "Not even your Auntie Em?"

He came and gave her a quick peck on the cheek. She was his favorite, and Missy figured he'd never say no to anything she wanted from him. He surprised her by coming to her, and pecking her cheek. "Love you, Mom." There went that damned lump in her throat again! She blinked away the happy tears. "Don't get carried away," he said. "I just couldn't leave you out. Can we go now, Dad?"

Emma smiled at her as the door closed behind them. "He really is growing up, isn't he?"

She nodded. "He'll always love his Auntie Em, though."

Emma smiled. "I hope so. So, what do we need to do?"

Missy sighed and sat down. "I don't even know where to start! We need to check on Megan."

Emma gave her a puzzled look.

"Michael seems to think there's something up with her. I don't know if there is, or if she's just nervous, and he's overreacting. Either way she must be stressed about something."

Emma nodded. "Michael's had a bee in his bonnet for a while now. I thought it was just him. I hope she really is okay."

"Me, too, hon. Have you seen anything of Holly? I'm worried about her and Pete. They seem to be getting worse instead of better."

Emma's face made Missy worry even more. She shook her head sadly. "I don't know what to do with them. They're both so stubborn! Pete's carried away and Holly has had enough. It's crazy though. They love each other so much. She even talked about calling it all off."

"Oh my God! She said that to you?"

Emma shook her head. "She said it to Pete. And he told me and Jack like it was just her being unreasonable—not like he was taking it seriously, or seeing how much she must be hurting to say that!"

Missy shook her head. "Are they here yet?"

"I think they should be. They waited to fly with Pete's mom and dad."

Missy smiled. "I'm so happy they're coming. And Gramps and Joe—that means the world to me."

Emma laughed. "Last time I saw Gramps and Joe, they were wandering through the casino like kids in a candy store."

Missy laughed. "I can imagine." She took a deep breath; she didn't need to go upsetting herself. "My dad would be with them if he was here."

Emma patted her arm. "I'm so sorry he can't make it, Miss. At least you've got Chance though."

Missy was determined to keep it light. She laughed. "Of course you see it like that, as long as Chance is here, you're quite happy."

Emma laughed with her. "Sorry, I can't help it! He's just dreamy!"

"I won't tell Jack you said that."

"Too late. He already knows. I can't help it; even the mention of Chance's name and I go all starry-eyed."

Missy laughed. "You're lucky Jack's not as insecure as you are. Can you imagine how you'd feel if he was like that over someone's big sister?"

Emma frowned. "Oh. I never thought of it like that. I wouldn't like that at all!"

"I know! So just think about that next time you go mooning over my big brother!"

Emma hung her head, even though she was smiling. "Yeah, I will. So where do you want to start? Is your dress ready? Is there anything you want to do here? Or do you want to go out on the prowl? See if we can find Megan, maybe Holly?"

Missy shook her head. "The first thing I want to do is call Charlotte."

"Oh crap! I completely forgot about that. When does she arrive?"

"She's supposed to get here tomorrow night. I said I'd check in with her, and it will be almost bedtime over there now. Her flight leaves early in the morning."

"Let's call her then! I'm dying to talk to her, and I can't wait to see her." She sighed. "Even though it makes me feel like a traitor to Ben!"

Missy nodded. "I know exactly what you mean. I feel the same way."

She dialed the number and waited. The line buzzed for a moment and then began to ring with that odd English tone.

"Hello?"

"Charlotte! It's Missy."

"Hiya!"

"I'm going to put you on speaker with Em, too!"

"Brilliant! Hi, Emma! I'm so excited to see you both!"

"And we can't wait to see you! What time do you get in?"

"I'm supposed to land at McCarran at twenty past four tomorrow afternoon. I'm a bit worried though, it's an odd routing. I have to change planes in Dallas, and I only have an hour."

"That should be plenty of time," said Missy.

"It's plenty of time to change planes, but since it's my first port of entry into the US, I have to collect my bag, clear customs and immigration, and put my bag back through. It's a pain in the arse."

Emma laughed. "Sorry. It's not funny. I just love the way you say that!"

Charlotte laughed, too. "I say it properly, you bloody American! You may as well call it a donkey the way you pronounce it."

Missy laughed as a thought occurred to her. "Well, I hope it's not too much of a pain in the donkey. I want you here as soon as you can."

"I want to be there, Miss. I wish I were there right now with you. But…"

The silence lengthened. They all knew what the but was, but none of them wanted to name him. Charlotte had thought it best to keep her visit short; she was flying in on Friday night and leaving on Sunday morning.

"How is he about me coming?"

Missy exchanged a look with Emma. "He's okay."

"Oh. Good. I…he…we… Shit, girls! I don't know what to say! I can't wait to see him. I'm dreading seeing him. I want to talk to him. I want to hide from him. I don't know if he'll want to talk to me." She sighed. "I'm being pathetic, aren't I? He'll be there with his date, he'll say a quick hello and that will be it. I'll be there crying into my champagne, wishing it was all so different."

Emma looked at Missy. "Won't you be wishing that Alastair was there with you?"

The sound of Charlotte's laughter crackling its way across the Atlantic had Missy looking back at Emma, wondering what the hell it meant.

"Oh, God, girls! You have no idea! I'll catch you up when I see you, but let's just say it will be a huge relief to be away from him for a couple of… Hang on."

Her voice was muffled for a few moments as though she'd put her hand over the mouthpiece. Missy had no idea what she'd meant about Alastair. Emma obviously didn't either from the look on her face.

Charlotte came back on the line. "I've got to go, girls. I'll call you from Dallas tomorrow. Bye."

The line buzzed when she hung up.

"Just like that, there she was gone!" said Missy.

"Well, that's what she's like. But what do you think she meant about getting away from Alastair? He's always given me the creeps!"

"I have no idea what she meant. I do know what you mean about Alastair, though. I mean, it's obvious he loves her, and he's good to her. Maybe we're just biased because he's not Ben?"

Emma giggled. "Or maybe it's just that he's a donkey-hole?"

Missy laughed with her. "Yeah, that could be it!"

Chapter Twelve

Dan smiled as he watched his mom chatting with Scot. She was so good with the kid. She'd welcomed him straight away as her own when she first met him. Dan had wondered how it must be for her to become a step-grandmother to a boy who was already fourteen years old. She'd laughed when he asked her about it.

"I'd have thought you would understand, Danny. How is it for you to become a stepdad to a boy who's already fourteen years old?"

He'd shrugged. "It doesn't feel that way, I'm not a step-anything. I love him. I'm his dad. That's how it feels."

"Exactly, I'm not a step-anything either, I'm his nanna, and I love him already."

Watching them now, as Scot explained one of the slot machines to her, Dan knew she really did love him. He was happy that she was talking about coming to live at the lake. Happy for himself, and for Jack, that they'd have her around, and even happier for Scot. He'd never known a grandmother before.

Missy came to join him. "I can't wait for her to move to the lake," she said, echoing his own thoughts. "I'm so happy she's here."

Dan met her gaze. "I wish your dad could be here, too."

She nodded. "It can't be helped." She smiled brightly. "At least Scot rigged him up so he can watch."

Dan loved that she always made the most of what was. She refused to let anything take her down. He'd always admired that about her. She'd lived a tough life but always battled through with a smile. He just wished that, for once, she could have everything she wanted and not have to put on a brave face.

She looked around. "I think everyone's here now. I guess we'd better round them up and make sure they all know what's going on. It's going to be like herding cats, trying to get everyone in the right place at the right time. But all we can really do is let them know what the plan is and hope they get to where they need to be when they need to be there."

Dan nodded. He found the logistics daunting. All he really cared about was that he, Missy, and Scot should be there at five o'clock on Saturday. He knew it wasn't that simple though. And it wasn't really all he wanted; he wanted their friends there, and he wanted Jack and his mom there. And that just brought it home even more that Missy wanted Chance and her dad there. His head filled with white noise. It just wasn't right.

She touched his arm. "Did I lose you?" she asked with a laugh. He shook his head. "No, I just get a bit overwhelmed when I think about it all." He smiled. "I almost wish we'd put Pete in charge of logistics."

Missy laughed. "I'm not so sure about that. Granted, everything would run like clockwork, but would anyone have any fun?"

Dan followed her gaze to where Holly was standing with a drink in her hand staring off into space. Pete was a few yards away talking to Ryan. "I wish they would work it out," he said.

"We all do. But short of locking them in a room together and not letting them out until they sort themselves out, I don't know what we can do."

Dan sighed. "I know; I just wish there was something."

He jerked his chin to where Michael and Megan were sitting at one of the tables in the lobby area. They each looked lost in their own thoughts. "I wish they looked happier, too."

Missy heaved a big sigh. "They should. They've got everything going for them. Unfortunately, Megan has got herself worked up. They'll figure it out."

Dan turned to her. "Worked up about what?"

Missy shook her head. "Don't say anything, but she's expecting. And she has this hang-up about not wanting to have to get married because she's pregnant."

Dan rubbed a hand over his cheek. "I don't understand. That's not why they're getting married—is it?"

She laughed. "No. And don't worry, you won't understand. It's completely illogical." She smiled up at him. "You won't get it no matter how hard you try. I'm an illogical female and I'm struggling with it."

He laughed. "In that case, I'll just go with accepting it. I have to do that a lot. I don't understand, but I accept."

Missy laughed. "So now you know how I feel with your computer-speak. It makes no sense whatsoever to me, but I accept that it's just beyond what my little brain can handle."

He wrapped an arm around her shoulders. "We're just different kinds of smart, that's all."

She smiled up at him. "We are."

Ben came to join them. "How we doing guys?"

Dan nodded. "We're just about ready to go through the schedule. How are you doing?"

"I'm okay. I'm a little worried about Megan. She's not right, but she's not talking about it."

Missy shook her head. "You just get her down the aisle tomorrow, they can figure it out from there."

Ben raised an eyebrow at her.

She shrugged. "Try talking to them. It's not my secret to share."

Dan was surprised how good it made him feel that she'd told him that Megan was pregnant, but she hadn't told Ben. She had such a special friendship with Ben, but Dan was her partner in life.

Ben shrugged. "I don't think I need to know." He looked around. "Shall we get them all into the room then?"

Dan nodded. "Yeah, it's about time."

Once everyone was congregated in the meeting room that Dan had rented for the weekend, Jack looked around. He loved seeing so many familiar faces brought together like this. He caught sight of Nate chatting with a pretty girl with short brown hair. For a moment he couldn't place her. Ah. She was the girl from the stables. Lily? Was that her name? He shook his head with a rueful smile. He'd have to have a word with Nate. He'd be better off staying away from the wedding guests if he wanted a woman to play with for the weekend—and knowing Nate, he did.

Smoke and Laura were standing at the edge of the room. Laura was smiling as she chatted with Leanne. Smoke stood a few feet back scowling to himself. That made Jack smile. It was quite something to see Smoke enduring the company of someone he disliked, just to keep his lady happy. The guy had come a long way since he'd met Laura. Jack was hoping they'd have a wedding announcement of their own soon.

He scanned the crowd until his eyes found their target. Pete. He shook his head. He'd been trying for weeks now to talk some sense into his partner. He wasn't getting anywhere though. Pete was being as bullheaded about their wedding as Jack had ever seen him—and that was saying something! Holly wasn't helping matters. She knew what Pete was like. Yet she wasn't making any allowances. He felt bad even thinking that. She was a woman; it was her wedding, too. He made his way over to them. Hoping yet again that maybe this time he'd find the words that would wake Pete up.

"S'up, partner?" Pete raised his glass to him.

Jack smiled. "Yo, bro. Just wanted to see how you're doing. Is this getting you excited for your turn?"

Pete scowled at him. "I'm not even sure I'm going to get a turn. Holly's talking about calling it off. After all the work I've done getting things set up…"

"Jesus, Pete!"

"What?"

"Listen to yourself! Holly, the woman you love, the woman you want to spend the rest of your life with, is considering calling off your wedding and all you're concerned about is how that will mess with your plans? I told you before and I'll keep telling you until you finally get it—Fuck the plan!"

Pete rolled his eyes. "That's easy to say, but not so easy to do when you need to get a couple hundred people out to the lake and have everything laid on for them. Not when you need to…"

"Stop it!" said Jack.

Pete stared at him in surprise.

"You don't need any of that! All you need is you and Holly! The rest is just detail."

Pete laughed. "But you're the detail guy! Surely you get it."

Jack shook his head, he wasn't laughing. "I'm the one who cares about crucial details. Not about peripheral bullshit. You need to get your head out of your ass and figure out what's really important. I don't want to be left picking up the pieces when Holly's gone. You do realize that's a very real possibility at this point, right?"

Pete looked at him. Jack started to feel as though he might finally be getting through, so he pushed on. "Look at her."

Pete followed his gaze to where Holly was now sitting—by herself—staring morosely into the drink in her hand.

"Does she look happy to you? Does she look like a woman who's excited to be getting married in a month? Or does she look like a woman who's just about reached the end of her rope?" He could see the pulse working in Pete's temple. Maybe he was getting through. "How are you going to feel, Pete, if she does call it off? If she decides she can't take anymore and gives up. How will you feel when she gives you that ring back and walks out the door and out of your life?"

~ ~ ~

Pete's heart was thundering in his chest. Holly looked up and met his gaze. She didn't smile. She just stared at him for a long moment before looking away. What the hell was happening to them? The thought of her giving him back her ring? That made him feel ill. He remembered the night he'd given it to her. They'd sat there in the hot tub outside the cabin at his folks' place. He'd thought a proposal was supposed to be serious and solemn. She'd proved him so wrong! He remembered the way her eyes had shone with tears as she'd cried, Holy shit, Bigshot! It's enormous! Even now he couldn't help but smile at how she'd thrown herself into his arms. It hadn't gone anything like he'd planned, but that was what had made it so special—so Holly. That was what he loved about her.

He looked at Jack. Realization was dawning. He'd even told her—once he'd finally let go of his life plan in order to let her in—that she made everything better than his plan ever could have been. Just by being her. By adding to his life in ways he could never imagine by himself. She made life so much better, because she was Holly. Because she was unexpected—because she wasn't bound up in or by a plan!

"Jesus, Jack!"

Jack gave him a knowing nod. "Yep! Jesus, Pete! What the fuck have you been playing at? And are you going to wake up in time?"

Pete looked over at Holly again. He'd almost lost her once before. That had been his choice. He'd thought he could go back to the life he'd had before he met her. He'd found out very quickly that he couldn't. He couldn't stand the thought of living the rest of his life without her. He looked back at Jack. "I'm awake!"

Jack grinned. "So what are you going to do about it, partner?"

"I have no freaking clue!" It was true. How could he bring them back from the brink of disaster, when he was the one who had taken them there. "What do I do, Jack?"

Jack shrugged. "That, I can't tell you. That's for you to figure out. But I will say you should probably figure it out with Holly, rather than for her."

Pete nodded. He could see now that he'd screwed up, by trying to plan everything for her. If they were going to fix things, they needed to do it together. He stretched his fingers out of the fist they'd been making at his side. Part of him wanted to make some grand gesture though. To show her how much he loved her. To show her he understood her and could give her what she wanted.

"Talk to me, Hemming? What are you thinking? I don't like that look on your face."

Pete smiled. "I don't know what I'm thinking yet, but when I do, I'll run it by you first."

Jack grasped his shoulder. "You do that. I want to see you fix this. Not make it even worse!

They both looked up as Dan tapped on the microphone. "Can you hear me?" he asked.

The speakers crackled with feedback.

Pete looked at Jack. "Shall we give him a hand?"

Jack shook his head and there was no mistaking the pride in his voice as he replied. "No, he's got this."

Dan tapped on the microphone again with a shy smile. "Okay, we want to make sure that everyone knows what the plans are for the next few days. I'm sure you'll want to go off and do your own thing, much of the time. But we've printed up sheets of what's happening where and when, so you don't miss any of the important stuff."

Pete watched as Dan looked around the room. He felt proud of him, too. He'd known Dan since he was Scot's age. He'd been just as quiet and shy. He'd come a long way.

"I guess the most important things to know are: Tonight is party night. Girls are meeting at the concierge desk at seven. Guys are meeting in the front lobby at seven. Tomorrow is a do-as-you-please day. We've got the spa booked out for anyone who wants to make the most of it. And then Saturday is the big day. Michael and Megan are getting married in the chapel at two. There'll be a reception afterwards, and then Missy and I have our ceremony at five out on the balcony." He looked around. "Does anyone have any questions?"

No one seemed to have any. The chatter started up again and Dan turned the microphone off. Ben came to join Pete and Jack.

"Are you guys ready to party tonight?" he asked.

Jack nodded. "I'm going to feel guilty drinking while Em can't, though."

Pete laughed. "She won't care. She's so hyped up on excitement she doesn't need the booze."

Jack smiled.

"It's true," said Ben. "She's happier than I've ever seen her."

"We both are," said Jack. "We've talked about babies for so long, and now it's really happening."

Pete scanned the room for Holly. She'd been so excited about babies, too. Early on. They hadn't talked about it in ages. They hadn't really talked about anything.

Ben punched his arm. "What's up, bud?"

He blew out a sigh. "Honestly? I'm wishing I could spend the evening with just Holly, instead. Take her out to dinner somewhere nice. Try to make things right between us."

Jack smiled at him. "You want to crash their bachelorette party again?"

Pete nodded, smiling to himself at the memory of Jack and Emma's bachelor parties. He remembered that he'd also started that evening wishing he could spend it alone with Holly.

"I don't think Missy would be too happy with us if we did that," said Ben.

Jack laughed. "You just want to make sure that it's a real guys' night, don't you?"

"I do! I've been pushing for someone to get us to Vegas for over a year now. I intend to make the most of it."

Pete watched him. Ben did a good job of making out he was ready to hit Vegas hard and party all night, but Pete knew him better than that. He was hurting. Pete realized that he'd been so caught up in his own problems he hadn't been there for Ben like he should. He raised an eyebrow at him now. "Is this a genuine desire to party? Or…" He didn't know how to say it. Didn't want to say Charlotte's name out loud.

Ben's smile faded as he met Pete's gaze. "What do you think?"

Pete nodded. He already knew. "When does she arrive?"

"I don't even know! It's driving me nuts! She could walk in that door any minute, or she might not show up until five o'clock on Saturday. I have no idea!"

"Jesus!" Pete was pissed at Missy. "Miss hasn't even told you?"

"It's my fault. I said I didn't want to talk about it. Subject closed."

Pete looked around. "Well, I want to know when she's coming. I'm going to find out!" He spotted Missy chatting with Michael and strode over to them.

Missy looked up at him. "Could you try smiling for once?" she asked.

He scowled at her.

"Turn that frown upside down, Hemming!" She laughed and stuck her tongue out at him. "What have I done now, anyway?"

He couldn't help but smile. "Sorry. I just get a bit too focused."

"Intense, is what you get. So, what's bothering you now?" She dug him in the ribs. "Is something not to sir's liking? Something not going to plan?"

He rolled his eyes at her then looked at Michael. "How have we put up with her all these years? She's mean!"

Michael smiled. "She is, but she only calls us out on what we need to hear."

Pete laughed. "Yeah, she's not just everyday-random mean, she's straight-for-the-jugular mean!"

"Excuse me," said Missy. "But she is sitting right here! And she is not mean! She just cares about you both enough to kick you in the ass when you need it." She held Pete's gaze. "And right now, you need it!"

"Too late, my ass is well and truly kicked. Jack just took care of that. I get it, I get how I've been screwing up, and I'm going to fix it. I'm not the only one screwing up though, Miss. You are. You need to let Ben know when Charlotte's coming. The poor guy can't relax; he's looking over his shoulder the whole time, wondering if she's about to walk through the door."

"Oh, shit! I didn't even think! He said he didn't want to talk about it, so I haven't mentioned her at all." She looked around. "Where is he? I'll go tell him. She doesn't get in till late tomorrow afternoon. He's safe."

Pete nodded. "I'll let him know."

Missy looked pained. "Shit, shit, shit! I feel bad now."

Pete put a hand on her shoulder. "Don't. You can't take care of everything and everyone. You need to take care of you."

She nodded. "Yeah, but it's Ben. It's not everyone. Or just anyone. It's Ben!"

"He'll be okay. Don't sweat it. Seems like we're all overlooking even the things that are really important to us at the moment. It's all fixable though."

Missy wrinkled her nose at him. "Have you come to your senses then?"

He nodded. "I have, and if there's one thing I do better than planning—it's fixing shit!"

Missy gave him a long, measured look. "I hope so, Pete."

Chapter Thirteen

Emma hurried down to the concierge desk; she was late. The girls were supposed to be meeting up at seven, and it was already ten after. She'd taken a nap. It seemed she needed one every afternoon these days, and her body refused to accept that being in Vegas made any difference. She smiled to herself when she reached the desk. Megan was there, April and Lily were there, but the rest of them seemed to be even later than she was. She smiled as she plonked herself down next to Megan.

"Are you excited yet?" she asked.

Megan nodded, but didn't reply. Poor thing! She must be really nervous. And Emma knew her well enough to know that a night out like this would be tough for her. She'd no doubt rather be curled up with a book in her room. Emma could relate to that, but she wouldn't miss this for the world.

"Never mind," she said. "Just have a couple of drinks and this evening will pass quickly."

Megan burst into tears.

"What's the matter?" Emma looked up at April and Lily who were sitting on the other sofa. Lily raised her hands in a helpless gesture. April shook her head sadly; they had no clue what was going on either. Megan pulled out a hanky and blew her nose loudly. "I can't drink," she mumbled.

"Why ever not?"

"Why can't you?"

"Because I'm pregnant, silly…." And then it dawned on her. "Oh!"

Megan nodded sadly.

"But Megan, that's wonderful news! Isn't it?"

"It should be." Megan sniffed. "It is really. I'm just being stupid. Ignore me. I'm fine."

"But you're obviously not fine! Why?"

She shook her head sadly. "I know it's stupid, but I don't want to get married because I'm pregnant!"

Emma didn't get that. "But you're not. You're getting married because you and Michael love each other and want to spend the rest of your lives together." She gave her an encouraging smile. "And now you're expecting a baby, too. It's all coming together at once. What could be better?"

"See, I told you. I'm just being stupid."

Emma patted her arm. "You'll be fine. You just need a little time to get used to the idea."

Megan nodded and looked up as Kenzie came out of the elevator.

"Hey ladies! Are we ready to do Vegas justice?" she asked.

Emma smiled. Kenzie and Megan could not be more different. Kenzie looked like she was born to party in Vegas. She wore a short black dress, split at the thigh. Her long blonde hair was piled up on top of her head. Just looking at her heels gave Emma vertigo. She looked like a million dollars. Megan looked beautiful too, but in a much more muted way. She wore a purple silk dress, with a mandarin collar. She looked demure, yet still sexy.

"I'm just hoping to survive the night," said Megan.

Kenzie's face softened as she came to sit beside them. "You'll have fun, sis. This is your big night. Relax and enjoy yourself for once. Be the wild little gypsy I know you can be."

Megan gave her a weak smile. "Okay."

Missy, Renée, Laura, and Jack's mom all emerged from the elevator, chatting and laughing. Emma smiled to herself. They were all so beautiful! Even Jack's mom. Maybe, especially Jack's mom. Emma knew she needed to get used to who Chris really was. She'd carried this image in her mind of a sad, downtrodden woman. She'd been widowed at a very early age, and no matter what Jack and Dan's father might have been, Emma knew that Chris had loved him. She'd never remarried. According to Jack, she'd never had an interest in finding a new relationship after their dad. That had made Emma imagine a dowdy, sad, old lady. When she'd met Chris, she'd realized how wrong she was, and the more time she spent with her, the more she came to respect and admire the strong, outgoing, bubbly character she was. In many ways, she reminded Emma of Missy, and looking at the two of them walking arm-in-arm to join them, she knew they were going to get along really well. Chris smiled. "Good evening, ladies. Thanks so much for inviting me along. I'm excited! I don't want to pee on your parade, so I won't stay out with you too late."

Missy laughed. "Ha! Don't think you're going to be able to wimp out early on us!"

Chris laughed with her. "I'll have to. I'm old and I'm out of practice. It's not the same for all you young things."

Emma grinned at her. "Nice try, but you're not old. That excuse isn't going to fly. And besides, Anne and Lizzie are coming too. Wait till you see them party; we'll have trouble keeping up!"

"Lizzie?" Chris raised an eyebrow. "Sorry, I haven't got everyone straight yet. I know Anne's Pete's mom, and I know I've met Lizzie, but I can't place her."

"Lizzie is Michael's mom." Missy shot a worried look at Megan. Emma caught her eye and shrugged. She was hoping that Lizzie might be able to talk Megan out of her funk. None of them had managed it.

Chris smiled. "I love that all of you grew up so close. I hope I'll be able to become a part of this big family of friends you have, even though I'm a latecomer."

Emma smiled at her. "You're already a part of the family. And after tonight I'm pretty sure you'll have a whole bunch of new friends."

Missy nodded. "And don't count yourself out as one of the oldies. It's a Summer Lake thing; the generations all party together. Always have, always will. You may as well get used to it."

Emma loved the way Chris smiled. With all the weddings and babies, they were all making new beginnings in their lives. Emma was happy that Chris was making a new beginning of her own. Emma hoped that she'd find her happiness in Summer Lake, like so many others were doing.

She spotted Holly walking down the corridor, accompanied by Anne and Lizzie. She was relieved to see Holly smiling as the two older women chatted away. If anyone could cheer you up when you were down, it was those two.

~ ~ ~

Holly couldn't help but smile to herself as she listened to Anne and Lizzie chatting away to each other. Anne had come to Holly and Pete's room at six thirty. She'd claimed she was nervous to go and join all the girls by herself and wanted to go with Holly. She'd kicked Pete out, telling him he could finish getting ready with his dad. It made Holly laugh to see Pete treated like a little boy—and meekly doing as he was told! It was such a nice change. Once he'd gone, Anne had pulled a bottle of champagne from her purse with a grin.

"Let's get this party started, darling!"

They'd giggled and drunk champagne while Holly finished getting ready. Anne had called Lizzie and told her to come join them. They'd had quite the little party going and Holly had loved it—that was why they were only just getting here to join the party proper, half an hour late. It didn't seem that anyone cared though. They were standing or sitting in little groups, chatting and laughing.

She spotted Lily standing by herself and went to join her; she didn't want anyone to feel left out this evening. She'd done enough feeling left out herself the last couple of months, and it sucked.

"You look gorgeous," she told Lily as she joined her.

Lily laughed. "I scrub up okay for a farm girl, don't I?"

Holly shook her head. She knew Lily's story, and she was pretty sure that the petite brunette felt just as at home in her gorgeous grey, satin off-the-shoulder number as she did in her Wranglers and work boots.

"Don't give me that crap."

Lily laughed. "Okay then, since it's you, I won't. I'll just say it's been far too long since I've been out and really let loose. Tonight may be the night. Girls just want to have fun, and this girl hasn't had any fun in a long time."

Holly raised an eyebrow at her. "What kind of fun are you talking about? Remember this is a girls' night—no men allowed."

Lily made a face. "We're bound to run into some guys. That's how Vegas works. A little drinking, a little dancing, a little…" she wiggled her ass and winked. "A little fun afterwards."

Holly shook her head. "I didn't think you were like that!"

"I'm not really. I'm just feeling frisky. I've been sadly single for over a year, and I want to have fun! Maybe even with that friend of Pete's. He's hot! And what happens in Vegas stays in Vegas, right?"

Holly frowned. "You mean Nate?"

Lily nodded and waggled her eyebrows. "I do! He's gorgeous! Don't you think?"

"He is a good-looking guy, but I wouldn't recommend going there."

"Oh, why not? I just want to play."

"Then play! Go find some random guy who you'll never see again. Nate just moved to Summer Lake. You don't want to have a one-night stand with someone you're likely to bump into at the grocery store, or at the Boathouse."

"Maybe I do. We might start something beautiful and go on to live happily ever after like the rest of you are!"

Holly shook her head. "If you're looking for the fairy tale, look elsewhere. Nate's no Prince Charming. He's a great guy, but he just wants to have fun."

Lily nodded. "Good to know. Maybe we can team up and go on the prowl together."

Holly laughed. "Just forget it. You'll be having far too much fun with the ladies to think about Nate, or any other guy."

Lily shrugged. "Are you just saying that because that's your own plan? To have so much fun with the girls it'll take your mind off your own guy for a while?"

Holly sighed. "Yeah, maybe. He seemed a bit better when we went up to the room. I thought he was actually going to talk to me..." she shrugged. "But then his mom came and threw him out." She laughed. "That's fine though, I have more fun with her than him anyway."

Lily shook her head. "I think you're supposed to marry the guy because you love him, not his mom."

"That's what I thought, too. I've been wondering whether marrying him is such a great idea after all."

Lily looked shocked. "I knew you two were having a rough patch, but…"

"Hey, ladies!" Missy was clapping her hands together to get everyone's attention. "We're all here now, so let's make our way up to the club."

Holly fell in step with Kenzie as they headed back to the elevators.

"It's good to see you smiling," said Kenzie. "I thought you must have forgotten how."

"It's hard to smile too much when your fiancé is taking over all your wedding planning and ignoring you and what you want."

Kenzie stopped walking and gave her an incredulous look. "And you're letting him get away with that shit?"

"You wouldn't get it; you don't know Pete."

Kenzie laughed and started walking again. "I don't, but I do know how men and women work. The woman tells her guy what she likes, what she wants, and the guy makes it happen for her."

Holly gave a bitter little laugh. "Not Pete."

"I bet he would if you gave him chance."

"I've tried and tried asking him to listen to me. Asking for what I want, he doesn't listen. He thinks he can do it so much better."

"Sugar, you're missing the point. I didn't say a woman asks for what she wants. She tells him what she wants. Men are simple creatures. They're like dogs. If you give them a clear command, tell them what you want, they go off and do it and they're all proud of themselves for pleasing you. If you don't spell it out in no uncertain terms, they go off and do things by themselves, and it's usually something you don't like. Then you're pissed at them, they're pissed at themselves, because they hate to screw up, and they're also pissed at you because they were trying to please you and you're still not happy."

Holly thought about that.

Kenzie laughed. "You're going to say something about Pete being smart or being used to running the show or whatever. Don't kid yourself. He's just like any other guy. He wants to please you. The best way for you to help him do that is to tell him exactly what you want—and what you don't."

She nodded. "Thanks, Kenzie. I think you might be right."

"I know I am. You should try it."

"I might just do that."

They'd arrived at the entrance to the club now. Missy talked to a hostess, and she led them through to the large private table they'd booked for the night. As they took their seats, Holly looked at Kenzie. "I can tell from the way Chase is with you that what you're saying works."

Kenzie looked even more beautiful as she smiled. "It does. It's not just a one-way street though. I do my best to make him happy as well."

"And he obviously is. Do the two of you have any plans to get married?"

Kenzie gave her a puzzled look. "Of course we do. We're engaged."

Holly nodded. "I know; I just wasn't sure what that means to you. You've never mentioned a date or any plans."

Kenzie laughed. "That's because we're not like that. We'll just wake up one day and know that's what we want to do, so we'll go off and do it."

Holly wished she and Pete could have done that.

~ ~ ~

Kenzie knocked back her drink. Her conversation with Holly earlier had set her thinking. Chase had mentioned getting married a couple of times over the last few months. She hadn't really given it much thought. She knew they'd get around to it one day. She wanted to marry him. That made her smile. Her! Wanting to get married! She'd come a long way since she met Chase. So had he. They'd changed each other for the better. She knew she wanted to spend the rest of her life with him. She should bring it up to him, maybe it was time.

She looked around the table, most of the women were laughing and talking. Laura and her friend, Leanne were out on the dance floor, fending off a couple of guys. The two of them were a hot ticket. Laura tall and slender with her long, dark hair. Leanne shorter and curvier with her blonde locks—she reminded Kenzie of Marilyn Monroe.

Lizzie was chatting with Megan and even had her smiling. Kenzie was glad to see that. Megan's soon-to-be mother-in-law was awesome. Kenzie just hoped she'd be able to help Megan past her hang-ups. God knew she herself couldn't. She loved Megan with all her heart, she'd do anything to help her, but she'd be the first to admit that she rarely knew what would help her.

Emma and Missy were laughing with Pete and Dan's moms. Kenzie hoped that one day she'd feel as comfortable with oldies as Emma and Missy did. It was different for them. They'd grown up at the lake where all the generations came together. They partied together, they worked together, they lived and laughed together. She envied them. In her mind she'd dubbed them the Summer Lake originals—the ones who'd grown up at the lake and whose families had been friends for years. They were almost like royalty in Kenzie's mind. She hoped that someday she and Chase would become a part of the place as much as the others were. For now, she still considered themselves to be newcomers.

She noticed that April was sitting by herself and checking her watch. She'd better not be thinking about calling it a night! Kenzie went over to her.

"Are you having a good time?"

April nodded. "Yes, thanks. I'm thinking I might turn in soon though."

"Well, you can think again." Kenzie beckoned to the waiter who was walking by.

April smiled. "I'm fine, thanks. I really should get going. I don't like to leave Marcus this long."

Kenzie rolled her eyes. "The kid will be having a great time with Ethan. Doc Morgan won't thank you if you show up and ask for Marcus back." She spoke to the waiter then turned back to April with a smile. "And besides, we're just getting started here. I've never had the chance to get to know you properly. If you duck out on me now, I might end up thinking you don't like me."

"Oh, no! It's not that. Not that at all. It's just that I…"

The waiter returned and placed two shot glasses in front of each of them.

Kenzie grinned, picking one up and handing April another. "Here's to making a new friend," she said, and then downed hers.

April watched her. "I'm not really…"

"You're not really used to having fun, are you? That's the trouble. Well, Auntie Kenzie's here to fix that. So down the hatch. There's a good girl."

April looked at the shot glass then back at Kenzie. "What is it anyway?"

Kenzie laughed. "You'll have to drink it to find out."

She was pleased when April smiled then shrugged. "What the heck. You only live once, right?" She knocked it back and immediately started spluttering.

Kenzie couldn't help laughing.

"What the hell is that?" asked April when she could speak again.

Kenzie smiled and downed her second. "That, my friend, is the taste of a good time." She handed April the last one. "Bottoms up and we're going to dance."

April shook her head. "I couldn't. I don't dance."

"I figured as much. That's why you need to down that. It has the miraculous effect of making anyone able to dance."

"That's what I'm afraid of!"

Kenzie stood up. "Come on. Live a little. When was the last time you had any fun?"

As April thought about that, Kenzie thought she might have lost her. She was thrilled when April downed it.

"I haven't had any fun at all in at least ten years!" she declared.

"Well, damn, girl!" Kenzie took her hand and led her out onto the dance floor. "You've got a lot of making up to do."

April giggled. "I guess I do, don't I?"

Chapter Fourteen

Chase grinned at Eddie. "This is more fun than I thought it would be."

Eddie nodded. "Me, too! I wasn't looking forward to tonight one bit. I'm glad we came now."

"I know. I was thinking we might have to duck out, but I don't want to."

Dan came over to join them. "Are you having fun guys?"

Chase nodded. "This is great. Thanks for inviting us."

Dan smiled. "Michael and I both wanted you here. Have you seen him around? We're both supposed to celebrating, but I haven't seen him in a while."

Chase shook his head. "Me neither." He was worried about Michael. He hoped that he'd been able to calm Megan down.

Eddie pointed out to the balcony. "I've been keeping an eye on him. He keeps going out there. He doesn't seem to be getting into the spirit of things at all."

Dan looked as worried as Chase felt. "Thanks Eddie. I'm going to go talk to him."

"Good luck," said Chase.

Eddie shook his head. "Do you know what's up with Michael? He hasn't seemed right for a while."

Chase blew out a sigh. "He's got a lot on his plate."

Eddie laughed. "Sorry, I forgot, he's almost family now, isn't he? Don't worry. I wasn't prying. Just hoping the guy's okay; that's all."

Chase slapped his shoulder. "You already are family to me. It's not that I think you're prying, just that I hate getting involved in other people's business. Period. And besides, this is supposed to be a bachelor party! We should be having fun, not standing around gossiping like a pair of old women. We should see if we can find you a piece of ass."

Eddie laughed. "I don't want to. I just want to hang with the guys."

"What's up? It isn't like you not to want to chase tail. Hell, we're in Vegas!"

"So, maybe I'm growing up a little. I just want to chill."

Chase gave him a puzzled look. "Okay, so we chill."

They stood in silence for a few minutes until Eddie turned to him. "What's April's story?"

Chase chuckled. "So that's it! You've already got your eye on a girl, huh?"

Eddie shrugged. "I'm just curious. She's new. She doesn't really seem to know anyone yet. She seems nice."

Chase narrowed his eyes at him. "And since when have you been interested in nice girls?"

Eddie shrugged again. "I'm not. Like I said, I was just curious. Never mind."

"Okay, sorry." He didn't want Eddie to clam up on him. "You know she came to the lake from Montana, right?"

"Yeah, there's some connection with Missy's brother?"

"He was the one who brought her. Sounds as though she was in a really bad marriage. Chance brought her to California for a new start."

Eddie nodded, but said nothing.

"You know she's a got kid, right? He's Ethan's new best buddy."

"Course I do, we met them at the airport this morning."

"Oh, yeah. We did. I just didn't want you going and getting interested in a chick who wouldn't work out for you."

"Who said I'm interested?"

Chase had to laugh. "You do! It's written all over your face."

Eddie gave him a sheepish grin. "She just seems nice."

"Yeah, right, nice!" Chase shook his head. "I don't see you settling down with anyone for a long time yet, let alone a battered wife with a kid!"

"Jesus, Chase. I'm not talking about settling down, but if I did it'd be less surprising than you and Kenzie. I don't know if you've noticed, but life in Summer Lake is kind of hard when you're single. I was thinking it might be the same for her, and maybe even harder with a kid to take care of, too. Unlike you, I know a middle ground with women. You only know how to fuck 'em or ask 'em to marry you. I know how to be a friend!"

Chase held up a hand. "Whoa! Sorry!"

Eddie rolled his eyes. "No, I'm sorry. I shouldn't have gone off on you. But all you couples are so caught up in each other; you have no idea how hard it can be to be single in a small town. You know what I'm like. I pay attention to people, imagine how life must be for them. I'm thinking it must be pretty difficult for April right now. She might need a friend; that's all."

"Yeah, sorry. I should have remembered it's you I'm talking to, not Robin." He raised an eyebrow. "So you're telling me you just want to make friends with her? Out of the goodness of your heart? No ulterior motives whatsoever?"

Eddie laughed. "I do have an ulterior motive, yeah. It'd be nice for me to have a friend, too!"

Chase felt bad. Eddie's life had changed a lot since the other band members had left the lake to go work a season on the cruise ships and Chase himself had moved in with Kenzie.

"Sorry. I didn't think."

Eddie punched his shoulder. "It's okay. She is pretty damned hot; I'm not denying that! Anyway, I'd just as soon change the subject. Who's that guy talking to Ben and Smoke. I keep thinking he's one of the bouncers by the looks of him, but I know he's with the wedding party."

Chase looked over. "He's a big buddy of Dan's, believe it or not!"

"Really?"

Chase nodded. "Apparently they go back a long way. His name's Ryan. He works some kind of top secret stuff. He could tell you, but then he'd have to shoot you, kind of thing."

"And he and Dan know each other how?"

Chase shrugged. "I dunno. It wouldn't surprise me if Dan was his boss or something. He's all mild mannered geek on the surface, but he's an international man of mystery, secret agent really."

Eddie laughed. "Yeah, I can see that!"

"Let's go say hi. See what the deal is really."

~ ~ ~

Smoke smiled as the two band guys came to join them. He liked Chase, and Eddie seemed like a good guy.

"Have you guys met Ryan yet?" he asked.

Ryan nodded and extended a hand. "You're the band, right?"

Chase nodded. "That'd be us."

"Awesome. Would you mind if I stop by to see your setup before the fun starts tomorrow? I used to play a little myself. I love checking out other guys' gear."

Smoke chuckled. "Sorry, but that sounds so, so wrong."

Ryan laughed with him. "Yeah. I should probably put that another way, huh?"

"I would if I were you," said Ben. He jerked his head toward a leggy blonde and her friend who were hovering nearby. "Your admirers might get the wrong idea."

Ryan laughed. "I wouldn't mind if they did."

"So you're not going to be joining Ben and Nate later when they go off to see what pleasures Vegas holds?" asked Smoke.

Ryan shook his head. "I need a break. Women are too much like hard work these days."

Smoke cocked his head to one side. "You surprise me. I thought you'd be up for anything and everything."

"I used to be."

"Can I guess that coming face-to-face with your ex has messed with your head?" asked Ben.

Ryan met his gaze. Smoke could tell he was searching for a witty comeback. He was a tough looking guy—built like a brick shithouse was the term that kept coming to Smoke's mind. He wouldn't want to get on the wrong side of him. It seemed he decided to drop the pretense and just be straight up honest. His face softened, he looked tired and older all of a sudden. He nodded. "You can and you'd be right. I don't think I knew it myself, until you pointed it out. Thanks."

Ben shrugged. "You're welcome, and I'm sorry."

"How did you know?" asked Ryan.

"Because that's exactly what's going on with me, too."

Smoke had to wonder how the hell a woman like Leanne could have gotten to a guy like Ryan. He liked Ryan. He was a straight shooter, obviously intelligent, funny, a real guy's guy. Leanne was.... well, she was just a piece of work as far as Smoke was concerned. "This is Vegas though, guys," he said. "The place where you come to escape. Where you can escape the past, escape the future, escape real life in general."

Ben rubbed his hand over his face. "Yeah. Not so easy to do when your past comes here to join you."

Ryan nodded. "I'd have to agree with that."

Smoke shook his head. He didn't know how to relate. The only woman in his past was one he'd been glad to escape! Not one whose presence would taunt him if he ever had to see her again. He was eager to change the subject. He pointed his drink to where the old guys were sitting watching one of the dancers shake her stuff. "Your granddad sure knows how to enjoy Vegas, Ben, even if you don't."

He regretted his words when he saw the hurt in Ben's eyes, but it was gone as soon as it appeared. He smiled. "Yeah, Joe knows how to have a good time anywhere. He and Gramps plan to live the hell out of this weekend."

"Good for them," said Eddie. "If I ever get to be their age I hope I'm just like them."

Smoke nodded. He hoped he might be like the old guys, except in one major way—they were both widowers. He couldn't imagine his life without Laura in it. He certainly couldn't imagine being happy and having fun with his buddy in Vegas.

As they watched, a third old guy joined Gramps and Joe. "Who is that?" asked Chase "I've seen him with the wedding party, but I can't place him."

Ben smiled. "That's Herb. He's a friend of Dan's. Actually, he's the doorman in the building where Dan lived in San Jose."

Ryan nodded. "Only our Danny, huh, guys? Who else invites his old doorman to his wedding and flies him out to Vegas for the weekend, all expenses paid?"

"Dan seems like an amazing guy," said Eddie. "I don't know him that well, but everything I hear about the guy makes me like him more."

"He's the best!" said Ryan. "You'll never meet a smarter, kinder, more genuine guy in your life." He stopped and then laughed. "Jesus, it sounds like I'm back to checking out other guys' stuff again, doesn't it?"

They all laughed at that.

"How do you know him?" asked Chase.

"We went to Berkeley together. Just for a semester, but you know how some people you just click with?"

"I do," said Chase.

Smoke nodded. Ryan and Leanne must have quite a history then. He knew Dan had met her at Berkeley as well. The three of them must have all been friends. He was intrigued by what their history might be, but he wasn't the sort to go nosing into other people's lives. He liked Ryan, the fact that he'd seen something in Leanne—something he'd liked enough to get engaged to—made Smoke wonder if maybe Laura was right, and Leanne wasn't that bad after all. He smirked to himself, then again maybe not—Ryan hadn't gone as far as marrying her!

He looked around. It seemed that all the guys were enjoying themselves in their own ways. The old guys were still ogling the dancers. Jack and Pete were deep in conversation with Gabe. They were no doubt talking business. Jack wasn't so bad, but the other two just didn't know how to leave work alone. It seemed any social event was also a potential business opportunity in their eyes.

He realized Nate was missing from their number. Where the hell was he? Smoke couldn't help but smile when he spotted him. He was out on the dance floor. Three chicks were practically cat-fighting over him as they danced. If only they knew, they didn't need to fight; Nate would happily take care of all of them, if they'd let him.

He realized the conversation had moved on without him. They were back to talking about music. Smoke's brain zoned out when it came to that. He wondered where Dan had gotten to. He spotted him out on the balcony talking to Michael. Ah. The two grooms together. That made sense. He wondered if he should go join them, but decided against it. He wondered again about how long it would be before he joined them in being a groom. As was always the way for him and Laura, their schedules made things difficult. In addition to that, they hadn't figured out what they wanted to do. Neither of them wanted a big wedding or a traditional one for that matter. The idea of a Vegas wedding didn't hold any appeal for them either. Smoke had suggested they sky dive and get married midair. Laura hadn't gone for that one. They'd figure something out. He looked at Pete's dad standing at the bar. He'd love to think that his own dad would come out on his stag night. It would really mean all the old wounds were healed if his dad and brother came. That made him think about Missy. He felt bad for her. She'd have her brother there, but not her dad. Smoke had offered to fly back and get him whenever she wanted, but apparently it wasn't an option. He watched Dan come back in, leaving Michael out on the balcony.

He made his excuses and followed Dan back to their table. "Is he okay?"

"Who, Michael?" asked Dan.

"Yeah. He doesn't seem right."

Dan shook his head sadly. "He's worried. Megan's upset about some things and he doesn't know what he can do to make her feel better."

"That's too bad."

Dan sighed and nodded. "It is. But there's nothing we can do, I'm afraid."

"How about you? How are you holding up?"

"I'm great."

Smoke was surprised to see a tinge of sadness in Dan's eyes even as he smiled.

"But what? Come on, this is me you're talking to."

Dan rubbed his hand over the stubble on his cheek. "Nothing I can do anything about. And that bothers me."

Smoke raised an eyebrow.

"I wanted all this to be perfect for Miss, but it's not. Not without her dad."

Smoke nodded. "I was just thinking about that. It's sad. It makes me sad for her. She's such a little trooper."

"I know. I just wish for once that she didn't have to be. That she could have everything she wants."

Smoke knew exactly what he meant. "And there's no way at all he can come?"

Dan shook his head. "Doc Morgan said four hours in the car wouldn't be good for him. I can see that."

"And thirty minutes in the air?"

Dan met his gaze. "That's all it would take? I told Doc Morgan I thought it would be about an hour."

Smoke nodded. "Nope. I can get him here in thirty minutes. Why don't you run it by Doc Morgan again?"

"I will. Thanks, Smoke." The smile on Dan's face made Smoke hope hard that the Doc would give the go-ahead. It'd mean so much to Missy, to Dan, hell to him! Even after his troubled past with his own family, he couldn't imagine getting married without his dad there.

Ben appeared at Dan's side. "What are you two grinning about?"

Dan turned to him. "We're hoping we might get Missy's dad here after all. It's less flying than I thought it would be. I'm going to ask Doc Morgan."

Ben grinned. "Damn! I hope he says yes. That'd be awesome!"

Michael came in to join them. "I think I'm going to call it a night guys."

Smoke's smile faded. "You can't do that! It's your stag night."

Michael shook his head. "I'm not even sure I should be getting married."

Smoke couldn't believe what he was hearing.

Dan put a hand on Michael's shoulder. "You should. You know it, Megan knows it. If there's any doubt at all it's only about when you should, not whether you should."

Michael looked as though he'd had a weight lifted from his shoulders. "You're right, Dan! They don't call you a genius for nothing, do they? You're absolutely right, mate! If she doesn't feel right about getting married now, then we call it off and just wait until she does."

Smoke looked from Michael to Dan to Ben; they were all smiling. Apparently they were all happy. Smoke had no clue what was going on, but as long as they were happy, so was he.

"I need to go find her." Michael seemed excited now. And though Smoke didn't understand why the thought of calling off his wedding might make him feel that way, he knew there was more going on than he was privy to.

Dan rubbed a hand over his cheek. "Well, we all went and crashed Emma's bachelorette party. Maybe we should make it a Summer Lake tradition. We can go crash Missy and Megan's too!"

Ben grinned. "I'll round everyone up or at least tell them what's happening. I don't think Joe and Gramps will want to come. The girls are at The Bank, right?"

"Yeah," said Smoke. "I'll come help you."

Chapter Fifteen

Megan stared out at the dance floor. Missy was dancing with the girls. She looked so happy, laughing and goofing around. Megan wished she felt the same way. She should be happy. She should get over it, she knew that, but she couldn't. Everything was so right; Michael and a baby—everything she wanted. But it felt so wrong.

She frowned as she watched a group of guys move in on the girls as they danced. A tall, dark-haired guy made straight for Emma and took her in his arms as they swayed to the music. Another guy moved in behind Laura, wrapping his arms around her waist as he moved with her. It looked almost indecent as he kissed her neck. Megan's anxiety subsided as she realized it was Smoke! The guy with Emma was Jack. But what were they doing here?

She didn't have time to ponder it as someone leaned on the back of her chair. Goosebumps ran down her spine as she remembered the first time she'd met him. She knew the feel of him so well, even before she heard his voice.

"I think you're in my seat, darl'," said Michael.

She smiled. He, too, remembered their first meeting.

"Didn't you say I could sit on yours anytime I like?"

He chuckled and came around to stand in front of her. "I did. And you can."

"What are you doing here?" she asked.

He squatted down in front of her and put his hands on her knees. "I had to come see you, little one. We need to talk."

She shook her head. "It's okay. I'm sorry. I know I'm just being stupid."

He sighed. "How many times do I have to tell you that you are not stupid, Meggie?"

"I came to tell you that we don't have to get married. I want our wedding to be happy, not stressful. I want you to be excited about it, not miserable."

She stared at him. "You're saying you don't want to marry me?"

He shook his head rapidly. "I want to marry you so much, but I want it to be right when we do. It's not going to be right if we do it now, so what do you think if we wait?"

"I...I...I..." She took a deep breath. "Wait until the baby's here?"

He nodded. "Is that what you want?"

She thought about it. The feeling of dread that had permeated her whole being since she'd first thought she might be pregnant started to dissolve. She knew it wasn't logical, but she would rather get married after the baby came. She nodded. She didn't know what to say. They couldn't call it all off just because she was being so silly.

Michael grinned. "Then that's what we'll do."

"But Michael! It's all wrong. All the arrangements are made. Everyone's expecting us to get married. What will they think? What will they say?"

Michael laughed. "Who cares? What matters is that you're happy. I can tell by the look on your face that you are. You're relieved, aren't you?"

She couldn't deny it. "I do want us to get married."

"I know. Just not now, not like this."

"What about you? How do you feel?"

"All I want is for my little Meggie to be happy. Course I want us to get married. But I know you'll marry me when you're ready." He waggled his eyebrows at her. "I mean, how could you resist? I'm adorable."

She laughed. "You are! You're adorable, you're wonderful, you're the best thing that's ever happened to me. I love you so very much. Thank you, Michael."

He took her hand and pulled her to her feet. "No worries, little one, no worries at all. Let's get out of here, why don't we?"

She followed him happily. She'd be more than happy to get out of here!

As they skirted the dance floor Michael put his arm around her shoulders. She loved it when he did that; she felt so safe. He grinned down at her and pointed to where Missy and Dan were dancing. They seemed oblivious to the world around them as if they were the only two people there.

"Let's go say good night. We'll tell them, and they can let the others know."

Megan followed him a little reluctantly; she didn't like to intrude when they were so wrapped up in each other. And she really wasn't looking forward to breaking the news that they were calling off their wedding.

When they reached them, Michael tapped Dan on the shoulder. He looked up and grinned.

"I'm not sure you two should be doing that out in public," said Michael with a laugh. "What will people think?"

"You've got to dance like nobody's watching," said Dan. "Isn't that right, Miss?"

Missy laughed. "It is." She looked at Megan. "Are you two okay?"

Megan nodded and looked up at Michael. She wanted him to say the words. She knew she wouldn't be able to.

Missy's smile faded. "What's going on?"

Michael grinned. "We're going back up to our room. We just wanted to share some happy news with you guys first."

Dan smiled, almost as though he knew what was coming.

"What?" asked Missy. She obviously didn't.

"We're calling off our wedding," said Michael. "We're going to wait until after the baby's here."

Missy looked at Megan. Megan nodded. "I'm so relieved, Miss."

Missy grinned. "Well in that case, congratulations!" She laughed. "That must sound odd, but I mean it. I mean congratulations on figuring out what's going to make you happy and having the balls to do it."

Megan smiled. She didn't know if she would have had the balls by herself. But Michael did, and he was making it right for her. She loved him more than she ever had.

"Would you guys mind letting the others know?" asked Michael. "We'll tell everyone officially tomorrow, but it'd be nice if the gang already knew."

"Of course," said Missy. "And don't worry, they'll understand."

"I'm not worried, darl'."

Missy laughed. "I know you're not! I'm trying to reassure Megan."

Megan nodded gratefully. Missy understood her. "Thank you. I guess we'll see you tomorrow."

"Good night, guys," said Dan.

~ ~ ~

Emma watched Michael and Megan talking with Missy and Dan. She wasn't too surprised when she saw them leave. She held Jack a little tighter as they danced and started to steer him toward Missy.

He grinned down at her. "Where are you taking me, Mousey?"

She smiled. "To your brother and his almost wife. I need to know what's going on with Michael and Megan."

Jack shook his head. "And here I was thinking you were lost in my arms."

She laughed. "I will be later, but right now I'm being nosey."

Jack laughed with her as they moved closer to Missy and Dan. "What's up with Megan and Michael?" asked Emma.

Missy grinned. "They just called off their wedding."

Emma didn't know what to think.

"They postponed it," said Dan. "They didn't call it off. You know how Megan didn't want to get married because she was pregnant? Well, Michael figured she didn't have to. They're going to wait until after the baby arrives."

"And they're both happy about that?" asked Jack.

"Couldn't be happier, by the looks of them," said Missy. "They've got to do what's right for them. They shouldn't go ahead if the circumstances aren't right for both of them."

Emma shot a glance at Dan. He looked wistful, perhaps even sad. Her heart hammered in her chest. She hoped to goodness that he wasn't thinking things weren't right for him and Missy!

He met her gaze and gave her that shy smile of his that she loved. It couldn't be anything like that, but something was bothering him, she could tell. She needed to know what it was. She looked at Missy. "Do you mind if I steal a dance with your fiancé? He's such a good mover, he beats my old man, hands down."

Missy laughed, "Of course you can. But don't keep him too long, I want to make the most of him, since he's not going to be my fiancé for much longer."

They traded partners and Emma moved Dan out into the crowd away from Missy and Jack. He smiled at her. "What's on your mind, Emma?"

She laughed. "Am I that obvious?"

Dan's eyes twinkled as he shrugged. He was too much of a gentleman to say yes.

"I just wondered if there's anything on your mind. It seemed there might be when you said Michael and Megan shouldn't get married if the circumstances aren't right for them both. It seemed as though you were talking about you and Miss, not Michael and Megan."

Dan nodded. "You got me."

Oh no! Emma's heart was hammering again. "What's wrong?"

"Nothing bad, nothing like that!" Dan sensed her concern and reassured her. "What's bothering me is that it's not going to be perfect for Miss, not without her dad there."

Emma's heart melted for him. He was such a sweet guy, and he loved Missy so much. "I know, it is sad, but she's accepted it. You know what she's like. She makes the most of what is."

"But I don't want her to have to. Not with something as important as this. Don't say anything, but I'm going to try to get him here."

Emma frowned. "But I thought the road trip would be too much for him."

"It would, but it only took us half an hour to fly here. Doc Morgan said the flight would be too much, but that was when I told him it would take an hour. Maybe half an hour would be okay. We spoke to Chance earlier, he said their dad's doing great. Improving every day." He shrugged. "All I can do is ask Doc. Don't say anything to Miss though, will you?"

"Of course not, and if we can help in any way just tell us. I'll be keeping my fingers crossed. Let us know as soon as you know, won't you?"

Dan nodded. "I will, and if he can come, I might want your help to keep it secret. What do you think? Do you think it would it be a good surprise, or do you think she'd rather know?"

Emma grinned. "She does love surprises." She thought about it. "Yeah. I think it would be a great surprise."

"You don't think she might enjoy the whole time more if she knows he's coming?"

"Of course she would, but I really think that the surprise of him being there would outweigh that. Can you imagine? She turns up thinking he's at least watching from home and then he's right there?" Emma blinked away the tears that threatened to fall at the thought of it. "I think it'd be awesome, Dan. I really do."

He nodded. "We don't know if he can come yet."

Emma held up her crossed fingers. "We can hope!"

~ ~ ~

Jack looked over Missy's shoulder and laughed at the expression on Emma's face as she waved her crossed fingers in the air.

Missy turned to follow his gaze. She laughed with him.

"What do you suppose they're up to?" asked Jack.

"I don't know, but my guess is that Em's got something up her sleeve that she doesn't want me to know about."

Jack grinned. Missy didn't miss a trick. He'd known from the look on his wife's face as she dragged Dan away that that was exactly what she was up to. He'd no doubt hear about it later.

Missy jerked her head to where Holly and Pete were sitting with Smoke and Laura. "Those two seem a little more civil with each other at least."

Jack nodded. "I'm hoping I had a breakthrough with Pete this morning."

"I hope so. Though how the hell you did, I don't know."

Jack smiled. "I just laid it out for him. I think I got through."

As they watched, Pete rested his arm along the sofa behind Holly. She turned and smiled at him. He said something and they both laughed.

"It looks like you might have," said Missy. "That's the closest I've seen the two of them in months!"

Jack nodded. "Me, too." He hoped his partner was finally seeing sense. Jack doubted he'd get any more chances, judging by the way Holly had been lately. She was just about ready to throw in the towel.

Gabe and Renée appeared, blocking his view. He smiled; he liked the two of them.

"Are you two having fun?" asked Missy.

Renée grinned. "Absolutely! But, I may have had one too many!"

Jack laughed. She did seem a little tipsy. He looked at Gabe; Jack couldn't imagine him ever getting drunk.

Gabe smiled back. "She's drowning my sorrows for me."

Jack cocked his head to one side, not understanding what sorrows Gabe might have.

"I don't get to be best man to my little brother anymore. Didn't you hear?"

Of course, that was it. "You will though," said Jack. "Just not for another nine months or so."

Gabe smiled. "Yeah, that's a better way to look at it." His smile grew even wider as a thought struck him. He looked at Renée. "We might even beat him to it now!"

Renée laughed. "That's the most excited I've seen you about it. You want to be careful! A girl could get to thinking that you care more about outdoing your little brother than you do about marrying a crazy redhead!"

Jack was always amazed at the way Gabe changed around Renée. When she wasn't there, he was serious, intense, always working at something. When she was, he was all fun and smiles.

"There's nothing I care more about than marrying you." He grinned at Missy and Jack and then spun Renée away, dancing off with her into the crowd.

Jack spotted Emma and Dan joining the others up at the table. "I guess they didn't wait for us," he said to Missy. "Do you want to go join them?"

She nodded. "Yeah. I can't wait to get off my feet."

~ ~ ~

April smiled at Missy as she and Jack came to join the group sitting at the table. This was quite a party! After Kenzie had made her drink those shots of whatever it was, she'd started to relax—maybe a little too much! She'd danced with Kenzie and chatted with Smoke and Laura for a while. She'd even chatted with the beautiful blonde woman who was one of Dan's friends. She was a lawyer. April felt bad about it now, but she'd asked her for advice. Advice about getting a divorce in the State of California! The woman—Leanne, that was her name—she wasn't even a divorce lawyer. But somehow April had poured out her whole story to her. Leanne had said she would help her. She seemed like she'd be a force to be reckoned with. As April had told her snippets about her life in Montana and about Guy, Leanne had gotten more and more angry. April chuckled to herself now; Guy wouldn't stand a chance in a battle with Leanne. Leanne had been so incensed by what she'd heard she was determined to help April—and take Guy down any way she could.

Maybe it was the shots, but April didn't even feel scared. Instead she felt as though, for the first time in her life, she was surrounded by good, strong people who wanted to help her. She wanted to help them, too, but she had no idea how she might do that.

Kenzie plonked herself down beside her. "Are you ready to come dance again yet, sugar?"

April shook her head. "My feet couldn't, even if I wanted to. And besides, Chase is here now. You should dance with him."

Kenzie laughed. "That's where I've been. I've worn him out. Look. He had to go get a drink."

April looked toward the bar where Chase was standing with a tall glass of water in his hand—that looked like a good idea! He caught her watching him and raised his glass. She blushed, though she had no idea why. Well, maybe she did, but it was nothing to do with his friend who was standing with him, smiling at her.

Kenzie poked her in the ribs. "Come over there with me. I need water, and you can't tell me you don't."

April was about to refuse, but changed her mind. She did want a glass of water and, embarrassed as she was, she would like to meet Eddie properly.

~ ~ ~

Laura watched Kenzie and April get up to go join Chase and Eddie at the bar.

Smoke slid an arm around her waist and pulled her against him. "What are you doing, lady? You're not eyeing up other guys are you?"

She laughed and pushed at him. "Get off, jerk."

He scowled at her, but she could see the laughter lurking behind it. "Jealous, possessive jerk, remember?"

She smiled up at him. He was so gorgeous, and that possessive side of his made her love him all the more. Any other guy wouldn't have seen her for dust if he behaved the way Smoke did, but with Smoke, she loved it. She didn't know why, but she did. "Actually, I was thinking we might be witnessing the beginnings of another Summer Lake romance." She looked back to where April and Kenzie were now chatting with Chase and Eddie. At least Kenzie and Chase were chatting and April and Eddie were smiling at each other.

Emma leaned in. "I thought that, too!"

Laura laughed. "Well if you say it, Em, it must be so; you've called every single one of us so far."

Emma nodded happily. "I have! My score is six to zero now. And I think we might just have our very next couple right there!"

Laura smiled. Emma was happiest when she was matchmaking.

"If you're so good at predicting, Em. Who do you think is getting married next? After this weekend it looks like all bets are off." It was Lily who spoke. Laura had to assume she wasn't aware of the cloud hanging over Holly and Pete and was simply referring to Michael and Megan.

Emma smiled. "That's too easy. It's Holly and Pete next." Laura had to hide a smile of her own as Emma grinned at Holly and Pete. Emma made out she was all sweet and innocent, but Laura knew she was making a point to the troubled couple and daring either of them to contradict her.

Holly smiled back at her. Pete grinned. Neither of them said a word and the awkward moment passed.

Laura was surprised, as the conversation moved on, to see Pete take out his phone and start texting. He wasn't doing anything to help himself, was he?

Holly looked at him and shook her head. Laura caught her eye and gave her an encouraging smile. "Men, huh?"

Holly rolled her eyes. "Yeah, who needs 'em?"

Pete looked up and pulled Holly to him, planting a kiss on her lips. "I'm sorry, sweetheart. That was something really important, I just needed to take care of it."

Laura watched the struggle on Holly's face, part of her wanted to stay angry with him, to push him away. Laura was relieved when she smiled and relaxed against him. "What's more important to you than being here with me right now?" she asked.

"Being wherever you are forever, and I was taking care of a little detail which might help me with that."

Holly smiled. "Good save, Bigshot."

Chapter Sixteen

When Pete woke up the next morning, he propped himself up on one elbow to look down at Holly. She was so beautiful. She looked peaceful as she slept. Her face was relaxed—something he hadn't seen for far too long. He couldn't believe that he'd been so blind—and dumb—about their wedding plans. Jack had really given him a wake-up call yesterday and he was grateful for it. He'd been happy that the guys decided to crash the girls' party last night. He'd wanted to spend the evening with Holly anyway. At least they'd had the latter part of it together. He felt as though they'd made up some lost ground, too. She'd danced with him, they'd laughed. It was still tense, but they were much closer than they had been. He loved her with all his heart, he wanted to get them back on track. He was prepared to do whatever it took to make her happy. To make her remember that she loved him too.

She opened her eyes and smiled up at him. "Good morning, Bigshot."

He dropped a kiss onto her upturned nose. "Good morning, sweetheart. I love you."

"I love you, too, Pete."

He relaxed a little as she reached her arms up and pulled his head down for a kiss.

"I really do."

When he lifted his head he smiled. "I'm sorry, Holly. I've been an idiot."

She nodded her head vigorously making him laugh.

"I love you. I want to spend the rest of my life with you. That's all that really matters. As far as the wedding goes we can do whatever you want. You tell me what you want, and I'll make it happen." He hesitated. He didn't want to say what he was about to say, but he needed to, for a couple of reasons. "If you want, we can call the whole thing off. Revisit it when we're in a better place."

She stared up at him. "You'd be prepared to do that? After all your planning?"

He nodded. He could see it now. All his planning meant nothing if it didn't make her happy. "If that's what you want, then that's what we'll do. The only plan I need to stick to is making you happy. And I can see now that I deviated from that."

She laughed, her amber-colored eyes shining. "You did take a pretty major detour."

He shook his head at her with a smile. "I know I can't expect you to cut me any slack here, but I am trying to say I'm sorry. I'm trying to make it right."

She looked sad now. "I know, Pete. And I'm happy that you are. I think we're saving us just in time."

His heart hurt to hear that. He knew he'd screwed up, but to hear her say that they'd been at the brink of breaking up really brought it home. "I'm sorry, sweetheart. Tell me what you need to make it better."

She hugged him. "I'm sorry, too, Pete. I could have handled it better, but it just hurt me so much. It felt like you didn't care about me, and what I want as much as you care about your plans. I started out so excited, thinking we were in it together,

then I just felt left out and ignored while you did what you
do."

He nodded. He could see that now. "I want to make it right.
Tell me what you want to do and we'll make it happen."

His heart hammered in his chest at her next words. "I don't
think we can make it right."

"What do you mean?"

She touched his cheek. "Sorry. I mean the wedding, not us.
We're going to be okay. We can learn and grow from this. But
the wedding you had planned. It won't ever feel good to me
now. I know it's wrong of me, but I've grown to resent the
hell out of it."

"Then we cancel it."

She looked at him questioningly. "And you don't mind?"

He shook his head. "Not one bit. Consider it done. Do you
have any idea of what you would like to do?"

She shook her head with a smile. "This is where I feel bad. I
destroy all your plans and don't have one of my own to offer.
It's just that," she hung her head and smiled out at him from
under lowered lashes. "I don't even really like plans. You know
that. I wish we could just do something spontaneous. I know
we can't, because we both want our families to be there, and
that takes organizing, but that would be my ideal. Do you
mind if I take some time to think about it? It's not fair of me
to bitch at you for doing what you think will make me happy
when I haven't told you what I think will make me happy and,
honestly, I haven't figured out what that might be yet."

Pete wrapped her in his arms. "You take all the time you
need." He chuckled. "If you decide you want to do something
spontaneous then maybe you can tell me what it is and I can
plan it in secret."

She laughed and slapped his arm. "You can't plan spontaneity,
dumbass!"

He laughed with her. "I know. I'm teasing you."

"It's been so long, I'd almost forgotten what that feels like."

He grinned as he started to tickle her. "Well, you'd better get used to it again, hadn't you?"

~ ~ ~

When April awoke she groaned at the throbbing in her head. She lay there for a few moments piecing back together why she felt that way. She needed to ask Kenzie what on earth had been in those shots! She was pretty sure that was all she'd had to drink. She'd danced with Kenzie, they'd gone to talk to Chase and Eddie. She'd only had water after that. Oh. Now she remembered. The four of them had gone to the function room. Chase and Eddie had wanted to check out the electrical set up. She squeezed her eyes shut. They'd had drinks, though again she didn't know what. She sat bolt upright. And Kenzie and Chase had decided they were going to get married! They'd asked her and Eddie to be their witnesses—she remembered now! She'd felt uneasy about it at the time. Kenzie had said that since her sister had called off her own wedding, they should probably just go off, find one of those Vegas chapels and do their thing quietly.

Surely it had just been the drink talking? They wouldn't do that? Would they? She scrabbled on the nightstand for her cell phone and texted Kenzie.

Are you really going to get married today?

She stared at the phone as she waited for a reply. Nothing came. What was she thinking? They'd still be asleep! She crawled out of bed and headed for the shower. She needed to get to Doctor and Mrs. Morgan's room to collect Marcus.

Half an hour later she was surprised that a smiling Dan opened the door to the Morgans' room. He must be here to collect Scot.

"Good morning, April!"

She smiled. He was chirpy. "Hi Dan, you don't seem any the worse for wear."

He grinned. "I don't drink much. And besides. I've just had some very good news." He looked back inside. "Thanks again, Doc."

"The pleasure is all mine. Just let me know what time I need to be ready."

"Come on in, April," called Lizzie.

Dan stood aside to let her pass. "Let's get going, champ," he said to Scot. "We've got some secret scheming to do."

April smiled as she watched them go. Whatever they were up to, they were happy about it. She loved the way the two of them were together. It made her wonder if she might ever meet someone who would become such a good father figure to Marcus.

"Hey, mom," called Marcus. "Do we have to go right away?"

She smiled. "Yes. Dr. Morgan must be exhausted from looking after the three of you last night." She smiled at the doctor. "Thank you so much."

He smiled back. "It's been my pleasure. In fact, it's me that wants Marcus to stay a while, if you don't mind? I have no interest in a spa day, and I wondered if the boys wanted to keep me company. I want to explore Vegas, but I don't think I can be trusted by myself."

April hesitated. She didn't want to abuse the Morgans' kindness, and besides, she didn't know what she'd do with herself without Marcus.

"Please, Mom?"

Lizzie smiled at her. "I'm going to get one of those hot stone massages, if you want to come with me? The boys will be much happier with us out of their hair."

Why not? She couldn't remember the last time she'd been to a spa. "If you're sure?"

"Absolutely!"

"Thanks, Dr. Morgan."

He smiled kindly. "Call me Doc. Everyone else does."

"Come on," said Lizzie. "Let's go get some breakfast and then we'll head to the spa."

April watched as she kissed her husband and said good-bye to the boys. She gave Marcus a quick hug and told him to be good. It felt strange to leave him, but she knew it was good for him, too. He had Ethan to play with and the…Doc was as good a grandfather figure as any kid could ever hope for.

As she and Lizzie waited for the elevator, Ben came strolling down the corridor toward them. "Good morning, ladies," he greeted them with a smile.

"Hi, Ben."

"What are you up to today?" asked Lizzie.

He smiled. "I've got a couple of things I need to take care of."

Lizzie wagged her finger at him. "You're not at work now young man. You're supposed to be enjoying yourself, slacking off."

He laughed. "I am!"

"Well, okay then. But don't go getting busy, just relax for once in your life. Did I hear right that your mom and dad are coming tonight?"

Ben smiled again, but April could tell it wasn't genuine. "I think so. It'll depend when they get here."

Lizzie laughed. "Or if the wind blows them in another direction first?"

Ben pursed his lips. "Yep."

Lizzie touched his arm. "They're free spirits, Ben. Don't be too hard on them. They may not have the work ethic that you do, but they could teach you a thing or two about how to relax and have fun."

April felt embarrassed to witness this conversation. She felt as though she was eavesdropping on stuff that was personal, just by being present.

Ben nodded. "Yeah." He smiled at April. "You'll understand when you meet them."

The elevator arrived and they all stepped in.

~ ~ ~

Ben stepped out of the elevator and made his way to the front entrance. He was meeting Dan and Jack and some of the other guys there. He was looking forward to seeing his parents—in a way. He loved them. They were just different. He didn't understand them—any more than they understood him. They were, as Lizzie had said, free spirits. They had a wanderlust that he hadn't inherited. They spent most of their time roaming the country in a motor coach; a life that held no appeal for him. The resort was his life; Summer Lake was his home. He liked to work hard, make the most of every day. They seemed to spend their lives chasing tomorrow, chasing the next adventure. He shrugged. He didn't. That was his problem. If he was honest, part of him was dreading seeing them, they always bugged him about finding a girl, getting married and settling down. Since all his friends had started doing that, his infrequent conversations with his parents had gotten more strained than usual. This particular visit promised to be excruciating—considering that Charlotte was going to be here. They adored her. They still talked about her. They never even considered what that did to him. It made sense, though; she was just like them, another one who'd wanted to chase tomorrow. He stopped dead, realizing that he'd overshot the lobby and was wandering away down a corridor. That was what thinking about Charlotte did for him. Got him lost and off track. He shook his head and turned around to retrace his footsteps. He needed to stay in the moment, find the guys.

He'd have enough to deal with later. Having his parents and Charlotte here was going to be tough, to say the least.

He put a smile on his face as he spotted Dan waiting by the doors. He didn't need to burden anyone with his problems. This was about Dan and Missy's big day, not about his own regrets at never having one.

"Thanks for coming," said Dan.

Ben nodded. Dan had called him as soon as Doc Morgan had said Missy's dad would be okay to fly to join them. "I'm glad to. I was thinking, I could go back with Doc if you like?"

Dan cocked his head to one side. "I think it'll be fine. I mean, Chance is there, between him and the Doc they should be okay."

Ben nodded. He shouldn't have even suggested it. He was trying to take the coward's way out and not be here when Charlotte arrived.

Jack and Pete came striding through the crowded lobby toward them. As always they turned the head of every female within a hundred-yard radius. Ben sighed. He didn't need to go feeling sorry for himself just yet. He still had a long weekend ahead; it was too early to start envying the others just because they had it all while he... He rubbed his hands over his eyes. He had a great business to run.

Pete came straight to him. "Are you okay?"

"Course I am, bud."

Pete gave him that hard stare that worked so well on most people.

Ben laughed. "This is me, remember? You can't intimidate me with the Hemming glare! What's up anyway?"

Pete smiled. "Sorry. I just know you too well. And I know how hard this weekend must be. I'm trying to look out for my old buddy, that's all."

Ben smiled, glad that Pete finally seemed to be getting back to normal. "Thanks, Pete. I'm not going to say it's easy, but I'll survive." He decided to come clean. "I was just telling Dan I'd be happy to go with Doc to collect Chance and Missy's dad."

"So that you're not around when Charlotte arrives?"

"And my parents. If they make it."

Pete blew out a sigh. "I can see why you'd want to do that. If you do decide to go, there's a couple of things I'd like your help with."

Ben raised an eyebrow. "Why, what are you up to?"

Pete gave him a mysterious smile. "I'll tell you later. I want to make sure I can pull it off first."

Smoke, Nate, and Ryan came to join them. "Morning," said Smoke. He looked at Dan. "Have you figured out how you want to work it yet?"

Dan shook his head. "That's why I wanted to get you all together to help me figure it out. When should we get him here? How do we keep it a secret until five o'clock tomorrow?" He rubbed his hand over the stubble on his cheek. "I don't know what's going to be best."

"Let's make a plan then," said Pete.

Jack groaned and punched Pete's arm. "Will you never learn?"

Ben laughed. "We do need to work out the details." He smiled at Michael and Gabe as they wandered up to join them.

"You look pretty happy for a guy who just called off his wedding," said Pete.

Michael grinned at him. "I couldn't be happier, but I'm sure you won't understand, Hemming. You'd be crying over all the wasted plans and lost deposits."

Ben hadn't even thought about those details. He'd just been relieved that Michael and Megan were going to do what made them happy.

Pete grinned. "Too right, I would! I think it's a crying shame. In fact, I wanted to talk to you about it. See if I can't help you out.

Michael laughed. "No worries, mate. It's all good."

Ben laughed as Pete put an arm around Michael's shoulders. "No really," he said as he started to walk him away from the others. "Let's have a talk. You know I can't stand to see a good plan go to waste."

Gabe laughed as he watched them go. "What does Pete think he can do?"

Ben had an idea, but it seemed a little too far-fetched. Pete wouldn't do that. He shrugged. "Who knows?"

"Knowing Pete," said Smoke, "he'll probably help Michael negotiate some kind of deal with the hotel and the caterers, move his deposits to a later date rather than lose them completely." He looked at Jack, "He won't be able to stand to lose a deal without renegotiating, don't you think?"

Jack nodded, but he looked thoughtful. Ben got the impression that Jack might be thinking along the same lines he was. He'd have to ask him when he got the chance. If he was right, they'd find out soon enough.

Chapter Seventeen

Missy sat with Emma and Holly in the foyer to the spa. They'd decided to wait and see who else showed up before they went in.

She smiled as she saw Lizzie and April step out of the elevator. Holly followed her gaze. "Michael's mom is a superstar, isn't she? She was so much fun last night, and she's always either taking care of the kids or rounding up the strays and making sure no one is left out."

Missy nodded. "She's always been like that. She's always been so good to us, hasn't she, Em? I think she wishes she'd had a daughter. I mean she absolutely dotes on Michael and Gabe—her angels, but she loves spending time with the girls, too. She's taken Renée in like a daughter, you'd think she really is Megan's mom, the way she is with her—and Kenzie, too. She's like the mother hen." Missy fell quiet as Lizzie and April arrived to join them.

"Good morning, lovelies," said Lizzie with a bright smile. "I thought there'd be more of us."

"There will be," said Emma. "I spoke to Chris; her sister came in early this morning. Laura's going to bring them in a little while."

Holly looked puzzled. "I struggle to keep up. Just let me get this straight. Chris is Jack and Dan's mom, so her sister is Laura's mom, right?"

"That's right, said Missy with a grin. "We're all becoming just one big, complicated family."

"What do you think?" asked Emma. "Should we wait to see who else is coming, or should we go on in?"

"We may as well go in," said Missy. "The only one I'd worry about would be Megan, but she'll probably come with Kenzie, and I doubt Kenzie will even be awake yet.

April gave her a worried look. It was obvious that something was bothering her. Missy didn't want to ask her in front of everyone. If it was something she wanted to share, she would have spoken up, wouldn't she?

Soon they were all sitting in their robes, sipping smoothies in one of the opulent lounges, as they waited for their treatments. Lily and Leanne had come to join them. Missy was pleased to see Pete's mom, Anne, come in and sit with Holly. She really hoped things were getting better there.

April came to sit beside her. "What's the matter, hon?" asked Missy.

April looked troubled. "Can I share someone else's secret with you?"

Missy wrinkled her nose. "You can if you feel you need to. It won't go any further."

April sighed. "I wouldn't normally share anyone's secrets, I hope you know that. It's just that, well, I think this one should go further. Even though I know it's not my call to make. I'd love to hear what you think."

Missy was intrigued. "Go ahead. I'll tell you what I think, you can always count on me for that."

"Thanks," April's smile was full of relief. "It's Kenzie. Last night, she and Chase decided that they're going to go off and get married today. They asked me and Eddie to be their witnesses."

Missy wasn't surprised at all. It was just like Kenzie and Chase to do something like that. "So what's the problem? We can fit it in. She'll need to drag her ass out of bed and let everyone know though."

April sighed. "That is the problem. Since Megan just called off her own wedding, Kenzie thought it best not to say anything. To just go off, her and Chase, with me and Eddie as witnesses. It seems such a shame. For one, I think Megan would be really hurt not to be there for her, and besides, everyone's here—in one place—together. Surely they'd all want to help the two of them celebrate their marriage." She stopped and looked at Missy questioningly. "Or am I just trying to impose what I think? Am I interfering?"

Missy shook her head. "You're not interfering; you're just wondering what to do for the best. I'm the one who's about to interfere! Kenzie has this thing that she and Chase are just outsiders, newcomers to the lake. She feels as though she doesn't quite belong, not as much as everyone else does. And it's stupid! It's only because she can't quite get used to the fact that she finally does belong, that she has friends and family who love her!" She looked around for Lizzie. Missy had only been saying earlier how Lizzie was taking in Megan and Kenzie as her own daughters. Well, Missy was about to ask for her help. If Missy had anything to do with it, Lizzie was about to be mother-of-the-bride! "Come on," she said to April. "You did right telling me; now we're going to ask for Lizzie's help in interfering!"

~ ~ ~

Dan pulled his phone out of his pocket and checked the text that had just come in. His heart hammered in his chest as he read Missy's words.

We need to talk! Secret scheming going on!

Holy shit! How did she know? He looked around.

Jack caught his eye. "What's up, bro? You look like you've just seen a ghost!"

"Missy knows!" he said.

"How? What makes you think that?"

Dan had no idea as to the how. He looked around at the guys, they'd all come to sit in the bar while they figured out the logistics of getting Missy's dad here. Surely none of them would have let it slip? "I don't know, but read this."

He handed Jack his phone.

Jack grinned. "Calm down, little brother. I think you're getting jittery. I read that as Missy is doing some secret scheming of her own and wants your help. Text her back. Ask her what she means."

Dan blew out a sigh as his heart rate slowly returned to normal. "Thanks, Jack. I hope you're right." He tapped out a reply

What's going on?

A few seconds later his phone rang.

"Kenzie and Chase are planning on sneaking off and getting married today. I want to get everyone there to surprise them." Missy was whispering; it sounded like she was locked in a closet. Dan had to smile.

"Oh. Okay. Where are they going? What time?" Dan was hoping this wouldn't clash with getting Smoke and the Doc out of here and back to Summer Lake.

"I don't know yet! You know what they're like, I don't think they even know themselves."

Dan bit back a chuckle. This was so Missy. "So, beautiful, how am I supposed to help you get everyone there?"

She laughed. "I'll tell you when I figure it out. I guess I'm just excited and I want your help. You're the genius, you can make anything work."

Dan's heart swelled with pride. She had so much faith in him, and he had no idea why. "Okay. I'll let the guys know what to expect, and you let me know when you figure out the details."

"See if you can get anything out of Eddie. He and April are supposed to go with them to be their witnesses."

Dan looked around. Chase and Eddie had not long come down to join them. He spotted them sitting with Ryan and Nate. "I'll see what I can do."

"Great. I've got to go."

He laughed. "Where are you?"

She laughed with him. "I'm hiding in one of the treatment rooms so Kenzie doesn't hear. But I think someone's about to come in."

Dan laughed harder. "Well, get out while you can, but don't get caught!"

Pete had come over to join them and was talking to Jack. As Dan hung up, Jack smiled at him. "So?"

Dan explained about Kenzie and Chase.

"Well, damn!" said Jack. "This is turning out to be an eventful weekend. One wedding got canceled. One springs up out of nowhere. I wonder what's going to happen next."

Dan shook his head. "Hopefully nothing. There's been enough excitement already."

Pete grinned at him. "Don't say that, Dan. This is Vegas. The excitement never ends."

Dan smiled, hoping Pete was just joking. "I guess I need to talk to Eddie. See if he knows what their plans are."

Jack nodded. "You do that. We can start telling the others they need to be ready for another wedding today."

~ ~ ~

Kenzie spotted Megan. She was by herself, leaning on the balcony overlooking the conservatory.

"How are you doing, sis?" Kenzie was feeling uneasy about going off to get married just after Megan had called off her own wedding.

Megan's bright smile surprised her. It seemed so genuine. "I'm better than I have been in weeks, Kenz. I'm so relieved."

Kenzie wanted to believe her, but she found it hard to. "Are you really? You're not just putting on a brave face?"

"I'm really not! I know it doesn't make sense to you or anyone else. But the thought of getting married pregnant was making me miserable."

Kenzie smiled and leaned on the balcony next to her. "It doesn't need to make sense to anyone else. All that matters is that you're happy."

"Well, I am. So relax."

Kenzie nodded. She almost relaxed enough to tell Megan her own plans, but it still didn't seem right. It felt selfish somehow. She'd love for Megan to come with her and Chase. Hell, she'd love for everyone to be there. But it wasn't the same for them. All these people were here for Missy and for Michael—two of their own. Summer Lake originals. These guys had been friends all their lives. She and Chase were newcomers. She was grateful for the friendship and the acceptance that they'd been shown, but she knew they didn't really belong. Not in the same way. She wouldn't be so presumptuous as to think any of them would even want to come to her wedding. She sighed before she realized she had.

"Are you okay?" asked Megan.

"Me? I'm always okay. You know this."

Megan gave her a puzzled look. "I hope so. What are you doing this afternoon? Ethan's out with Doc this morning, but we were thinking of taking him over to the mall later. He'd love it if you came, too."

Kenzie shook her head. "I'm going to help Chase and Eddie practice. We invited April along." That was the cover story they'd come up with to explain their absence while they went downtown to the Marriage License Bureau and then ran across the street to the wedding chapel. Chase had researched it all online this morning. He'd even filled in the forms.

Megan looked sad. "Okay. You know, I was really looking forward to you being my bridesmaid tomorrow."

Kenzie nodded. She'd been looking forward to that, too. She wondered again if she should ask Megan to come. But no.

Missy came and leaned on the balcony on the other side of Megan. "What are you two up to? Got any plans for this afternoon?"

"We're thinking about taking Ethan to the big mall," said Megan. "Do you think Scot would like to come? I was going to ask you, and ask April about Marcus too." She looked at Kenzie. "Is he going to the practice with you?"

The way Missy looked at Kenzie made her nervous, for some reason. "You're going to practice?"

She nodded. She knew the best way to lie was to give as few details as possible. That way there was less to remember—and less to trip herself up with!

"What time?" asked Missy.

Damn! "I don't know yet. When the guys are ready."

Missy made a face. Apparently she was looking for a more specific answer, though Kenzie had no idea why it should matter to her.

Megan looked up at the big clock on the wall. "It's almost time for my massage. I'll catch up with you later."

Once she'd gone, Missy smiled. "Megan seems so much happier now they've decided to wait, doesn't she?"

Kenzie nodded.

"I don't think we need to worry about her, do we?"

Kenzie felt as though Missy was trying to get at something, but she didn't know what. It was weird, Missy was the most direct person she knew. Why would she be beating about the bush now? "Whatever it is, just come out and say it, Miss."

Missy laughed. "Don't mind me. I'm just trying to make sure that you're not worried about her. You know her better than anyone. She seems great, but if she wasn't, you would know."

Kenzie smiled. "Yeah. I think she's fine."

"So do I. I don't think anything would upset her right now."

Kenzie held Missy's gaze. It was almost as if Missy knew. And she was saying that Kenzie should tell Megan. No. That couldn't be right. It was more likely her own guilty conscience getting paranoid because she didn't want to upset Megan and she wasn't sure that keeping her own wedding a secret wouldn't hurt her more than telling her and inviting her would. "She'll be fine." Kenzie knew her words were aimed more at trying to reassure herself than Missy.

~ ~ ~

Missy went back through to the lounge where she found Emma, Holly, and April. "I was hoping to get Kenzie to tell me, but she's not going to. I think she feels guilty about not telling Megan, though. We are doing the right thing, aren't we?" She knew she was butting in where she shouldn't, but she couldn't just stand back. She knew in her heart that Kenzie would love to have the others there, if she could. Or at least she thought she knew, she wanted some reassurance from the others.

Emma nodded. "I think so. I think Kenzie would love to have everyone there. I don't think it's a case of they want to go off by themselves. It's more like they're just spontaneous people. Kenzie wouldn't want to bother anyone. She doesn't believe anyone would want to go out of their way for her. And Chase, well, he just goes with the flow. They both feel as though they're a little bit different from the rest of us, as though they're not quite part of the gang."

"Exactly!" said Missy. "And what better way to prove to them that we see them as part of the family?"

Holly smiled. "I think it's the right thing to do, too."

Missy raised an eyebrow at her. "But what?"

Holly laughed. "But nothing. Not about them anyway. I was just wishing that Pete and I could have done something like that."

Missy smiled. "You two will figure out what's right for you now." She turned to April. "See, your instincts were right. Thank you."

April smiled. "Thank you! I hate to break a confidence, and I hope Kenzie doesn't hate me for it. But I had to say something."

Emma patted her arm. "Kenzie will love you for it."

"I hope so." She pulled her cell phone out of the pocket of her robe. "That's her," she said as she read a text. "I'm supposed to meet her at their room at one thirty."

Missy looked out to where Kenzie was still leaning on the balcony. Renée was chatting with her. She turned back to April. "Well, you've got my number. Keep me updated. Let me know everything you can. Especially about times! It's going to take some doing to get everyone to the chapel, but I'm going to try!"

Chapter Eighteen

Ben grinned at the sight of everyone congregated outside the main entrance. He was happy that they all wanted to be there for Kenzie and Chase. April and Eddie had been willing accomplices in leaking back the details as they learned them.

Ben had gone ahead and hired a shuttle bus. It was waiting outside, on standby to get everyone to the church on time. Wherever the church was—and whatever the time might be!

Missy looked up from her phone with a big smile on her face. "They got the license and Chase just called the chapel across the street from the Marriage Bureau. They can fit them in at three! We need to get moving, people!"

Everyone started making their way toward the shuttle bus. Ben stopped as he passed Missy. "Do you think you'll make it back in time?" he asked.

She nodded. She knew what he meant. "These wedding chapels try to get people in and out as fast as they can. I doubt we'll be there more than fifteen minutes. Dan got the caterers onto it and they're putting on a reception in our function room when we get back here. I'll just slip away and pick Charlotte up at the airport. She's due in at four twenty."

Ben nodded. Pete had told him what time she was landing. He just wished he could find some reason to be out of here by then.

Michael stuck his head back out of the shuttle bus. "Come on, you two! Get a move on!"

Ben followed Missy onto the bus. "You've done us proud, mate," said Michael gesturing around the plush interior of the mini-coach.

Ben smiled. "We needed something that could get us all there in one group—and fast!"

Michael laughed and held on as the coach pulled out. "I see what you mean!"

Ben moved along and took an empty seat in front of Megan. He'd been a little concerned how she might feel about all of this. "Are you okay?" he asked.

She beamed at him. "I'm wonderful." She held up a big bag. "I even brought my wedding dress, in case she wants to wear it."

Ben grinned. Megan was an amazing little person.

She gave him an inquiring look. "I'm going to see if she wants to borrow it. I wondered if she might like to borrow the guy who's supposed to walk me down the aisle, too."

Ben hadn't even thought about that.

"She'd love it, you know. You're her boss, but you're so much more than that. You're the person who made it possible for her to stay at the lake. You're more than a friend even, you're more like a brother, to both of us. It means the world to me that you're going to give me away. I think it would mean just as much to Kenzie."

He nodded. He knew it would. For all her worldly ways and street smarts, Kenzie looked up to him, as Megan had said, more as a brother than as a boss. "I'd be honored to."

~ ~ ~

Kenzie looked around the waiting area of the wedding chapel. She was excited. This felt right. Chase had managed to get them into a room called The Wedding Garden. From the pictures it looked like a Mediterranean courtyard, except it was inside. It looked lovely. It had white chairs for guests to sit, and a little aisle between them. It was perfect. Part of her wished that they'd have some guests, she shrugged. It wasn't as though she'd ever even dreamed of a wedding growing up. She had what mattered—the man she loved, and who loved her. Having guests and someone to walk you down the aisle—that was for other girls. Girls who'd lived very different lives than she had. She was fortunate she even had friends now. She'd never had real friends before. Family had never been part of the picture for her. She'd been as good as dead to her parents since she was seventeen.

Chase put an arm around her shoulders and smiled down at her. "Are you happy with this?"

She reached up to plant a kiss on his lips. "I am. I'm happy with you and that's what it's all about. We're not the kind to do anything traditional. This is right for us."

"As long as you're sure."

"I am. I love you. I want to marry you. Right here, right now." She turned to look at April and Eddie.

April was texting someone, no doubt checking up on Marcus. She looked guilty when she caught Kenzie watching her.

"Is everything okay?" asked Kenzie.

April nodded. "I hope so. I have a confession to make."

Kenzie frowned. "And what's that?"

April went to the door and looked out. She beckoned to someone, before turning back to Kenzie. "I told Megan."

Kenzie's eyes filled with tears when her sister came in through the door. She smiled and held up a large bag. "Sorry if you don't want me, but I wondered if you want to borrow my dress?"

Kenzie swiped at the happy tears that were rolling down her face. "I do want you! This is amazing! I'm sorry I didn't tell you." She looked at April. "And I'm glad you did! Thank you."

April was visibly relieved as she smiled back.

Kenzie looked at Chase. He was beaming.

"Did you know?"

He shook his head. "I had no idea." He grinned at Megan. "But I'm so glad you're here. Is Michael with you?"

Megan nodded as Ethan peeked his head around the door. "Is it safe yet?" he asked.

Kenzie laughed. "Come on in, monkey, and bring your dad."

Ethan grinned. "What about the others?"

Kenzie stared at Megan. "What others?"

Megan grinned. "Um, all of them?"

"All of them?" Kenzie's heart felt as though it might burst. She went to the door. She felt as though her knees might buckle under at the sight of all the smiling faces that greeted her. Ethan reached up for a hug. "I don't know why you thought you could get married without me here, Auntie Kenzie." He gave her a hurt look. "That was pretty dumb of you."

She sniffed and smiled at him. "You know me. Sometimes I can be a bit dumb."

He patted her arm. "That's okay."

She laughed as she looked back up at the crowd waiting outside.

"So, are we invited?" asked Missy.

"Of course you are! Come on in! This is wonderful!" She couldn't quite believe it as they all trooped in. Emma and Jack, Pete and Holly, Missy and Dan, Smoke and Laura, Michael came to join Megan, and Gabe and Renée. Even the oldies. Ben's grandpa, Joe. Emma's Gramps. Pete's parents, who she always thought must be stuck up, but had found out this weekend were awesome. Jack and Dan's mom, Laura's mom. She tried to swallow back a fresh wave of happy tears as Doc Morgan came in and gave her a hug.

"Thanks for being here," she mumbled.

He hugged her tight. "We wouldn't miss it for the world. We consider you girls family."

Kenzie wiped her sleeve over her eyes as Lizzie stepped up. "And that makes me mother of the bride," she said. "So I'll give you a minute with Ben, and then we need to get you ready."

Ben brought up the rear. He smiled and held his arms open to her. She couldn't stop the tears that were streaming down as he hugged her. He patted her back and stroked her hair. Eventually she sniffed and looked up at him. "Sorry, boss. I guess I'm a bit emotional."

His smile was so kind. "Quit with the boss shit, would you? We're family. Or at least I feel like we are. So, I was wondering…" It seemed as though he was pretty choked up himself.

"Wondering what?" she asked.

"If you'd like me to walk you down the aisle?"

Kenzie sobbed. She couldn't keep it in! This was all too wonderful. It was so much more than she'd ever dreamed of, certainly much more than she felt she deserved.

Ben smiled. "Hey, no need to cry. If you hate the idea that much, just say no."

She slapped his arm. "Asshole! I'd love it. I would absolutely love it. Thank you."

He nodded. "It'll be my honor."

He gestured toward Lizzie and Megan who were waiting for her outside the little changing room. "Since we messed up your makeup with all those tears, you might want to go get ready."

She nodded and went to join them, wondering if she might be dreaming.

~ ~ ~

Chase stood at the front of the chapel with Eddie by his side. He couldn't quite believe how this had all worked out. He was thrilled. For himself as much as for Kenzie. He loved Summer Lake, he loved the life he and Kenzie had started there. He loved that they had such a great group of friends, though like her, he didn't feel they were part of the group. He'd always felt just that little bit apart from them. They had so much history together. This though? Today? They were proving it, leaving no room for any doubt whatsoever that they saw him and Kenzie as two of their own. It meant the world to him. It meant so much more than he had words for.

"Are you all right?" asked Eddie.

He nodded. He didn't want to risk words, the lump in his throat might not let them out.

He looked around the now crowded room. They were all smiling back at him. He could feel the love and support coming off them in waves. It was amazing. He caught Smoke's eye. Smoke grinned and nodded at him. Dan smiled and gave him the thumbs up. Michael winked at him. Over on the other side, Emma gave him a little wave. He had to laugh as Jack scowled at her then gave Chase a mock stern look. It seemed a lifetime ago that he'd been new at the lake and had had his eye on Emma. Jack had soon set him straight about that. Emma was nice, but she was no Kenzie. She and Jack were perfect together. Just like him and Kenzie.

He turned to watch Kenzie as she came out and took her place at the other end of the short aisle, with Ben at her side. He had to swallow around that lump in his throat. He even wiped his fingers quickly over his eyes as the canned music began. He, and everyone else, burst out laughing when instead of the Wedding March, the theme tune from Jaws began to play. That was so Kenzie! He had no idea when she'd set that up, but he was glad she had.

After the first few bars, it changed to the Wedding March. He felt like he'd been sucker punched. All the air rushed out of his lungs as she held onto Ben's arm and walked toward him. She was so goddamned beautiful! He knew it was Megan's dress she was wearing, but it looked as though it had been made for her. It was much more modest than anything she would have chosen for herself, but it suited her perfectly. It matched her soft, sweet smile as she met his gaze. He felt like the luckiest man on earth. She was his. She loved him, and she was about to marry him.

When they reached the front, Ben smiled at him. He bent down to kiss Kenzie's cheek and stepped to the side. Chase wanted to hug him. That guy had made everything possible for the two of them.

The minister stepped up. "Friends and family. We are gathered here today..."

Chase looked at Kenzie and they both smiled through the tears. They really were surrounded by friends and family, something neither of them had expected. Something neither of them would ever forget.

~ ~ ~

Jack smiled at Emma. In some ways it seemed like yesterday that they'd taken their own wedding vows. In other ways, it seemed like a lifetime ago. They'd come so far in their first year together, and now they were expecting their first child. She smiled back up at him, making his heart swell in his chest. Whenever she smiled at him, her eyes shone with love. It had taken him a long time to earn it, but they shone with trust, too. He vowed again to himself that he would never do anything to break that trust. He'd spend the rest of his life taking care of her and their baby. He looked across at Pete, wondering if the wedding ceremony might make his partner feel as sentimental as he did himself. It sure looked like it!

~ ~ ~

Pete slid his arm around Holly's shoulders as he listened to the minister's words. "To have and to hold. To cherish and to protect…"

Her smile told him she remembered the way he'd proposed to her. He breathed a happy sigh. They'd put each other through some shit these last few months, but they were out the other side now. They could make it right. He knew it. He couldn't help smiling to himself. He even had a plan!

~ ~ ~

Dan closed his hand around the back of Missy's neck. She looked up into his eyes. Tomorrow this would be them. He couldn't wait! He was even more excited now that her dad was going to be here. His mind was already racing on to how he was going to manage things so she wouldn't find out.

"I think the risk paid off, don't you?" she whispered. "This was a good surprise for them."

He nodded, hoping that she'd like his surprise for her even more tomorrow.

~ ~ ~

Smoke squeezed Laura's hand and smiled when she squeezed right back. Weddings normally bored him, but he was really touched by this. He squeezed his eyes shut for a moment. Kenzie had come such a long way since she first came to the lake. He couldn't help feeling a sense of pride that he and Laura had been the ones who had taken Chase to rescue her from what she'd been living in Nashville. He sure as hell wouldn't call it a life. He was happy for the two of them. And for the first time, he felt impatient. He wanted to be the one standing up there with his lady. He wanted to stand before God and their friends and families and vow to Laura to love her and make her happy for the rest his life.

Her blue eyes shone as she smiled up at him. She looked around the room and raised an eyebrow. He followed her gaze, not understanding. Did she mean the people or the décor? He knew she loved everybody here. The room itself was a pleasant surprise to him, for a Vegas chapel. It was done up to feel like a rustic courtyard in Tuscany. He raised an eyebrow back at her.

"Let's get married in the Mediterranean somewhere," she whispered.

~ ~ ~

Megan rested her head against Michael's shoulder as Ethan squirmed in between them. He hoped she really was all right with this. It had to be weird for her, going to her sister's surprise wedding the day after she'd canceled her own. Nah, postponed her own.

She quelled all his fears when she turned to smile at him. "I'm so happy for them, Michael!" she murmured.

He grinned. "Me, too." He really was.

"Me three!" Ethan piped up. They both shushed him as those around them chuckled.

~ ~ ~

Gabe watched Renée dab at her eyes. He'd always wondered why women cried at weddings. Today brought him much closer to understanding. He felt a little sentimental himself. Kenzie and Chase were both good people. They deserved happiness as much as, if not more than, anybody here. He knew Kenzie felt like an outsider, and when he first met her, he'd considered her to be one. He was glad to admit now that he'd been very wrong. She'd become one of them. One of the gang. One of the family. Chase had, too. If anything, they belonged more than he himself did. He got a free ticket because he was a born Summer Laker. Watching Kenzie and

Chase have their first kiss, he determined that he would earn his place, just like they had.

Renée blew her nose and looked at him. He knew what she was thinking. "Not long now," he said quietly.

She smiled and he smiled right back. He couldn't help it when she looked at him like that.

~ ~ ~

Ben stared straight ahead. He started taking inventory in his head. He needed to go down in the cellar at the lodge when they got back and... And what? Even his usual fail safe mind tricks to help him not think about Charlotte couldn't help him now. He was happy for Kenzie and Chase, was proud to have been a part of their special day. But now he just wanted to get out of here. Even though he put on a brave face, he hated weddings at the best of times. And this sure as hell wasn't the best of times!

Chapter Nineteen

Missy stood with Emma outside the arrivals point at the airport. Charlotte's plane was a little late, but at least she was on it. Emma was practically bouncing up and down with excitement.

"This has been such a great day, and it's going to get even better when Charlotte gets here. I can't wait to see her!"

Missy nodded. She was excited, too, but she was feeling bad about Ben. "I hope Ben's going to stick around," she said. "Did you notice how quiet he was on the way back from the chapel?"

"I did." Emma sighed. "I wish there was some way they could just be friends. You know, be happy to see each other after all this time. Maybe they'll get talking and everything will be okay. Do you think?"

Missy didn't. She remembered her conversation with Ben earlier in the week. "I don't. It's too hard for him. He's not over her, and I don't think he ever will be."

Emma sighed again. "I wish I had a time machine and could go back and change what happened between them. Make it right."

Missy smiled sadly. "Life's not like that though, is it. We'd all go back and change something." She shrugged. "A year ago I would have gone back and changed things, and look what I would have missed out on. I would never have met Dan. And nothing I went back to could make me as happy as I am right now. If there's one thing I've learned in life, it's that there's no point wishing we could change yesterday. All we can do is our best to make a better tomorrow."

Emma smiled. "Well, aren't you quite the philosopher?"

Missy laughed. "You get a diploma in that stuff when you graduate from the School of Hard Knocks…. Oh my God! There she is!" Missy started waving madly when she spotted Charlotte.

Emma squealed and clapped her hands together before she too started waving like a crazy person! "Charlotte!" she shouted so loudly that people around them turned to look.

Charlotte grinned and waved back. When she reached them, the three of them stood there squealing and hugging.

When they'd calmed down enough to actually speak, Charlotte grinned at Missy. "Have you grown, shrimp? I'm sure you're taller than you were last time I saw you."

Missy laughed. "No, you're just shrinking in your old age, beanpole. I can't believe you're finally here."

"You can't? How do you think I feel? It took forever! I needn't have worried about having enough time in Dallas. I ended up sitting there for ages waiting for this second flight."

"Well, you're here now," said Emma. She took hold of Charlotte's case and started pulling it toward the exit. "Come on! You're missing a perfectly good party."

Charlotte looked at Missy. "You're partying? I thought I missed the hen night?"

Missy laughed. "You did. This is a reception for two of our friends who made the most of being in Vegas to sneak off and get married themselves."

"Well, they tried to sneak off," said Emma, "but our Miss was on the case. You know what she's like. She rounded everyone up and got us all there. And now she and Dan are throwing a party for them."

They walked outside and Charlotte started heading toward the line of people waiting for taxis.

"This way," called Emma.

Charlotte gave Missy a puzzled look as they kept walking. "We have our very own shuttle bus," explained Missy.

"Oh wow, this Dan of yours is sparing no expense is he?"

"It wasn't Dan, it was Ben," said Emma.

Missy watched Charlotte's face for a reaction, but she wasn't giving anything away. "He rented it to get us all to Kenzie and Chase's wedding this afternoon, then decided we may as well keep it for the rest of the weekend. It seems someone is always needing to go somewhere. This makes life much easier."

The driver took Charlotte's bag from Emma and the three of them climbed on board. Charlotte looked around. "I guess I don't need to ask if the resort is doing well. This must have cost him a pretty penny."

Missy nodded. "The resort does very, very well. I just wish I could say the same for Ben. He works his ass off."

Charlotte nodded. "No surprises there. He always has." She held Missy's gaze. "How is he?"

Missy shrugged. "He's okay. His parents are supposed to be coming tonight. But whether they will or not is another matter."

Charlotte smiled. "Oh, I hope they do. I'd love to see them."

Missy nodded. She knew how much they loved Charlotte. It bothered her that they seemed to care more about her than they did Ben.

"How are you anyway?" asked Emma. "And where's Alastair? Why didn't he come?"

Charlotte rolled her eyes. "It's good to see you're still as nosey as ever, Mousey."

Emma hung her head, "Sorry. I'm just excited to see you. I want to hear all your news, that's all."

Charlotte shrugged. "We decided it'd be best if he didn't come."

Missy wrinkled her nose. "Why though?"

"Good God! You're as bad as she is!"

Missy grinned. "That's what friends are for."

"What? To bug the shit out of you until you divulge every detail of your personal life?"

"Pretty much. So spill. What's going on with you two?"

Charlotte stared out of the coach window for a few moments. "We've been going through a rough patch recently."

Missy knew she shouldn't, but she felt a rush of happiness at that news.

Emma apparently felt the same way, but she had no qualms whatsoever about saying so. "Well get rid of him then and come back home to the lake with us!"

"Emma!" Missy gave her the look she usually saved for Scot when he was misbehaving.

"What?" Emma was unrepentant.

Charlotte laughed. "It's okay, Miss. Part of me wishes I could do just that. But I can't."

"Why not?" they both asked at once.

"Well, aside from all the practical details of having a life in London. I can't just get rid of him as Emma puts it. I married him. I made a commitment. And if I left him, it would be for all the wrong reasons."

"What reasons?" Missy asked. Though she had a feeling she already knew.

Charlotte shrugged. "There's no point getting into it, because it's not going to happen. Oh look! There it is!"

They were almost back to the Bellagio. Charlotte pointed through the window to the beautiful building, fronted by the pool where later the fountains would dance.

"Are you really excited to see the hotel, or is that just a diversion tactic to end this conversation?"

Charlotte gave Emma a wry smile. "You figure it out. And if you don't mind, Miss, I want to go check in and go up to my room. It's been a long day for me already. I need a shower and a couple of minutes to pull myself together before I can start partying."

"Of course. We'll come with you."

"Don't you need to get back to your guests?"

"They're fine. And besides, they're not my guests right now. They're Kenzie and Chase's guests."

"I'll go tell them you're on the way," said Emma.

"Thanks, Mouse."

~ ~ ~

Emma made her way back to the function room. She wished with all her heart that Charlotte and Ben could somehow find their way back to each other. She knew it wasn't possible. Their paths had separated so abruptly, so long ago. They'd both built a life for themselves that didn't include the other, but in Emma's mind at least, they still belonged together. She so wanted for Ben to be happy. He deserved it more than anyone she knew. She didn't believe he ever would be happy with anyone who wasn't Charlotte, though. And Charlotte was married. To someone else. And lived on the other side of the Atlantic. But still. For all Emma loved to predict happily-ever-afters for her friends, she couldn't ever see Ben finding his without Charlotte.

The function room was crowded. Everyone was talking and laughing, eating and drinking. She'd wanted to come back here rather than go with Missy and Charlotte for a couple of reasons. She wanted to let Ben know to prepare himself. She wanted to let Dan know that Missy was back, so anything that was going on with getting her dad here needed to be shushed up. She looked around the crowded room—she wanted to find Jack. She loved that man with all her heart.

Ben found her before she found anyone else. He looked stressed. She hugged him tight before he could say a word.

He gave her a grateful smile. "Thanks, Em. I take it she's here?"

She nodded. "She's going to check in and take a shower before she comes down."

"I'll probably miss her then."

"Why? Where are you going?"

"I'm going back to the lake with Smoke and the doc."

"Oh. Okay. You are going to come back with them, aren't you?"

"Of course I am. I wouldn't miss the wedding for the world. It's just that I don't want to be around here tonight. My folks called and they're not going to get in until really late, so there's no need for me to be here."

"And you need to not be here, right?"

"Yup. Besides, Pete asked me to…." He stopped short.

Emma frowned. "To what?"

"Nothing." He shook his head.

"Come on, Ben. What's perfect Pete up to?"

"Are they back?" Emma hadn't even noticed Dan come to join them.

"Oh, sorry Dan. Yeah, they've gone up to Charlotte's…" Emma watched Ben take advantage of her being distracted and walk away. She sighed.

"Are you all right?" asked Dan.

She nodded. "I am. I'm not so sure about Ben though."

"Me neither, but I don't know what we can do. He wanted to go get Missy's dad."

"Yeah. He wants out of here is what he wants," said Emma.

"And who can blame him?" asked Dan.

"I know," said Emma. She shrugged. "I guess he has to cope however he can. I came to let you know that we're back. Missy will be down soon, so if you've got any arrangements left to make, you'd better hurry up."

"Thanks. Everything's sorted. Smoke is already out at the airport getting Papa Charlie ready. Ben and the Doc wanted to be here for Kenzie and Chase for a little while, but now Charlotte's arrived they'll be on their way too."

"And what are they going to do when they get back here? How are you going to keep Missy's dad a secret?"

Dan smiled. "I talked to my friend, George on the concierge desk. We're going to sneak them in the back. Gramps and Joe are looking forward to hanging out with him and George has cleared one of the smaller VIP lounges for them. Missy will never go in there, and it means he won't have to stay hidden cooped up in his room."

"So he's well enough to be out and about then?"

"He is. According to Alice, apart from the muscle weakness on the one side, you wouldn't know there's anything wrong with him."

"Oh, that's good! Will he be able to walk her down the aisle, do you think?"

Dan shook his head sadly. "He's in a wheelchair. He can take a few steps, but he's very unsteady. I need to talk to him when he arrives. Figure out what he wants to do. He was adamant before that he wouldn't go down the aisle in a wheelchair. I'm hoping he's changed his mind, but somehow I doubt it."

"So do I!" Emma loved Missy's dad. She'd always called him a grumpy old bear. He was gruff to say the least, but he was as kind as he was stubborn.

Jack came to join them as they talked. "You're back, wifey," he said with a grin.

She reached up to kiss his cheek. "I am. I missed you."

Dan smiled. "I'll leave you two to your reunion then. I've got stuff to do."

"Is everything set?" asked Jack. "Do you need me for anything?"

"I think I've got it all covered now, thanks. I just want to give Chance a quick call before Miss gets here."

They watched him walk away. Jack smiled down at her. "That little brother of mine has come a long way in the last year."

"I think we all have," Emma replied. She watched Kenzie and Chase chatting and laughing with Gabe and Renée, and April and Eddie. "The bride and groom certainly have. Come on, let's go see them. I haven't officially congratulated them yet."

~ ~ ~

Eddie smiled when Jack and Emma came to join them. He watched as they congratulated Kenzie and Chase. He liked the two of them; they were his kind of people.

Jack turned to greet him. "And I believe we need to thank you for making sure we could all get there."

Eddie shook his head. "Not me. It was April's idea. I was just a mole in the camp."

Chase laughed. "Yeah, what kind of friend are you?"

Kenzie smiled. "The best kind," she said. She smiled at him then at April. "And you. You're the best, both of you. I'll know to keep my eye on you in future."

Laura came to join them and brought Leanne and Lily with her. Soon the talk had turned to girl stuff. Eddie excused himself from the little group and went to the bar to get a fresh drink. He stood there, surveying the room. This was such a great bunch of people. He was happy to be a part of it. He spotted the boys sitting at a table in the corner. Poor little guys looked bored silly. He went over and pulled out a chair to join them. Scot was fiddling with his phone and barely looked up. Marcus gave him a wary look and then went back to staring at his shoes while he kicked his feet together. Ethan grinned at him.

"I can play guitar, too, you know."

Eddie had to laugh. "I know. I remember when Chase taught you."

"Uncle Chase!" Ethan corrected him. "He's married to my Auntie Kenzie now."

Eddie smiled. He wasn't really sure how to talk to little kids. Especially one as precocious as Ethan. He turned to Marcus. "Do you play guitar?"

The kid still looked wary. He shook his head, but didn't speak.

"You should teach him," chimed in Ethan.

That hadn't been in Eddie's plan. Marcus looked up at him again. He looked scared and hopeful at the same time.

"Would you like that?" Eddie asked, before he'd considered the implications.

Marcus nodded and for the first time, Eddie saw him smile.

"We'll have to see what we can work out then, huh?"

The smile faded. Eddie guessed that the kid was used to being let down. He'd had a pretty tough start in life by the sounds of it.

"Come on. Let's go find your mom and we'll ask her."

Marcus's eyes were wide. "For real?"

Eddie nodded. "For real!" He wasn't too sure how he'd gotten himself into this, but now he had, he was determined not to let the kid down.

Ethan jumped up. "Yeah, let's go."

Eddie hadn't been banking on that; he couldn't exactly tell him no though.

Scot saved him. He looked up over his phone. "Hey, Ethan. Can you show me how to unlock the next level? I'm stuck again."

Ethan snatched the phone. "Course I can. It's easy, you just…"

Scot gave Eddie a knowing smile while Ethan chattered on. "See you later, I guess."

Wow, Scot was pretty damned perceptive for a teenager! Eddie jerked his head at Marcus for him to join him and they went off to find April.

~ ~ ~

"Are you ready for this?" asked Missy.

Charlotte nodded as the elevator doors opened and they stepped out. "Ready as I'll ever be. By the sounds of it he's not going to talk to me anyway."

"Probably not."

Charlotte brought both hands up to cover her face as she took a deep breath. Her heart was hammering; her hands were shaking. She stopped walking.

Missy raised her eyebrows. "Are you sure you're okay?"

"No. I'm not. But I don't have any choice do I? I'm being ridiculous. I'm about to see a guy I dated when I was a teenager. So what? Big deal, right? I mean, honestly!"

Missy wrinkled her nose. "It is a big deal though. He's not just some guy you dated years ago. He's Ben. He's…."

"My soul mate," finished Charlotte. She scrabbled in her bag for a hanky. "I don't believe this, Miss."

Missy looked worried.

"I don't believe I'm messing up my mascara."

Missy laughed. "Don't worry, you look fantastic."

Charlotte hoped so. She'd spent weeks figuring out her wardrobe for this weekend. She'd bought so many outfits, finding fault with each of them before going out and buying another. The dress she'd chosen for tonight made a statement, all right. It was a simple sheath that clung to her slender figure, the pushup bra, she'd paid a fortune for, gave her more cleavage than she'd ever have imagined her less than ample breasts could muster. The dress was a bright blue that made her eyes seem ever bluer. Her light brown hair fell in soft curls around her shoulders. She looked good and she knew it. She just hoped Ben would think so. Even though what he thought shouldn't matter at all! She looked at Missy.

"Why am I doing this, Miss?"

"Because I asked you to. I invited you to my wedding, remember?"

Charlotte shook her head. "I know that much. But why I am I getting so worked up about Ben? It's stupid. He doesn't want to know me. And even if he did, what would that look like? It's not as though the two of us could ever make polite conversation about nothing. The only way we know how to be together, is to be together." She sighed. "And those days are over."

"Are they over forever?" Missy raised an eyebrow.

"Of course they are! How can you even ask me that? Even as she said it, she knew Missy was only asking the question she kept asking herself.

Missy shrugged. "You just said he's your soul mate."

"I did, didn't I? I don't think I've ever admitted that to anyone before. Including me."

"I could tell. You looked as shocked as I felt when you said it."

"But Miss. It's over. It's been over for years. Even if there wasn't this minor detail of me being married to someone else.

There's too much history between us. You know what happened."

Missy shrugged. "Isn't that the nature of a soul mate? They're a part of you. They share your history. They also share your future and your present. Even when they're not there."

Charlotte thought about that. Ben was certainly a part of her. He may not have been there in her life all these years, but he'd certainly been there in her mind, in her heart. She sighed. "Let's just get on with it, shall we?"

Missy smiled. "That's my Charlotte. Just rush in and get on with it, right? See how it pans out."

She nodded. "That would appear to be my usual M.O., yes."

Chapter Twenty

Pete saw Missy and Charlotte come in and stop just inside the doorway. He was glad Ben had already left. What would it do to him to see her standing there? She was a beautiful woman, no question about it. She'd been pretty when they were kids. Now? Now she was…

"Well, hello, gorgeous!" Nate stood beside him. He sounded as though his tongue might be hanging out. "Why did Missy never tell me she had a friend who looked like that? Come on, Hemming. You have to introduce me. My weekend just took a turn for the better."

Pete shook his head. "Forget it, Nate."

"How could I forget a woman who looks like that? I intend to spend the rest of this weekend making beautiful memories with her."

Pete had to laugh. "Weren't you saying that about Lily last night?"

Nate looked put out. "Yes. But Lily wasn't interested. She turned me down flat—four times! She broke my heart."

"I wasn't aware that you had one?"

"Oh, that hurts."

"Yeah, right." Pete watched Missy and Charlotte make their way over to where Dan was chatting with Laura and Leanne.

"Come on," Nate tugged at his sleeve. "I need to meet her. She might just turn out to be the love of my life."

Pete pursed his lips. "No."

"What do you mean, no? She might."

"I doubt it. You don't know who she is."

"Who? Tell me! I need to know!"

"You're right, you do need to know. You see, she's the love of Ben's life."

Nate's lecherous grin disappeared in an instant. "That's Charlotte?"

Pete was surprised. "He told you about her?"

Nate nodded. "I'm staying at the resort remember. We hung out after he closed the bar the other night. He was drowning his sorrows."

Pete felt bad again that he'd been so caught up in his own mess, he hadn't been there for his friend like he should. "I should have been there for him."

"That's okay, boss. I stood in for you."

"Thanks, Nate. Come on. I'll introduce you, now you know."

Nate followed him.

Charlotte looked up as he approached. "Oh my God! Pete Hemming!" she cried. "Just look at you. All grown up."

Pete grinned as he looked her over. "Same back at ya, Charlotte. It's good to see you."

"You too, old friend." She reached up to hug him.

"It's been too long."

She stood back and met his gaze. "It has, but we both know why."

Pete nodded. "He's not here tonight."

"Yeah," she looked disappointed. "Dan was just telling us."

Missy looked upset. "I hate it. I bet he's just hiding in his room. I think I should go up there."

Pete exchanged a look with Dan. "He said he wanted to be by himself. I'll check on him later. He's not going to come down."

Missy sighed. "I know, you're right."

Charlotte shook her head sadly, but said nothing.

Pete looked around at them. "Well this is awkward, hey? How about we change the subject?"

Missy smiled.

So did Charlotte. "Good idea, Pete. How about you? I hear you've got a wedding of your own coming up in the not too distant future?"

He couldn't help grinning. "That's right. Not too distant at all."

Missy gave him a puzzled look. "Have you two got it all worked out now?"

"I have!" And he couldn't wait! His phone buzzed in his pocket. He checked it. "Sorry. I just need to deal with this. Give me a minute? When I'm done I'll find Holly and introduce you." He went to the doors and out into the corridor before he hit the speed dial.

"Where the hell is it?" asked Ben. "I feel like a freaking burglar sneaking around your house."

Pete laughed. "It's exactly where I said it was. Hanging in the closet in a big bag thing."

Ben was quiet for a few moments. "Oh. Shit. This thing! It was in front of my nose the whole time. Okay. Panic over."

Pete laughed. "Thanks, bud. I appreciate it."

"Sure thing. I'm going to ask you again though, are you absolutely sure about this?"

"I've learned better than to be absolutely sure. If it doesn't work out, so be it. I'm not going to try to impose it. I'm just going offer it as a possibility."

"Okay. If that's how you're approaching it, then I'm with you."

"Thanks, Ben."

Pete wondered whether he should say anything about Charlotte.

Ben made the decision for him. "Have you seen Charlotte yet?"

"Yeah, she's here now."

Ben was quiet for a long moment. "How does she look?"

"I'd love to tell you that she looks old and frumpy and that you did well to get out of that situation."

Ben heaved a loud sigh. "But really she looks even more beautiful than she ever did and you feel sorry for me that I fucked up the best thing that ever happened to me?"

"I wouldn't put it like that. Well, apart from that first bit. She does look stunning!"

"That's okay. I knew she would."

"Do you think maybe it's time to let the past lie? She's one of us. She always will be."

Ben sighed again. "I can't, Pete. I... Ask Missy why."

Pete was puzzled by that. "You can tell Miss, but you can't tell me?"

"It's not that, bud. It's just that I don't want to say it out loud again. Ask her. You'll understand. I'd better get going. I said I'd meet up with the others back at the airport. Smoke went with Doc to pick up Chance and his dad."

"Okay. I'll let you go. Give me a shout when you get back here."

"Will do. See you later."

Pete made his way back inside. He spotted Holly, sitting with Michael and Megan and Lily. Michael winked at him. "What are you up to, Pete? Anything you want to tell us about?"

Pete scowled at him. Just because he was in on it, didn't mean he should go risking anything. "Actually, I came to find Holly," he smiled at her. "I'd like you to meet Charlotte."

"The Charlotte? Ben's Charlotte?" she asked.

He nodded. "She was one of the gang when we were growing up."

Holly stood to join him. "I know that much. I'd love to meet her!"

~ ~ ~

Chance took his dad's arm as they waited for Smoke to let the plane steps down when they landed at McCarran. "Do you want me to go ahead of you?" he asked.

His dad nodded. "Thanks, son."

Chance swallowed, hard. He was glad to step in front, so his dad couldn't see his face. Couldn't see the tears he was blinking back. When they made it to the bottom, his dad leaned on his arm for a moment. "See, I did it under my own steam."

Chance nodded and looked at the wheelchair the doc had waiting. "What do you think? Do you want that?"

"Want it? Hell no!" He shuffled in front of it and let himself plonk down. "But even I can't deny that I need it."

When they reached the shuttle bus, Chance exchanged a look with Doc Morgan. Now they had to get him up another set of steps. Getting him onto the plane had been tough, at least this was just a couple. His dad looked up at him. "You're a strapping fella. I bet between you, you, Ben, and Smoke can lift this chariot of mine up there."

Chance nodded. He knew they could. It would be easiest. He just hadn't wanted to subject his dad to the indignity.

When they were all settled on the bus, Chance called Dan.

"We're on the way from the airport now. So make sure Miss is busy."

"Yeah," called his dad. "I don't want to go through all this and then blow the surprise."

Chance smiled. His dad was going along with all this in much better spirits than he had expected. It made Chance realize now just how important it was to him to be here. They'd had quite a time this last couple of days. It was the first time they'd been alone together in who knew how many years. They'd made up a lot of ground. Not that either of them had actually said much, openly. They'd made their peace with each other. In the way only two taciturn men could.

"Did you hear that?" he asked Dan.

"I did. He sounds good."

Chance nodded. "He is."

~ ~ ~

Lily smiled at Megan and Michael. "I think I might call it a night."

"Oh, no you don't," said a voice from behind her. "I was just looking for you. I've rounded up all the singles to go party."

She looked up over her shoulder at Nate. Damn, he was a good-looking guy. He was fun, too! She knew better than to think anything might happen between them. But he was fun to hang out with. "Who's going?" she asked.

"Ryan, Eddie, Leanne, me, and you."

"What about April?"

"She turned me down." Nate gave her that disarming smile of his. "If you can believe that! She got a better offer from another guy. I can handle it, since the guy in question is ten years old, and he's her son."

Lily smiled. She knew this whole weekend was way out of the ordinary for April. She was probably glad to use Marcus as an excuse for an early night. "I was thinking I might turn in early myself."

"Well, think again. You can't do that to me. It would destroy me to be turned down by two beautiful women in one night."

She laughed. "And I'm supposed to feel bad when I was your second choice anyway?"

He hung his head and grinned out at her. "Actually, I have to come clean. You were the third. I wanted to ask that English chick, Charlotte, but apparently she's off limits."

Michael laughed. "You can say that again!"

Lily couldn't wait to catch up with Charlotte herself. She hadn't seen her for years. They used to ride together when they were kids. She was biding her time, though, until she could get Charlotte on her own. Lily was more of a one-on-one kind of girl. Superficial group conversations did nothing for her.

Nate came around to stand before her. "Come on. The clock's ticking. We've only got so many hours before the sun comes back up, we need to make the most of them. Party till dawn. We may as well since we don't have to be anywhere until five o'clock tomorrow now."

Lily shot a look at Megan. She didn't seem in the least upset that Nate was referring to her canceled wedding.

"I wouldn't bank on that," said Michael. "Don't go thinking you can sleep all afternoon."

"Why, what's happening?" asked Nate.

Michael shrugged. "I can't say. But keep your afternoon free."

Lily didn't have time to wonder what might be in store tomorrow afternoon as Nate took her hand and pulled her to her feet. She laughed, why not? She happily followed him over to where Leanne, Ryan, and Eddie were waiting.

"Let's go, party people."

~ ~ ~

Kenzie watched the group of singles make their way toward the doors. Chase slid an arm around her waist and smiled down at her. "Are you wishing you were still single?" he asked.

She laughed. "No way! I am a very happily married woman thank you."

"That's good to know, because I am a very happily married man."

Kenzie looked around at all their friends. The crowd was thinning now, but it had been one hell of a party. She'd never even considered having something like a wedding reception, but this had been special.

"What are you thinking?" asked Chase.

She grinned up at him. "Can you guess?"

She loved the way he narrowed his eyes at her. "I think I can."

"And do you want to?"

He nodded. "You know I do. Just because we're married now, it doesn't mean we're old and married and boring."

"I don't think we ever could be, even if we tried."

"We'll need to say our thank yous before we go."

She nodded. "Come on then. Missy and Dan are just there, let's start with them. They laid all this on for us."

"Other than them, April's gone to bed. Ben's not here. They're the ones we really need to thank. I think everyone else will understand if we just disappear, won't they?"

"I think so. They know us well enough."

Chase grinned. "Let's be quick then. Thank Missy and Dan and we can go catch up with the others and party."

~ ~ ~

After Kenzie and Chase had left, Dan smiled at Missy. "You made this really special for them, you know."

Missy smiled. "I'm just glad we could. They would have been happy enough to go off and do their thing by themselves, but I'm glad we were all there for them."

"So were they."

She shrugged. "I get to have this amazing wedding; I just wanted to share the love, you know?"

Dan nodded. He did know. He knew that she always went out of her way to do nice things for other people. She saw ways to make people happy and she went out and made them happen. He was so glad that now he was able to do that for her. He was proud of himself that he hadn't just accepted that her dad couldn't be there.

She caught him off guard. "What are you smiling to yourself about?"

He could hardly tell her. "I'm thinking how lucky I am. How much I love you."

She smiled up at him. "I hope so, because this time tomorrow, I'm going to be your ball and chain!"

He laughed. "You could never be that."

She laughed with him. "Don't bet on it. I'll be chasing you around with a rolling pin before long."

Laura laughed at Missy's words as she joined them. "I was just coming to say goodnight. Am I interrupting a domestic before you're even married?"

Dan shook his head. "No, we're only playing."

"How's Smoke?" asked Missy.

Laura shot a look at Dan. "He's feeling much better. He just texted, that's why I'm going up."

Dan hated that they'd had to lie to Missy and say that Smoke had gone up to his room with a bad headache, but they'd had to explain his absence somehow.

"Oh good. Well you two enjoy the rest of your evening." Missy looked up at Dan. "I was thinking we might go up in a little while? I'm pooped!"

"Do you want to go on ahead then?" he asked. This might be his opportunity to slip up to the VIP lounge and check on her dad.

"I want to wait for Chance to get in. I'd really like to see him. He texted a while ago to say that he should be here in half an hour or so."

Crap! Dan had forgotten that Chance would have to come out and say hello, since he was supposed to be arriving tonight— by himself. "Why don't you go on up anyway? He can come up to our suite when he gets here. It's not as though he's likely to want to hang out with everyone is it?"

He loved the way she smiled. "Yeah. I think I'll do that. Are you going to round Scotty up?" Dan nodded. "I want to check in with Mom, too. I haven't had much time with her today."

"Of course! Do you want me come?"

Dan shook his head. He really didn't! He could hardly say that his mom and all the oldies were no doubt having a party of their own up in the VIP lounge by now—with Missy's dad!

"No. You go and have a soak in that big tub. I'll take care of it."

He knew that sealed it. Whenever they stayed here Missy loved to find time to soak in the huge tub in their room with a glass of wine in her hand. "Okay. I'm off," she said with a grin. She reached up and pecked his lips. "Don't be too long."

He hoped he wouldn't.

~ ~ ~

Laura opened the door to her room and smiled when she saw Smoke standing there waiting for her.

"How did it go?" she asked.

Smoke nodded. "The old guy's holding up pretty well. He's not saying much, but I think he's damned glad to be here."

"That's good. And I'm glad you're here. It seems even this weekend we're not going to get much time together."

He nodded and came to put his arms around her. "I'm sorry, lady. Tomorrow morning's going to be the same."

Laura grinned. "I know, but like tonight, it's so worth it. I don't mind missing out on our time so much when it's for such good reasons. I can't wait to see Missy's face when she sees her dad." Her grin faded. "I just hope tomorrow's trip is going to work out like he hopes."

Smoke raised an eyebrow. "You don't think she'll go for it?"

Laura shrugged. "I hope she will, but I wouldn't want to put any money on it."

Smoke pecked her lips. "Well, that's for them to figure out, not us. We've got the rest of tonight to ourselves, what do you say we forget everyone else and just go out and have some fun?"

As Laura smiled up at him, her hands found his belt buckle. "I was thinking more along the lines of staying in and having some fun."

His hands closed around her waist and pulled her against him. "Persuade me."

She pulled his head down to kiss him—she intended to!

Chapter Twenty-One

Pete paced the room while Holly took her shower. He was starting to think he might be crazy. Was he about to screw up even more than he had been doing before? No. He had to believe he wasn't. He'd been listening to what she said. Taking notes about what she wanted. He was trying to give her exactly that. And he wasn't going to force it on her. He was going to give her the choice.

She smiled at him as she emerged from the bathroom. "Shall we go up and say hi to Missy's dad later?" she asked.

He nodded. They should. But he didn't want to leave it until much later—for a number of reasons. "Yeah, let's go there first shall we?"

"Oh, okay. I was thinking we could go out and walk down the Strip. I haven't had a chance to do that yet."

"Then we will. Why don't we stop in to see him on the way out?"

"Sounds good to me."

After they'd seen Missy's dad they wandered through the grounds. Holly looked up at the balcony where later this afternoon Missy and Dan would take their vows.

Pete watched her, wondering what she was thinking. "Penny for them?"

She smiled. "Just thinking about this afternoon."

He nodded. He was too!

"And yesterday was pretty cool, wasn't it? Kenzie and Chase were thrilled that we all showed up like that."

"They were. It was quite a surprise for them. How do you think you would have felt if you were in their shoes?"

She laughed. "I don't know. And it's not a scenario I need to worry about, is it?"

He shrugged. "But how do you think you would have felt?"

"I don't know, Pete. It's different for me, isn't it? I mean we would never sneak off by ourselves. I wouldn't want to get married without my family there. It's just not the same situation at all. Why do you even ask?"

Pete backed off. "I don't know, I was just wondering, that's all." He took hold of her hand as they walked and she smiled up at him.

"Sorry, I know you're only trying to get ideas, and it's sweet of you. But come on, we're not into spur of the moment stuff or surprises, are we? We'll figure out what we're going to do. For now, let's just enjoy being here."

He nodded.

~ ~ ~

Ben stood on the walkway watching Pete and Holly wander through the grounds. He hoped to hell they were going to be okay today. He sighed. He hoped he was going to be okay today. He was skulking around trying to stay out of everyone's way. He turned at the sound of his name being called.

"Hey, Ben!"

It was Chance.

Ben smiled. It was hardly surprising to run into Chance when he was avoiding people. Chance was the master at that. "Hey. How's it going?"

Chance nodded. "It's going. You know me, I'm keeping a low profile until showtime."

"Me, too."

"Yeah. Charlotte's here, right?"

Ben nodded.

"That's got to be tough."

He nodded again. He felt bad admitting that to Chance. Things were a lot tougher for him. Whatever Ben's history with Charlotte was, however much pain he felt, it had to be so much worse for Chance. Charlotte was here, much as that hurt Ben. Chloe was dead.

Chance shrugged. His words made clear he was thinking the same thing. "Where there's life, there's hope."

Ben sighed. "Yeah, sorry."

"Don't go feeling sorry for me. But don't go feeling too sorry for yourself either. No matter how black things look, there's always the possibility that something might change."

Ben didn't see it that way. It was too late.

"Anyway. Since we're both hiding out, want to hide together?"

"Sure."

"Then, follow me. There's a little café a couple of blocks over. This lot will all stick to the Strip if they venture out at all. We should be safe."

Ben fell in step beside him. If his parents called to say they were here, he'd come back. He wasn't going to stick around just in case.

~ ~ ~

Jack smiled at Dan. "Are you all ready for your big day?"

Dan nodded. "I am. I just want five o'clock to be here now."

"It'll come soon enough," said his mom with a smile. "I can't believe that I'm going to be the mother of two married men."

"And grandma to two, soon enough," said Jack.

"Nanna," she corrected him. "I'm too young to be a grandma. I mean look at Emma's Gramps, he's a lovely man, but he's twenty years older than I am."

Dan grinned as he watched Gramps and Joe take their place in line at the cash register. They were sitting in one of the self-service restaurants having a late breakfast.

"He is, but he's going to be a great grandpa to our baby," said Jack.

"And I'm going to be a wonderful nanna," joked their mom. "How are the girls doing this morning?" she asked.

Dan nodded. "Missy's great. She has no idea about her dad. She and Em are having a girly morning."

"Charlotte's with them, too," said Jack. "I think they're trying to keep her out of Ben's way."

"But how are they going to manage that this afternoon?"

Jack shrugged. "I don't know. I don't think they'll be able to."

Dan nodded; he was worried about Ben. He waved when he saw Laura and her mom come in. Smoke must be on his way to LA by now. Dan had to wonder how that surprise was going to go down.

~ ~ ~

By eleven thirty, Pete couldn't contain himself any longer. He and Holly had spent the morning wandering up and down the Strip browsing the stores. Now they were back in their room and it was time to do it. Smoke had texted him to say he was back. The VIP lounge where Missy's dad was hiding had to be pretty crowded now.

He had a bottle of champagne waiting and wished he had a bottle of whiskey in case this didn't go the way he hoped.

Holly came to stand before him and took hold of both his hands. She looked up into his eyes. "What is it, Pete? I know something's going on with you. You've been on edge all morning."

And he thought he'd hidden it so well! He relaxed and smiled back at her. "You know me so well."

She nodded. "I do. So out with it. What's bothering you?"

It was time. He dropped to one knee in front of her and took hold of her hand. "I want you to marry me."

She gave him a puzzled look. "I'm going to. We're back on track. We're going to be okay."

He smiled up at her. "I mean today."

"What?"

"You heard me. Holly Hayes, would you do me the honor of becoming my wife, today?"

"How? Pete I know I said I wanted to do something spontaneous, but a Vegas chapel isn't quite what I was thinking of."

He grinned. "I know. It's not what I'm thinking either."

"What then?"

"There's a wedding already set up for this afternoon. The chapel right here at the Bellagio. The reception afterwards. We can even go off to Aruba for ten days afterwards if you want to."

She stared at him. "Michael and Megan's wedding?"

He nodded. "When Michael said they were going to cancel I asked him not to. I took over all the deposits." He held her gaze. "And I'm perfectly fine to lose them, if you don't want to do this. It's just an idea, sweetheart, that's all."

She looked sad. "I love the idea, Pete. I really do. It's so sweet of you. But I don't know if I can. I'd want my family here. I'd want my dress. I'd…"

Pete grinned and got to his feet. He led her to the closet and opened it. Her dress was hanging there ready.

"How the hell did you do that? I know you didn't bring it with us!"

"I had Ben go pick it up last night when he was back at the lake."

She was beaming at him. "But what about…"

"Your family?" he asked. He couldn't help grinning at her. "There are some advantages to being a planner, you know. Every time you've gotten pissed at me for being on my phone, I've been taking care of details. Your family are hiding out in the VIP lounge with Missy's dad. That's why I needed to get you in and out of there before they arrived."

Tears were glistening in her eyes. "Oh, Pete!"

He wrapped his arms around her. "Roberto and John are here, too."

She let out a sob as she hugged him tight. "Pete! You never cease to amaze me!"

He planted a kiss on the top of her head. "I know; I'm just hoping that this time it's in a good way?"

She nodded as she sniffed. "In the best way."

"So what do you say? Do you want to marry me?"

She nodded as the tears streamed down her face. "You can bet your ass I do!"

He kissed her again, before he popped the cork on the champagne.

When he handed her a glass she raised it to him. "Here's to being spontaneous."

Pete grinned as he raised his own glass. "I'll drink to that. And we won't talk about all the sneaky planning I did."

She laughed and shook her head at him. "I love you."

"And I love you, sweetheart. Shall I call your family and the girls, tell them you said yes and they can come help you get ready?"

Holly wiped at her eyes again. "Yes, please.

~ ~ ~

Ben took his seat with his parents. He could do this. He just needed to focus on being happy for Pete and Holly that they'd finally managed to work it all out and they were here. About to get married.

His dad put an arm around his shoulders. "How much longer are you going to make us wait, Ben?"

His mom leaned over. "Yes, just look how happy Anne and Graham are."

Ben did look to where Pete's parents were sitting at the front, beaming. He knew how shocked, but also happy they were to be seeing their son get married today—in Vegas of all places! It was hardly their style, but they were so supportive of Pete. He knew Anne especially was thrilled that Pete had let go of his need to plan the big traditional wedding up at their house at the lake and instead follow his heart, and more importantly Holly's heart. He looked at his mom and was shocked to hear the words that came out of his own mouth. "They're happy that their son is doing what makes him happy. You should try it sometime."

His mom shook her head at him. "All we wanted was for you to do what made you happy. But what made you happy was Charlotte. And you still won't admit that."

Ben took a deep breath. He couldn't handle much more of this. "I admit it, Mom. She did! But guess what. It's over. It's been over for years, and you keeping talking about it, rubbing my nose in it—it just makes me even more miserable. So would you do me a favor and leave it?"

They both stared at him.

"I'm sorry, but this is hard enough for me. Why won't you see that?"

His mom patted his arm. His dad squeezed his arm a little tighter around his shoulders. "We do, Ben. We just feel helpless. That's hard for a parent, you know?"

Ben nodded. He just wished they'd at least try to understand how much harder it was for him.

"There she is!" said his mom.

Ben didn't even want to look. He'd been dreading the moment he would see her. Now it seemed it was finally here. He stared straight ahead. Hoping Holly would make her entrance soon and they could get on with this, so he could get out of here.

He must have wished so hard that someone heard and took pity on him. The first chords of the Wedding March sounded and everyone turned to look at the bride.

~ ~ ~

Holly clung to her dad's arm. She couldn't quite believe this was really happening! This morning she had been out walking the Strip. Now here she was getting married. Her family was all here. She was wearing her dress. And Pete was standing up at the front waiting for her. Waiting to make her his wife. She smiled through the tears that welled up when he smiled at her. He was such a good man. He was her man, and he was about to become her husband.

"Are you ready?" asked her dad.

She nodded and they began to walk down the aisle. She held Pete's gaze the whole way. His smile was so full of love. She hoped hers told him she felt the same way. She realized as they got closer that they didn't even need anyone else here. It was just about the two of them. She felt the love and support of their family and friends. She loved Pete for making this happen. But she loved him even more just for being him.

When they reached the front, her dad smiled at her. She smiled back and kissed his cheek. He took her hand and placed it in Pete's.

Pete smiled at her and she couldn't help it, she pinched him.

He laughed out loud.

"Are you sure you're for real?" she whispered.

"I am. And I'm about to prove it."

The minister looked from her to Pete and back again. "Are we ready?"

They both nodded. They were. Holly knew that they hadn't left all their troubles behind them. Life didn't work that way. It would no doubt have more storms to throw at them. What she did know now was that they would be able to weather them together. They'd learned so much from what they'd put each other through the last few months. One of the vows she was making today was to make sure they didn't do that again. As man and wife they would work together, not against each other.

~ ~ ~

Jack slid his arm around Emma's shoulders as they stood off to the side. She smiled up at him. She knew he was as glad as she was that their friends had finally worked it out. By tonight all but one of her group of childhood friends would be married.

All but Ben.

She scanned the faces sitting there watching. She found Ben's. He was smiling, but his smile looked as though it was frozen in place. He stared at Pete and Holly taking their vows as though he didn't dare look away.

Emma understood why. She kept on searching and spotted Charlotte a few rows farther back, sitting with Lily. She, too, was smiling, but hers was a sad smile, and her focus wasn't on Pete and Holly. She kept stealing glances at Ben.

Emma wished with all her heart that somehow she could bring the two of them back together. Growing up, they'd all believed that Ben and Charlotte would be the first of them to get married. Who would ever have believed that it would turn out like this?

Jack poked her in the ribs. She gave him an apologetic look and turned her own attention back to Pete and Holly. She was so happy for them!

Chapter Twenty-Two

Chance looked around the function room. It was weird for him to be in the same place with so many residents of Summer Lake. He watched Pete and his fiancée, Holly, for a moment, as they stood hugging their parents. He was pleased for Pete; he'd always liked that guy. Last time Chance had been back, things had been looking strained between him and Holly. He was glad they'd worked it out. He smiled as he corrected himself—she wasn't his fiancée anymore—she was now his wife.

It seemed that he was surrounded by wedding fever wherever he went these days. Back at home in Montana his friends were finding good women and getting engaged. Pete just got married, and in a couple of hours, Missy would do the same.

As he looked around the room, observing all the happy couples and smiling faces, he saw one couple he wanted to check in with. He hoped that they'd be joining the ranks of the married someday soon.

Gabe caught his eye and raised a hand. Chance made his way over to where he and Renée were sitting.

"You made it then?"

Chance nodded. "We got in last night. But I've been keeping a low profile."

"How's your dad doing?" asked Renée.

"Better than you might think. The Doc is pleased with his recovery so far. I think much of it has to do with the fact that he really wanted to be here for Miss."

Renée grinned. "She's going to be so happy when she finds out he's here!"

"She is."

"Is he going to be able to walk her down the aisle?" asked Gabe.

Chance shrugged. "We're going to play it by ear. I don't know yet."

Gabe nodded. "That makes sense. And how long are you sticking around for?"

Chance shrugged again. "Same answer. He's doing well, but..." He turned to Renée. "It's done us good to spend the last couple of days together. I'm not sure I want to leave straight away."

Renée grinned. "That's great, Chance! Stay awhile. It'll do you good."

Maybe it would.

"And besides, if you do, you can come to the grand opening of the women's center."

Chance raised his eyebrows. "You still haven't come up with a better name?"

She made a face at him. "No. I thought you were going to help me!"

He laughed.

"Sorry to interrupt." Dan had come to join them. "But can I steal you for a minute, Chance?"

"Sure."

"We'll catch up with you later," said Gabe.

Chance nodded at them as he walked away with Dan.

"What's up?"

"Nothing's up. I just want to make sure we know what we're doing later?"

"We sure do. While Miss is getting ready, I'm going to bring Dad down. We're going to wait in one of the little dressing rooms. Emma is going to text me when Miss is ready, and I'm going to meet her to walk out onto the balcony."

Dan looked concerned. "And what's he going to do?"

Chance shrugged. "We're still working on that."

"Okay. But let me know if you need me to change anything up, won't you?"

Chance smiled and grasped his shoulder. "Relax, Danny. It's all going to work out. Don't worry."

~ ~ ~

Dan blew out a big sigh. "I know, you're right, but I don't think I can relax. I want so badly for it to be perfect for her."

"It will be," Chance reassured him.

"I'm working on it," said Dan. He was, too. He needed to get back to Missy. They needed to go and congratulate Pete and Holly and then he needed to round up Scot so they could go and get ready.

Scot didn't seem to be nervous at all. At least not yet. Dan still had to wonder about how he would do tonight. At the reception. When the time came for him to make his speech. He kept saying he was fine about it. He was going to sit next to Jack, and Jack was on standby to help him out if the need arose.

Missy smiled up at him when he made it back to her. "It's nearly our turn."

"I know. Where's Scotty?"

She pointed to where he was chatting happily with Gramps and Joe. "The old guys are keeping him busy. I think they're trying to build his confidence in their own way."

Dan smiled as he watched. Scot laughed at something Gramps said. "I think we should go see Pete and Holly and then get out of here."

Missy nodded. "Come on then."

Pete grinned as they approached. "We beat you to it!"

Missy laughed. "You never could be outdone, could you Pete?"

Holly shook her head. "I'm not going to complain about it this time though."

"And you know I don't mind," said Dan. "I don't feel outdone."

Holly laughed. "You're not. I mean Pete's surprise was awesome, but yours is…" her hand flew up to cover her mouth.

Dan couldn't believe that she was about to blow it.

"Your wedding is going to be amazing!" Pete stepped in, in an attempt to cover for her. He grinned. "I mean you've had all this time to plan it and everything!"

Missy laughed. It seemed she hadn't picked up on Holly's mistake at all. "Yours was amazing because it wasn't planned Pete! You'd do well to remember that."

Holly nodded at him. "See! It's not just me!"

Pete grinned at Dan. "It's not fair, is it? None of these ladies seem to appreciate planning and preparation, do they?"

Dan smiled. He was relieved that they hadn't blown it, but he didn't want to stick around any longer than they had to. Anyone could let the cat out of the bag at any moment. "I don't know, Pete. I think when it comes to planning dresses and makeup they get it. I know Miss here wants some time to prepare herself."

Missy grinned at him. "I do. We should get going." She hugged Holly. "Congratulations, hon. I'm so happy for you."

Dan nodded. "Congratulations to you both. Now if you'll excuse us, we need to go get ready."

~ ~ ~

Missy pecked Dan's lips. "I guess I'll see you out on the balcony."

He smiled down at her. "You will. Don't go changing your mind before you get there, will you."

"No chance! You just make sure you're there waiting for me."

"Oh, I will be. You've got no worries there. Are you nervous?"

She smiled. "I think I am. Maybe it's just excitement, but either way the butterflies are swirling like crazy in my tummy."

She looked at him, she knew he didn't experience emotions in the same way she did, but she was curious.

"What?" he asked.

"Do you even know what butterflies feel like?"

He smiled, the smile she wanted to wake up to every day for the rest of her life. "Believe it or not, I do. But mine don't swirl."

"No?"

She loved the way his eyes twinkled when he smiled. "No, I've trained mine to fly in formation."

She laughed. She had no doubt that he meant it!

He slid his arms around her waist and she clung onto his shoulders as she kissed him again.

Scot laughed as he joined them. "I keep telling you two, you need to stop that!"

Missy laughed and went to hug him. Not only did he let her—he hugged her right back!

"Okay, then," he said. "I'll let you off since I get one as well."

"Come on, champ," said Dan. "Let's go do our thing."

Missy's heart filled up as she watched them walk away. They were her world. And the three of them were about to make their little family official. In some ways she'd felt almost left out the last few months, since the adoption papers had come through and Dan was legally Scot's dad. Now she and Dan would be bound together in the eyes of the law—as well as in love. They already had that, and she knew they always would.

Emma came to her side. "Do you want to go yet?"

"Yeah, let's go, hon. It's time. Do you know where Charlotte is?"

Emma sighed and jerked her head to where Charlotte was sitting with Ben's parents.

"Oh, crap!" said Missy. "Where is he? That's all he needs!"

"I know. And I can't find him."

Missy sighed. "I feel so bad about this. But I swear I'll kill him if he doesn't show up!"

"Calm down. You know he'll be there. You need to forget all about him for now. You've got more important things to think about like getting into that beautiful dress of yours and marrying Dan!"

"I know, hon. But I can't just forget about him, can I?"

Emma shrugged. "He's going to be fine. And much as we love him, I really do think you should put him out of your mind. Focus on the good stuff. Come on. Let's go get Charlotte and get you ready."

~ ~ ~

"Have you decided what you're going to do yet?" Ben asked Missy's dad. He'd decided to come hang out with him while they waited for five o'clock to come around.

He shook his head. "It just doesn't seem right to roll out there in a wheelchair. That's not who I am, Ben. You know that."

Ben nodded. He didn't know what to say. He could imagine how it must feel.

"But then, it seems even worse to not do it at all."

Ben could see that, too. He decided to take a risk and say what he thought. "Do you mind if I ask you something."

"Go ahead."

"If you do it in a wheelchair, what's wrong with that?" He watched as Missy's dad thought about it. He decided to make the question a bit more leading. "What gets hurt if you do that?"

"I know where you're taking me. The only thing it hurts is my pride. And if I don't do it at all, I hurt Missy's feelings, right?"

"Wrong. I didn't mean you'd hurt Missy's feelings. I meant that you'd hurt yourself. You'd deny yourself the chance to do something that every father thinks they'll do for their daughter someday."

Chance came into the lounge and walked toward them. "Missy's gone to get ready. It's almost time."

His dad nodded at him, a thoughtful frown on his face.

Chance looked from his dad to Ben and back again. "What's going on?"

"I want to do it."

Ben smiled to himself as understanding dawned on Chance's face.

"You do?"

"Yeah." There were tears in his eyes as he said. "Well, I want us to do it. I want you to push me, so I can hold her hand. The three of us. Together. As a family. Like we haven't been in twenty years."

Ben felt like an intruder now as Chance and his dad hugged each other awkwardly. He stood up, he should go.

"You stay right there, son. You're the one who made me see that my pride doesn't count for much. That I'd be a fool to let it get in the way."

Chance shot him a grateful smile.

Ben nodded. He knew he was pretty good at helping other people get over their shit. Why couldn't he do the same for himself?

~ ~ ~

Dan grinned at Scot as he straightened his cravat for him. They were getting ready in one of the changing rooms by the hotel chapel. "You look great, champ. How do you feel?"

Scot nodded. "I feel great!" He checked his inside pocket. "I've got the rings. I'm good."

Jack smiled at them both. "I'm so proud of you guys."

Dan nodded. It was totally illogical that happiness should make a person cry. But he still had to take a breath before he dared reply. Even then he didn't trust his voice not to crack, so he simply nodded.

"What do you think?" asked Scot. "Is it time to go out there yet?"

Dan checked his watch. He shook his head. "Not yet."

Jack raised an eyebrow at him. He shrugged in reply. He wasn't nervous about getting married. Wasn't nervous about committing the rest of his life to loving Missy and Scot. But he was nervous about standing out there in front of the crowd while he waited for her to arrive. He didn't want to be on full display for everyone while he felt so emotionally transparent.

There was a knock on the door. Jack went to open it. He grinned as he stood back to let Missy's dad come through with Chance behind him, pushing his wheelchair. Ben brought up the rear.

"Poppy Jim!" Scot said with a grin.

Dan knew there was something different about him as he reached his good arm out to Scot and hugged the kid tight.

"What's the plan?" asked Dan.

Chance looked at his dad and they both smiled.

"I'm going to let my son push me around."

Dan cocked his head to one side, not sure he understood.

Chance grinned. "The three of us are coming out there together." He put a hand on his dad's shoulder. "As a family."

Dan had to swallow the lump in his throat again. He was so happy that his and Missy's special day appeared to be bringing her dad and brother together. Healing the rift that had kept them apart for years. He nodded. "That's awesome."

"It is. And we've got this fella to thank for it," he jerked his head toward Ben.

Dan wasn't at all surprised to hear that. Or to see him here instead of out with the other guests, where he might run into Charlotte.

"Thanks, Ben."

Ben nodded. "Do you mind if I wait here with you? I want to see Missy's face when she sees her dad."

"Of course."

~ ~ ~

Missy held her breath while Emma pulled her zipper up, wishing the whole time that she'd made more of an effort to lay off the doughnuts these last few weeks.

"Oh my God! Just look at you, Miss!" cried Charlotte. "It's beautiful. You are beautiful!"

Missy smiled as she looked at herself in the mirror. She didn't consider herself to be beautiful. She hung out with too many truly beautiful women to go kidding herself about that. But even she had to admit that today, in her wedding dress, she did at least look beautiful.

Emma laughed. "Even you can't argue, Miss. Not today. Not looking like that."

Missy laughed with her. "Okay, so I'm gorgeous!"

"You are. I can't wait to see Dan's face!" said Emma.

"He hasn't seen the dress at all yet?" asked Charlotte.

Missy shook her head. "I wanted to do some of the traditional things. I mean, yeah, we didn't spend last night apart, and we've been together most of today, but I didn't want him to see the dress. And I wanted to do the something old, something new thing.

"That's wonderful," said Charlotte. "So what are they?"

"Well, the something new, is my dress. Isn't it gorgeous?" she wiggled her ass making the others laugh. "The something blue, is this." She picked up a garter, slipped her foot through and rolled it up to her thigh."

"Nice!" said Charlotte.

Missy picked up the box Michael had given her. "You're going to love this," she told Charlotte.

"Oh, you will," agreed Emma. "I do!"

Missy took out the pearl earrings and necklace.

"They're lovely!" exclaimed Charlotte.

"They are," said Missy, "and what's even lovelier is that they're Michael's grandmother's. She told me when we were little kids that they could be my something borrowed. He remembered and let me have them!"

"Oh, that's so nice! He's such a good guy, and Megan's lovely! But hold on. You've got new, borrowed and blue. What's your something old?"

Emma looked at her, too. "Yeah. What is it?"

Missy was determined not to cry. "The something old is my ring." She held out her right hand so they could both see.

Emma nodded. Missy knew she would recognize it immediately.

"I'm sure you remember, I had a pretty rough time with my dad when I told him I was pregnant at seventeen."

Charlotte nodded. "Of course I do."

Missy hesitated, wondering what memories this would bring back for Charlotte.

Charlotte smiled as if to reassure her. "I might not have been here, but we did used to talk all the time. Go on, though. Tell me about the ring?"

Missy looked down at it. "He came through for me though when Scotty was born. He bought me this ring and brought it to the hospital when he came to meet his grandson for the first time. I know how hard it must have been for him to accept that I'd screwed up my life. But he did. He gave me this ring. Told he me loved me no matter what. And now that Scot was here, he would love him, too." She had to blink away the tears. She shouldn't have gotten into this right now.

Emma patted her arm.

She swallowed. "And he told me that he'd always be there for us, no matter what." She finished on a sob. "And he always has been. Until today!"

"Oh, Miss. Don't cry!" said Charlotte.

"It's going to be okay," said Emma.

"How can it be okay?" she wailed. "He's not here!" She didn't understand the look Emma and Charlotte exchanged. They probably thought she was over emotional. Well, dammit she was! And she had every right to be! She grabbed a tissue and blew her nose. "Sorry. I just wish he was here. All this is wonderful, but if my dad was here, it'd be perfect. I should know better than to hope for perfect, though. That's not how my life goes, is it?"

Emma put an arm around her shoulders. "Maybe today is the day that all that changes."

"What do you mean?'

Emma looked panic stricken for a moment.

"I think she means that today you marry your lovely Dan. And from now on your life will be perfect," said Charlotte.

Missy nodded and blew her nose again. "I like the sounds of that. Anyway. I don't have time to sit around here blubbing. It's time to work your magic with hair and makeup, ladies."

As she got ready, Missy had to keep dragging her mind away from thoughts of her dad. She had to focus on what she did have. Dan and Scot, and Chance, and all their wonderful friends.

Chapter Twenty-Three

"Will you put your phone down, Mouse! I'm ready. It's time to go. I don't want to be late for my own wedding because you're too busy texting. Who are you texting anyway?"

Emma gave her that odd panicky look again.

Charlotte laughed. "I'll bet it's Jack. She hasn't seen him for a whole hour!"

Emma hung her head. "Sorry. I'm done. Let's go."

"Thank you!" said Missy with a grin. She was excited now. The time was finally here.

When they got close to the chapel Emma stopped. "Just wait here a minute would you?"

"Are you kidding? We're almost late! I need to find Chance."

"I know! I'm going to get him. Just wait here, would you? And stop panicking."

Missy looked at Charlotte as Emma went on ahead. "Is it me, or is she the one that's panicking? I'd swear she's more nervous than I am!"

Charlotte shrugged. "She just gets excited. She hasn't changed much has she?"

Missy shook her head. "Not in some ways, no." She picked up her skirt. "But I can't be standing around here waiting for her. Let's go." She started out toward the corner that Emma had just disappeared around. When she reached it, she stopped.

There was no sign of Emma, or Chance. Or anyone. She'd thought they were supposed to meet Chance here!

The chapel attendant who had helped with all the arrangements popped her head out of the reception area. "There you are. Your guests are all out on the balcony. Your brother said he'd meet you there, too."

Missy looked at Charlotte. "Great! He's supposed to walk me up the stairs and out onto the balcony!"

Charlotte smiled. "Never mind." She offered Missy her arm. "I'll be happy to take his place for the stairs at least."

Missy linked arms with her and grinned. "We did say we'd be there for each other's wedding day, didn't we?"

"We did. And I wouldn't miss this for the world!"

When they reached the top of the stairs Missy smiled at the sight of all their friends sitting there. They didn't spot her yet. They were all facing the front where Dan and Scot were waiting. Dan saw her first and smiled. All heads turned to follow his gaze and she was met by a sea of smiling faces. Chance stood off to the right behind the last row of chairs. Missy had to chuckle that Emma stood beside him. Even in a moment like this she couldn't resist being around him. It dawned on her though that they were standing too close together. Almost as though they were hiding something behind them.

She gave Chance a puzzled look. He smiled. He looked as though he might be on the verge of tears. Then he and Emma stepped aside and she understood why. Her dad was sitting there in his wheelchair, smiling at her. Missy couldn't hold back the tears as she ran toward him. "Dad!" She squatted down beside his wheelchair.

He folded her in with his good arm and she sobbed into his chest.

"You're here!"

He patted her back. "I couldn't miss my little girl's big day, could I?"

"But how? The Doc said…"

He smiled at her. "The Doc came back to get me, with your friend Smoke…"

"You flew?"

He nodded. Missy searched the watching faces until she found Smoke. She'd never be able to thank him enough! He smiled and nodded. He even looked a little teary eyed himself.

"And Ben," her dad continued.

Missy searched for him. He stood in one of the last rows— what was he doing all the way back there? He, too, was smiling and nodding at her.

"There'll be time to explain it all later," said her dad. "For now the man responsible for me being here is starting to look a bit lonely up there at the front. What do you say, shall we go see him?"

"You're going to walk me down the aisle?" Her heart felt as though it might burst.

Her dad looked sad for a moment as he patted the wheelchair. "I can't, Miss. But this works out even better."

She couldn't believe the look he exchanged with Chance, the way the two of them smiled at each other. "We decided we're both coming. Chance is going push me, so I get to hold your hand."

Missy had to wipe away the tears. This was perfect! It was even better than she could have dreamed. Having her dad give her away was what she'd wanted. Now she got both her dad and her brother, and better yet, the two of them had obviously made their peace.

She looked up at Dan. He stood there with Scot at his side, smiling at her. Waiting for her. He was the one who had made it all possible. And she could not wait to marry him! "Come on, then," she stood up. "Let's go."

Missy stood to the left of her dad, so she could hold his good hand. He smiled up at her and squeezed her hand. Then the music started and Chance pushed the wheelchair forward. Missy had to hurry so she wasn't left behind. She looked up at Chance. She wanted to savor every step of this walk the three of them were taking together.

Chance understood and slowed down.

She felt her dad run his finger over the ring on her hand. He looked down at it and then up at her. The happy tear that rolled down his face brought a fresh wave of her own. She wiped at her eyes with her free hand and then smiled at her friends as she passed them. She really wished Ben wasn't sitting all the way at the back here. But she knew why he was. Gramps and Joe sat with him. Other faces went by in a blur; she could only pick out some of them here and there.

Michael winked at her as she passed. His mom, who had been like a mom to Missy, blew her a kiss, and then wiped the tears from her eyes. Pete grinned at her. They'd shared all their major life events since Kindergarten and now they were sharing their wedding day.

As she got closer to the front she saw Dan's mom, Chris. She was such a wonderful lady. Missy was looking forward to getting to know her better—to having her become a part of their lives. Chris's smile was so encouraging, so loving. Missy knew how thrilled she was that Dan had surprised them all by falling head over heels in love.

And then she was there. Standing face to face with Dan. Scot stood by his side. His smile was solemn. He was taking this very seriously.

Her dad squeezed her hand again and she bent down to kiss his cheek. He smiled at Dan as he placed Missy's hand in his then looked up at Chance. Missy had to kiss Chance's cheek, too, before she'd let them go. When she had, Chance wheeled her dad a little way to the side then squatted down beside him and held his hand as they watched. Seeing that, Missy had no idea how she'd be able to hold in the tears.

Dan smiled down at her. He was so handsome! His eyes twinkled. As the minister began to speak, Dan ran his hand over his cheek and Missy realized for the first time that he hadn't shaved. She grinned, and he grinned back, knowing that she'd understood what he was telling her. She loved his sexy scruff, and he always said he didn't feel like himself without it. He used to feel he had to shave for any formal occasion, but she'd kept telling him that he didn't. That what mattered was how the two of them felt about it, not what anyone else might expect. The fact that he hadn't shaved it off today told her that all he cared about was the two of them and what they wanted.

~ ~ ~

Charlotte slid into the last row of seats. Arriving with Missy as she had meant she was too late to take a seat up the front. This was probably better anyway. Miss and Dan had so many friends and family members here, people who were part of their everyday lives. She knew she herself was just a blast from the past. In that moment she wished she was more than that. Wished she could return to life at the lake. Wished that she'd never taken the detour that had led her so far away from the place she still considered home. She felt tears prick behind her eyes when Missy's dad placed her hand in Dan's. She took out her hanky when Chance pushed his dad's wheelchair to the side and squatted down beside him. When he took hold of his dad's hand, the tears began to stream down her face. If the two of them could put the past behind them, then anything was possible. Well, almost anything.

As the minister led Missy and Dan through their vows, Charlotte let her eyes rove over the guests. Where was he? He wasn't with his parents up near the front. He wasn't with Pete, where she might have expected to find him. As she worked her way back down the rows, her heart started to race. Please let him be here! He'd managed to avoid her ever since she'd arrived. She understood that. But she'd never forgive herself if he missed the wedding because of her.

Then she spotted him. In the second to last row. He was almost directly across from her. God he was gorgeous! The years had been kind to him. His dark blond hair skimmed his collar. He'd always liked to wear it a little long. He was well muscled, the cut of his suit made that very clear. He was beautiful. That was the only word to describe him. He was watching Missy and Dan with the tiniest hint of a smile on his lips, and the tiniest hint of pain in the lines around his eyes. How she wished they could turn back the clock, go back in time and change the decisions they'd made. The decisions that had changed both of their lives and caused them both so much pain. She brought her hanky up to her face and tried to blow her nose quietly.

Of course that was the moment Ben chose to turn her way. His gaze locked with hers. She felt frozen in time and space. She tried to tell him with her eyes all the many things she wanted to say to him and had never had the chance. She felt as though he was doing the same, but she had no idea what he wanted to tell her. The seconds felt like hours as they stared into each other's eyes.

"And now, you may kiss the bride."

Ben turned away to look at Missy and Dan. Charlotte turned, too. They looked so perfect together, standing there in front of the stone balustrade along the balcony with the grounds stretching out behind them. Dan took Missy in his arms and as he kissed her, the famous fountains sprang to life, shooting high up into the air.

Charlotte looked back at Ben, but the seat he'd been sitting in was empty.

~ ~ ~

Dan smiled around at everyone as he sat there at the reception. The day had been even more perfect than he'd hoped. He'd never forget the expression on Missy's face when she'd seen her dad. It had backed up his firm belief that you should never accept the impossible. It was a lesson he'd faced so many in times in life. As the awkward geek in high school, as the quiet shy guy who'd needed financial backing for his first business. As the unlikely suitor for Missy's hand. So many times the outcome he'd desired had seemed impossible, but he'd always pursued his dreams and won out in the end. His dream for today had been that it should be perfect for Missy. He was so glad that he hadn't accepted defeat and they'd found a way to get her dad here.

She leaned her head against his shoulder and smiled up at him. "You once told me that you never would, but you can't argue that you achieved superhero status today."

He smiled back down at her and dropped a kiss on her lips. "I don't know about that. But I did achieve husband status today and that's what I wanted most."

Scot leaned in from his other side. "Guys!" He said with a laugh, "You're married now, you really do have to stop that!"

Dan shook his head. "You'd better get used to it, champ. We don't ever intend to stop." He wrapped his arm around Missy's shoulders and pulled her to him to kiss her deeply.

"Ew! Enough already!" laughed Scot.

~ ~ ~

Ben sat with his parents. He was happy for Missy and Dan, but all he was doing was biding his time until he could leave. If it weren't for Scot, he would have slipped away already. He knew how important making the best man's speech was to the kid. He couldn't bring himself to miss it.

He looked up as Jack stood and dinged his spoon against his glass to get everyone's attention. It was time for speeches. He'd only have to endure a little while longer. He risked a glance over to where Charlotte was sitting with Michael and Megan. She was beautiful. She'd grown even more beautiful with the years. She turned in his direction and he looked away quickly. He couldn't afford to let his mind go to all the could-have-been, should-have-beens. He'd destroy himself if he did that. Instead he tried to focus on Scot as he stood up and looked around the room nervously.

The kid pulled out a bunch of notes and looked down at them. Then he sighed and looked up.

"Thank you all for being here today. It means a lot to me, and it means a lot to my mom..." he shot a glance at Dan, "...and dad."

A round of applause rippled around the room at that.

"My speech is going to be short, because I'm not very good at this." He smiled at Jack. "My Uncle Jack is up next and he'll say all the right things and make you laugh. I just wanted to stand up today and say thank you. Thank you for being here with us as we make our family official. Life hasn't always been easy..." Scot looked at Missy, and Ben had to swallow as he watched her wipe her eyes. She got rid of the tears, but the love and pride in them shone strong. "...for my mom. She's been the best mom on earth and she's made life as good as she can for me. And then she met Dan. Life hasn't always been easy for him, either." Scot hesitated then looked out at Ryan and grinned. "Even though you might find that hard to believe of a guy who owns a Lamborghini!"

Ryan nodded and everyone laughed.

"But what I've learned from both of them is that just because life isn't easy, that doesn't mean that it's not good. And if you work at it, you make it great. It isn't about what you've got or what you don't have. It's about who you have in your life and how you treat them. I've learned from my mom and dad that the way you care about the people in your life is what matters. The way you care for and look after the people you love is what makes life great."

Ben was surprised to see the kid turn toward his grandfather and then Chance. "And even when things have gone bad between you and someone you love, it's never too late to put it right if you still love them."

Ben swallowed hard. Scot's words for his poppy and his uncle, were hitting him hard. If only they were true in his case.

Scot looked around the room. "I know I'm not doing a very good job of this, so I'll shut up in a minute and let Uncle Jack take over."

"You're doing great, shortie!" called Chance.

Everyone clapped again in agreement.

Scot smiled and looked down at his notes. "I wrote this whole speech, and that might have been better." He looked out into the crowd. The expression on his face sent goosebumps racing down Ben's spine. "But I'm telling you what I've seen and learned. I hope that you all might learn something too. And that is, that no matter how hard life is sometimes, it will always get better if you believe in yourself. And if you're lucky you'll meet someone who believes in you too. And then, if you love each other, anything and everything is possible. That's what I've learned from my mom and dad. They are the best people I know. I'm proud of them both." He looked around the room and shrugged. "And I guess that's all."

He sat down, then stood back up again quickly and held up his glass of orange juice. "To Mom and Dad!"

"Mom and Dad," the whole room echoed.

Ben knocked back his own drink. That may not have been your standard best man's speech, but it had certainly hit home. Everyone was smiling and nodding.

When the chatter had quieted down, Jack stood. He smiled at Scot. "My nephew is a tough act to follow."

Ben didn't hear most of what Jack had to say. He was still pondering Scot's words: ...even when things have gone bad between you and someone you love, it's never too late to put it right if you still love them.

He sighed. It was too late for him though, wasn't it?

Chapter Twenty-Four

Pete made his way over to Ben; he could tell that his friend was watching the door and judging the moment when he might make his escape.

"Come on, bud. Let's go congratulate them and then you won't feel bad about it when you sneak out."

Ben met his gaze. He didn't make any attempt to deny that was his plan; he just nodded.

Michael tapped Pete's shoulder as they passed him, on their way to congratulate the happy couple.

"Did you get the tickets transferred all right?"

Pete grinned. "Holly wasn't keen on the idea of Aruba. We're going to head home with everyone else and take a couple of days. She still likes the idea of the Seychelles, so we're going to put the travel agent on it."

Michael grinned. "Good on you, mate. Let her do exactly what she wants to." His grin faded. "But let me give you the money back for the tickets. You shouldn't have to lose out on the deal."

Pete shook his head with a grin. "Don't worry about it. I was thinking we should give them to Kenzie and Chase."

Michael laughed. "You're right. We should. They'll love it. Let's at least go halves though?"

Pete nodded. "Sure. Hit me up when we get home."

Ben smiled at him as they continued on their way to the happy couple. "That's pretty decent of you."

Pete shrugged. "I'm not the asshole people make me out to be."

Ben smiled. "I know, asshole!"

When they got to Missy and Dan, Jack and Emma and Holly were standing with them. Missy smiled. "I was wondering where you two were. Now we're all together again."

"Yeah, the gruesome foursome reunited," said Emma with a laugh.

"And all happily married," said Ben.

Missy gave him a worried look, but he laughed. "Don't worry. I'm happy for you. I'm here to say congratulations."

Pete watched Missy hug him tight. "Thank you," she said. "Thanks for everything, Ben."

He nodded. "I'm glad to have been a part of it." He looked around, "But if you don't mind. I'm not going to stay long."

Missy nodded sadly. "I wish you would."

"I wish I could. I'm going to go have a quick word with my folks and I'll be on my way."

Emma hugged him. "I'll call you later, okay?"

He nodded. "And when we're all home, can we do a whiskey night soon?"

They all nodded.

Pete shook his head as they watched him walk away to go look for his folks.

"Is he okay?" asked Chance as he came to join them.

"I don't think so."

"I'm going to go after him," said Chance.

Missy nodded. "Thanks, Chancey. If anyone can get through to him, you can."

Pete realized that was true. Chance would understand better than any of them how Ben was feeling.

~ ~ ~

As he followed Ben, Chance did understand how he felt—at least to some extent. It was different for him. Chloe was dead. It wasn't as though he'd ever find himself in the situation Ben was in right now. And hard as it was for Ben, Chance would give anything to be in the same room as Chloe again. He wanted to help Ben, but a part of him wanted to shake him, too. Charlotte may not be his anymore, but at least she was alive.

He watched as Ben joined his parents. He decided to give them a minute. He'd follow when Ben made for the door. He turned around when someone tapped his shoulder.

It was Renée. She grinned at him. "I'm so happy for you, Chance."

He knew what she meant. He'd caught her gaze when he'd been walking down the aisle with his dad and Missy this afternoon. She of all people knew the history. The pain they had overcome to make that moment possible. He nodded. He'd thought he was done with the prickly eyes for today. "Thanks."

"Do you want to come sit with us?" she asked.

He shook his head. "I can't. I need to...." He needed to follow Ben and make sure he was going to be okay. "I'll catch up with you when we're back at the lake."

She smiled. "I'll look forward to it. And don't forget, I still need your help naming the center."

As it hit him, Chance knew that his scratchy eyes and lumpy throat were far from over. He swallowed and wiped his sleeve over his face.

Renée touched his arm. "Chance, are you okay?"

He nodded, "It just hit me what you need to call it. It made my eyes leak." It was true, two fat tears rolled down his cheeks.

She looked worried. "What do I need to call it?"

"Prepare yourself, it's going to make you cry, too."

"Just tell me then! What?"

"Chloe's Place."

He watched her face crumple as the tears came. "Oh, Chance! It's perfect."

He nodded. "I know. I've gotta go."

He walked away, leaving a startled Gabe to comfort his sobbing girlfriend.

He couldn't see Ben anywhere. His parents were talking to Dan's mom, but he was no longer with them. When he finally spotted him, he was almost to the double doors that led out into the corridor. Chance froze. He wasn't the only one following Ben.

~ ~ ~

Ben had no idea where he was going. He had half a mind to go up to his room and pack his bag. Head to the airport and catch any flight he could, just to get out of here. He'd done what he said he would, he'd been here for Missy. In the process he'd managed to be here for Kenzie and Chase and for Pete and Holly, too. But enough was enough. He couldn't stand anymore. Ever since he'd locked eyes with her out on the balcony this afternoon he felt like he couldn't avoid Charlotte any longer. He needed to talk to her, he needed to touch her, to hold her, to kiss her. He needed to put the past behind them, and get on with the future that was supposed to have been theirs.

He shook his head. What he needed was to get a grip and get out of here! As he reached the double doors that would open up to the cool corridor and to his escape, he felt a tap on his shoulder. He didn't want to turn around. He grasped the handle and began to open the door before his body betrayed him. He did turn around, and there she stood. He was face to face with Charlotte...his Charlotte. All he could do was smile.

"Hello, Ben."

~ ~ ~

Missy nudged Emma and pointed toward the door where Ben and Charlotte stood smiling at each other. Emma watched wide-eyed, then turned back to Missy.

"What do you think is going to happen now?"

Missy shook her head. "All we can do is wait and see."

;

A Note from SJ

I hope you enjoyed visiting Summer Lake and catching up with the gang. Please let your friends know about the books if you feel they would enjoy them as well. It would be wonderful if you would leave me a review, I'd very much appreciate it.
To come back to the lake and get to know more couples as they each find their happiness, you can check out the rest of the series on my website.

www.SJMcCoy.com

You can find out more about Ben and Charlottes history in the next Book in the Series "Chasing Tomorrow"
WARNING!!! This is not Ben's happily-ever-after story, but a look into his past. Chasing Tomorrow is a shorter story than the other Summer Lake books.

Additionally, you can take a trip to Montana and meet a whole new group of friends. Take a look at my Remington Ranch series. It focuses on four brothers and the sometimes rocky roads they take on the way to their Happily Ever Afters.

There are a few options to keep up with me and my imaginary friends:

The best way is to Join up on the website for my Newsletter. Don't worry I won't bombard you! I'll let you know about

upcoming releases, share a sneak peek or two and keep you in the loop for a couple of fun giveaways I have coming up :0)
You can join my readers group to chat about the books on Facebook or just browse and like my Facebook Page.

I occasionally attempt to say something in 140 characters or less(!) on Twitter

And I'm always in the process of updating my website at www.SJMcCoy.com with new book updates and even some videos. Plus, you'll find the latest news on new releases and giveaways in my blog.

> I love to hear from readers, so feel free to email me at AuthorSJMcCoy@gmail.com.. I'm better at that! :0)

I hope our paths will cross again soon. Until then, take care, and thanks for your support—you are the reason I write!
Love
SJ

PS Project Semicolon

You may have noticed that the final sentence of the story closed with a semi-colon. It isn't a typo. Project Semi Colon is a non-profit movement dedicated to presenting hope and love to those who are struggling with depression, suicide, addiction and self-injury. Project Semicolon exists to encourage, love and inspire. It's a movement I support with all my heart.

"A semicolon represents a sentence the author could have ended, but chose not to. The sentence is your life and the author is you."

- Project Semicolon

This author started writing after her son was killed in a car crash. At the time I wanted my own story to be over, instead I chose to honour a promise to my son to write my 'silly stories' someday. I chose to escape into my fictional world. I know for many who struggle with depression, suicide can appear to be the only escape. The semicolon has become a symbol of support, and hopefully a reminder – Your story isn't over yet

Also by SJ McCoy

Summer Lake Series
Love Like You've Never Been Hurt (FREE in ebook form)
Work Like You Don't Need the Money
Dance Like Nobody's Watching
Fly Like You've Never Been Grounded
Laugh Like You've Never Cried
Sing Like Nobody's Listening
Smile Like You Mean It
The Wedding Dance
Chasing Tomorrow
Dream Like Nothing's Impossible
Ride Like You've Never Fallen

Coming next
Live Like There's No Tomorrow

Remington Ranch Series
Mason (FREE in ebook form)
Shane
Carter
Beau
Four Weddings and a Vendetta

Coming next
Chance

About the Author

I'm SJ, a coffee addict, lover of chocolate and drinker of good red wines. I'm a lost soul and a hopeless romantic. Reading and writing are necessary parts of who I am. Though perhaps not as necessary as coffee! I can drink coffee without writing, but I can't write without coffee.

I grew up loving romance novels, my first boyfriends were book boyfriends, but life intervened, as it tends to do, and I wandered down the paths of non-fiction for many years. My life changed completely a few years ago and I returned to Romance to find my escape.

I write 'Sweet n Steamy' stories because to me there is enough angst and darkness in real life. My favorite romances are happy escapes with a focus on fun, friendships and happily-ever-afters, just like the ones I write.

These days I live in beautiful Montana, the last best place. If I'm not reading or writing, you'll find me just down the road in the park - Yellowstone. I have deer, eagles and the occasional bear for company, and I like it that way :0)

Made in the USA
Middletown, DE
14 April 2020